The Might Series

Becoming One

The Might Series

Becoming One

W.W. MORSE

W.W. Morse

Published by W.W. Morse, Battle Creek

ISBN-13: 979-8-218-17611-2 (paperback)

ISBN-13: 979-8-218-17612-9 (eBook)

First Edition

Contents

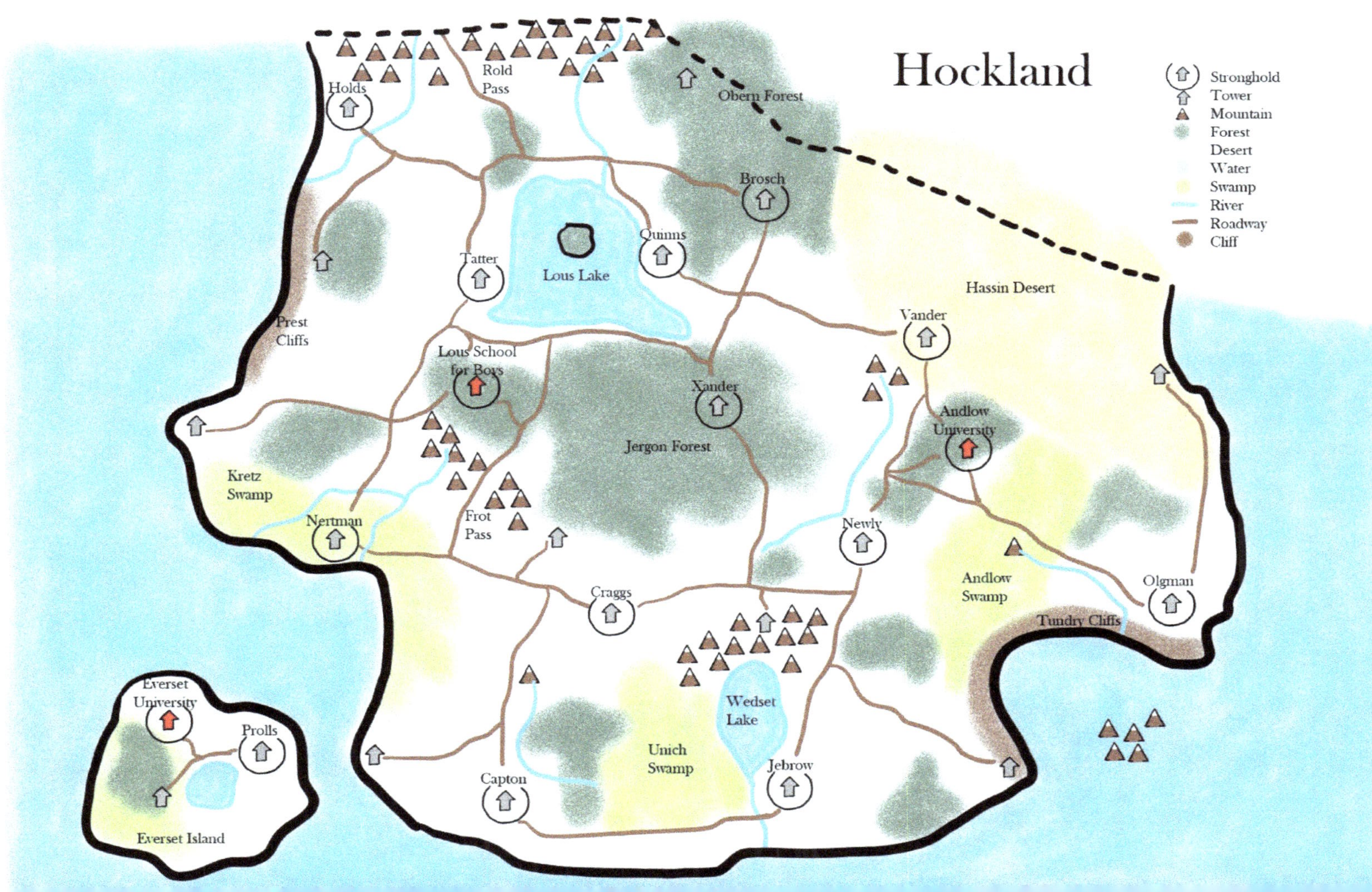

Hockland
Holds
Rold Pass
Obern Forest
Brosch
Quinns
Tatter
Lous Lake
Prest Cliffs
Hassin Desert
Vander
Lous School for Boys
Xander
Andlow University
Jergon Forest
Kretz Swamp
Nertman
Frot Pass
Newly
Andlow Swamp
Olgman
Craggs
Tundry Cliffs
Everset University
Prolls
Wedset Lake
Unich Swamp
Jebrow
Capton
Everset Island
Stronghold
Tower
Mountain
Forest
Desert
Water
Swamp
River
Roadway
Cliff

Prologue

Seraphim ran through the dark tunnels, her breath sawing in and out from exertion. Her people were being slaughtered and their cries echoed along the halls. She reached the end of a tunnel that to the untrained eye looked to be a dead end. Her hands felt along the surface of the wall until a stone depressed. With the mechanism engaged she pushed on the wall, and it swung open, leading her into the depths of the mountain.

She pushed the wall back into place hearing the screams and cries muffled through the stone. She held back the tears that forced their way to the surface. She had known what would happen to her people, but they were confident in their abilities and weapons. How wrong the Elders were.

She groped along the wall and found the torch waiting for use. She lifted it from its scone and placed it on the ground. She pulled out her flint and stone from her skirts and lit the torch. Placing her items back into her pocket she hurried along the empty passage with the torch lighting the way.

Some would think that she took the cowardly way out, leaving her people and saving herself. She needed to live. It was her fate that she survived. The knowledge she carried was needed. If she didn't use this escape route, then there would be no hope for the others that would come after.

She made her way down into the middle of the mountain. Her path led her past empty mining equipment, never to be used again. No other people would mine the treasures the mountain offered. She was alone. Only her quick steps and breathing was all that she heard. The flickering light of the torch illuminated the buckets and pulleys along the path. Soon she slipped into another tunnel leading her away.

Her steps slowed as she made her way among the intricate tunnel system. Only the people of the mountain knew of these tunnels and knew how to navigate them. She paused after several hours. She leaned back against the smooth stone surface and closed her eyes. Her thoughts were all over the place.

As a young seer, she was still learning about what her visions meant. When she went to the Elders to tell them of her visions of death and the mountains would lay empty for many centuries to follow, they listened, but felt that this would not come to pass for many years. And that is where they went wrong. Instead of thinking this would happen in a few years, it happened a few weeks later.

Alone standing in the tunnel thinking about all her family that she left, she couldn't hold the tears any longer. Her sobs were the only sounds echoing through the network of tunnels. She slid down the wall and the torch slipped from her fingers and clanked on the stone floor beside her. Her knees were drawn up and she hugged them to her.

All her memories swirled together, faces flitted across her mind. Her mother's sweet caring smile, sister's fun laugh, each of her friends and then a face popped in that she didn't recognize. It was of a young woman, close to her age with the same hazel eyes. Seraphim opened her eyes and looked around her. She swiped the back of her hand against her runny nose and sniffled.

She needed to keep moving. She needed to find the way through the mountain. She stood and lifted the burning torch. She continued, twisting, and turning along through the mountain. That face she saw was so like her own. She had a feeling that she was being followed, but when she looked behind her no one was there.

A fork in the tunnels had her pause briefly. Which way? As she stood debating which way to take, she was overcome with a vision. Except, this vision was nothing like she had experienced before.

Seraphim found herself in a white world. She looked around her and there was only a clear bench behind her. She looked to the left and as she looked right a person stood there. She jumped not expecting to see the person since there was no one there a second ago. Her eyes widened as she realized who it was.

The woman with the same hazel eyes stood before her. Her dark hair was pulled back into a thick braid. She wore leather and were those pants? It seemed like she was also assessing her trying to figure out who she was.

"Where are we?" Seraphim asked.

"The Station," the woman answered. "It's where Sparks meet, or at least that was what I was told."

"You're not from here?" The woman shook her head back and forth. "Who are you?"

"Eva. I'm from Hockland."

"I am too."

"What's your name?"

"Seraphim."

"You seem familiar," Eva said stepping closer.

"I thought the same thing." The likeness was uncanny. The only difference was that Seraphim had blonde hair. "Did you say this is where Sparks meet?"

"Yeah, that's what the last person told me when I was here."

"Why'd you come the last time?"

"I was looking for help. Are you here to help me?"

"I don't know. What do you need help with?" What could she know as a young seer? She wasn't worldly. She's lived in the mountains all her life.

"Is there a different way out of the mountains?"

"Which mountains?"

"Wedset Mountains. There are people coming and I know they won't spare anyone. Is there a different exit?" Eva looked at her with such hope.

"There is."

"Can you show me?" The woman stepped up to her with her eyes sparkling and grabbed her hands. It was an immediate connection. There was something they shared but she couldn't put her finger on it.

"I think I've done that already." Eva's brow scrunched. But then her eyes widened.

"Oh." Seraphim gave her a small smile. Eva had already appeared in her mind's eye, which means she was able to see what Seraphim had seen.

"Traveling through the mountain will not be easy, but you'll stay safe. Think of me by name and you will see the path."

"Thank you." Eva squeezed her hands and let go. As soon as she let go of her hands Eva disappeared. The area around her started to fade.

Seraphim blinked her eyes, and the fork was still before her. The dark-haired woman, Eva, was counting on her to make it through the mountains. The feeling of someone following her was not so bad now that she knew it was only Eva.

She went left at the fork which spiraled down. She had to make it out. Not only did her people need to live through her, but she also needed to help Eva. She had a suspicion that she just met a future descendant. Of course, only seers from the same family line could connect, even across time. So much depended on Seraphim making it out of the mountain, the future depended on it.

Chapter 1
Wedset Mountains

Eva opened her eyes and blinked several times to adjust to the low lighting. The last thing she remembered was standing in a field at the base of the Wedset Mountains surrounded by people she didn't recognize. All she knew was they were not the enemy, but Jace could protect her if they became hostile.

It shouldn't have surprised her that she had passed out. She seemed to not be able to stay awake once her energy was drained. She had to make a note to herself the next time she used her ability in large quantities to at least save some to make it to a bed.

She sat up on the thin straw mattress that was on the stone floor. From her first glance around the room, it was all stone, like it had been carved out of the rock. The room had a dome shape with an arched doorway chiseled out leading to a darkened path. She suspected that with all the same stone around her they were inside the mountain.

When she sat up, Jace stood and came over to her from a chair that he had been sitting in. His blue-green eyes searched her face, looking like he was making sure she was good. Not that he needed to since she was sure he could feel what she was feeling through their connection. Ever since he found her on the rooftop of Newly's house, they developed this link.

Right now, she could feel his concern for her. It was a little sweet, but he needed to be on his guard in this place. He probably wanted to trust these people as much as she did. They haven't been killed yet so that was a plus.

"You alright?" Jace asked, kneeling on the floor beside the bed.

"Yes. You should feel that I am."

"Well, I was getting a different weird feeling before you woke up. Were you having a dream or something?" That's right, she couldn't forget about taking another impromptu trip to the Station. That place was strange, all white as far as the eye could see. Maybe it was an unconscious thing that her Spark did, and she had no control over it.

This time she didn't meet the same person as before, but a different individual with the same hazel eyes as hers. The only difference was that the person, Seraphim, had fairer skin and golden curls. Whereas Eva was slightly darker from her time in the sun and her hair was black as raven feathers. Although Eva was sure she had never met her before, she still felt familiar. It was also weird that her subconscious asked questions for her or was that the Fates doing? Of course, more puzzles to figure out.

"Not exactly a dream," she answered. She caught a bit of movement by the entrance. Jace saw where her eyes were directed and looked also. "Is that what I think it is?" He slowly nodded his head.

"Yep. Looks like they have a couple brutes guarding us. Not like that will stop us if we want to get out of here."

"They're cautious of us. It's to be expected. We are inside the mountains, aren't we?" His gaze turned back to hers and a small smile showed on his face.

"Yes, we are. It's ingenious. I can't believe man created these tunnels. Just the little bit I've been through has been impressive."

"At that time there were people with Might among them." She was certain of it. Thinking back on when she had a vision of the past, those visions showed her these very tunnels and a few of the people that appeared in them had ability.

"Perhaps," Jace shrugged. "Anyway, it looks like this group isn't staying." He lowered his voice and leaned in, "I think we found the Ren." The Ren was a group of people with Might that had gone underground very soon after the Great War ended fifteen years ago. People with Might were hunted and killed by the tyrant Brosch. He also began to take children with the Might and building his own army that no one could win against. The only hope that this country has are the people currently hiding away, afraid for their very lives.

What Eva saw in the battle they had with the small Brosch army; the Ren could hold their own. If this group was backed with a few strongholds for support, they could turn the tide. If Brosch wasn't concerned yet with these people, he should be.

The click on the stones of approaching feet shifted Eva's attention to the room's only entrance and exit. She didn't want to be sitting if a threat was approaching. Jace must have thought the same thing. He rose slowly extending to his full height of six foot three. As she stood up next to him, a lady with snow white hair with a cloak about her shoulders stepped into the small room. A soft violet aura emanated from her.

"Ah, I see you are awake," she directed her gaze at Eva, assessing her. "Please forgive the inconvenience," she waved her hand behind her. "My name is Willow. Follow me," she turned and led the way out of the room.

Jace looked at Eva and raised a brow. She shrugged in response, might as well. They followed Willow out and down the narrow tunnel. It was wide enough that Jace and Eva could walk side by side behind the interesting lady.

Her eyes were so light in color. She'd never seen anyone with the like. She wondered why they were so pale. Even in the dark tunnels, Eva could see the soft pulsing of Willow's aura. That pulse meant that this lady had the Might. What ability was violet?

"As you can see, we are quite busy at the moment," Willow said over her shoulder. "It shouldn't be too much longer, and we will be on our way." They stepped into a large cavern and Eva's mouth dropped open at the sight. Two large stone pillars reached up into the air disappearing where the light was unable to touch. Intricate carvings graced each pillar and along the outer walls. Eva was tempted to walk over and touch each one. As her gaze swept across the enormous space, many of these people walked with purpose, some carrying what looked to be provisions.

She continued following Willow into another tunnel with Jace at her side. When they reached the end, it opened into another large hall. A stone table sat in the center with stone benches where each item looked to be carved out of the very ground of the hall. Scones along the walls lit the hall and illuminated the space within. Eva glimpsed more carvings on the wall before her attention was diverted back to Willow.

"Have a seat," the older woman said as she sat at the head of the table opposite the entrance. Eva took a seat around the center and on the left side of the table. Jace lowered himself next to her closest to the opening. His gaze was fixed on the tunnel where others were filing in and taking their seats around the table as well.

Many Eva noticed had blue auras and a couple green. It made her wonder if blue was a common aura color, even among people without ability, blue seemed to be a norm. A woman stepped into the room with a deep red aura. Both Jace and she watched the woman's path around the opposite side of the table where she sat in the chair next to Willow. Eva could only guess that she held some importance as well.

Jace leaned in and whispered in her ear, "Is her hair, maroon?" Eva turned to him and lifted an eyebrow in response. "What?" he asked acting innocent. The knowing playful sparkle in his eyes gave him away.

Eva whispered back, "In all seriousness, this looks like a war counsel." Her brows drew together in concern.

"I don't think you are far off the mark," Jace agreed, sitting straighter and masking his face once again into a stern expression.

"Once we all get settled, we will begin," Willow announced as the last of the group entered and took their seats. She continued after the last individual sat. "Our Elites have just returned confirming what we were suspecting. A group of Chasers along with many cronies, twice as many as yesterday, have left Brosch territory and are heading in this direction." A low murmur started. "I know this was an ideal location, but we are now compromised, and our only option is to leave."

Chasers were men that tracked down people with Might. They used dogs specially trained to detect the lingering effects of a person's aura that used their ability. The hounds were able to track this like a trail leading to the person who used the ability. Just thinking about what the Chasers would have done to her friend Gene Newly if she hadn't ended their lives put Eva in a sobering mood.

"This exit is a death trap," a man at the far end of the table chimed in. "There is only one way out, and it'll be right into the hands of that army." Many nodded their heads in agreement.

Willow slowly nodded and even looked dejected. "It is true, we will have to fight our way out."

"There's no possible way any of us will survive!" a younger man on Eva's right said. Many more joined his response. It seemed that many were unhappy with the situation they were put in.

The maroon haired lady stood and yelled above the chatter, "Enough!" The men and women around the table quieted until the room was silent once again. The woman sat resting her gaze back on Willow.

"I have led this company of young men and women for many years," Willow said. "You have trusted me to keep you safe. You have all learned and grown in skill and I am proud of the sacrifices you have made. It's not easy to know that you are hunted for your ability. There was a time that people respected your extraordinary gifts. If you haven't noticed, I am getting old in years and my visions grow few and far between. I was not able to foresee this coming fate. And in that, I have failed you."

"Willow, please don't think that of yourself," the maroon haired lady placed a comforting hand on top of Willow's. "We all owe you our lives."

"Is there no other way?" one of the men asked. Everyone looked around at each other then rested their hopeful eyes on Willow. She was their support; her ability gave these people the courage to continue to live outcast lives and the hope that they would prevail.

Before Willow could speak the words Eva knew the woman dreaded saying, she answered. "Yes." All eyes swung to Eva, some with a look of confusion, some hopeful and others untrusting. She was an outsider, and she couldn't blame them for not trusting her.

"What was that?" the red aura around the lady pulsed and snaked out. Eva didn't know what her ability was, but she knew that she wouldn't succumb to her influence. She had enough practice from Jace's persuasive ability that she wouldn't be affected. In a stronger voice Eva answered.

"Yes, there is another way out of the mountains." She could see Jace out of the corner of her eye look at her with a questioning expression. She could feel his curiosity.

"Explain," Willow gestured for her to proceed.

"The mountain people that lived here created a passageway that led out the other side of the mountain."

"And how did you learn this information," the older woman asked. Eva wasn't going to reveal to these people that she was a seer. She could see Willow's tired eyes. If this group of people knew that of Eva, they would possibly want to make her their leader. She wasn't having it.

The vision that she had on the way to the Rens' location was painful. Not physical, but emotional. Her vision took her into the past to a time when the Wedset Mountains still held their inhabitants. These people mined iron and crafted weapons that no other group of people could emulate. The story goes that centuries ago, the mountain people were slaughtered by a hoard of invaders. There were no survivors. Well, that wasn't entirely true.

Her vision showed a false wall. Beyond this wall was a path that led into the bowls of the mountain and a tunnel was cut into the mountain that led to the south. But this vision came at a price. When Eva was showed this, she had to glimpse a part of her own past. Her carefully constructed walls chipped away to reveal the image of her mother's vacant eyes. The images of her mother's death came to the forefront of her mind.

Even now, she was trying to force those images back. She felt Jace's hand on her knee and he gave her a little squeeze. He probably felt her anxiety and he did have a worried look on his face when she looked at him. She had to think of something.

"I have been told this information through my family," she blurted. Well, she was sort of telling the truth. When she met Seraphim at the Station, she felt this family connection to her, even though Eva had never met her before. In the vision that she had, she was sure it was her that led her through the mountain.

"Impossible. There are no descendants of the Wedset Mountain people," the maroon haired lady spat. "Are you just trying to get our hopes up for a good laugh?" A sneer spread across her features.

"I have no reason to lie," Eva said. She saw the red tendrils of aura skim across the surface of her skin. She could feel a sensation to tell the truth. It was an evasive feeling, so she pushed at it and blocked the aura from entering. Even though she couldn't see Jace's aura, she got that same evasive feeling with him, persuading her to do something. She just applied the blocking she learned to the red aura, and no surprise to her, it had worked.

The lady that she had blocked scrunched her brow in confusion. "Who are you to have any say in these matters anyway?"

"I am Eva, descendant of the Wedset people."

Chapter 2
Secret Tunnel

Jace

Jace could feel the certainty in Eva's response. He still had his hand resting on her knee. Even though he need not touch her any longer to feel their connection, he still wanted to lend her the strength to face any of these people's questions.

The main reason he went searching for the Ren was because of their leader. The seer was who he was searching for and there she was, sitting at the end of the table. He had many questions regarding the prophesy about a child who would be a savior to all. He wanted to know if she had any prophesies about the child or if she had heard any. Being an older lady, she would have met people before the Great War and would have heard this prophesy.

The main question Jace had, was he the child? He didn't feel like there was anything special about him. He still couldn't believe that his Nanna would sacrifice her life to save his because she believed he was the one.

People murmured around the stone table after Eva's announcement. He could hear that some did not believe her. One such woman voiced her opinion further down the table. "That's impossible. The Wedset people were slaughtered centuries ago. There were no survivors."

"So the records say," Eva said. "They can be wrong, and this instance, they are."

"What proof do you have?" the maroon-haired lady asked, still looking irritable.

"Only a descendant would know about the other passageway, and I do."

"I'll believe that when I see it," the lady growled, not very becoming of her.

"Ruby," Willow turned and admonished the maroon-haired lady with a look. The silver-haired woman turned her gaze to Eva and stared at her, probably contemplating on how much she believed Eva. She finally spoke. "I'm willing to believe this." A few voices murmured around the table at this pronouncement. "However," she said a little louder so the underlying talking would cease. "I would have to see this passageway myself to determine if this would be a better option of escape or not. I will not change the plan to evacuate. How we evacuate, could change with this new information."

"You're not taking this seriously, are you?" Ruby leaned in and spoke low to Willow, although not low enough for everyone around the table to hear.

"Why shouldn't I? She has every right to say something, just like everyone else that is here." Ruby didn't like this answer and she sat back in her seat and folded her arms in front of her with a frown on her face. "For now, continue with the preparations to leave," Willow addressed the others in the room. "We will reconvene in about an hour to discuss the route we will take. You are dismissed."

People started to stand and exit, talking in hushed voices as they left. Jace stood as well, with Eva by his side. "Eva. You and your companion please stay a moment. I'd like to discuss something with you," Willow rose and made her way to where they were standing beside the table. Ruby stayed where she was, sitting there with slits for eyes.

Willow sighed and turned toward the stubborn maroon-haired woman. "I do not need your assistance, Ruby."

"You can't make me leave, I cannot allow you to be unprotected," Ruby said through gritted teeth.

"Leave," Willow sternly said. "You were given an order to prepare for evacuation. You were included in that order." Ruby stared at Willow a moment longer until she finally stood and left, not without throwing a very menacing look at Jace and Eva.

"Now then," Willow said to them with a smile. "Eva, is it? I am surprised that there was a descendent of the great Wedset people. How can I be certain that you are telling the truth?"

"I did not wish to keep this passage a secret," Eva answered. "That is truly the only other way out of this mountain." Willow stepped closer, eyeing Eva with curiosity.

"And how could you know that?" Jace looked down at Eva, seeing her keeping her composure against this lady. He didn't know what ability she was capable of, but he hoped that it wouldn't affect Eva.

"Like she said," Jace interrupted. "She is a descendent. She would know every corner and path in these mountains."

"Even I know that is not possible," Willow turned her attention to Jace, and raised an eyebrow in question. "These mountains have not been occupied by one group of people for many years. Sure, a few gypsies now and then, but not for any length of time."

"I trust Eva is telling the truth," he said very protectively. Eva must have felt his emotion and placed a calm hand on his tensely crossed arms. He didn't even realize he had crossed them.

"Jace, its fine," Eva said softly. He knew she was okay. He just didn't want Willow to find out that Eva was a seer. He was the only one who knew this information. Eva turned to Willow. "I would be happy to show you the tunnel now."

"Excellent," Willow smiled. "Please, lead the way." She gestured with her hand toward the exit. Eva dropped her hand away from Jace's arm and started toward the archway into the tunnel system. Jace fell in step next to her. He didn't know if he should say anything or not.

"Is something wrong?" Eva asked next to him.

"No, why do you ask?" Jace replied.

"I'm getting this uneasiness with you right now. I don't mind helping these people, especially since if we don't, we could be slaughtered right along with them."

"I know, I just," he sighed and continued in a lower voice for Eva to hear only, "I just don't want them to know everything about you." She smirked at him and chuckled slightly.

"Then how will I make friends?"

"Friends? I didn't think now was the time to make some."

"Oh, Jace. Lighten up! I was only teasing." He must be wound up tight if he didn't realize she was just messing with him. He shook his head to try and clear the tension away.

Eva led them back out to the large cavern and turned down a tunnel the opposite way they had been staying. The tunnel was like all the others, with little alcoves and rooms branching off, until the tunnel ended.

"And we have come to the end of this tunnel," Willow said behind them. "I should have told you before you took it that nothing lies this way." Jace looked behind him and saw the white-haired lady stop just behind Eva, who was still staring at the wall intently. She was staring so much that Jace was wondering what she was possibly looking at. He placed his hand on her shoulder.

"Eva?" That's when he noticed in the faint light that her eyes flickered. She must have had a vision. He sent a quick glance Willow's way, but it didn't look like she saw what he did. Eva stepped forward and placed her hand on the wall. Her fingertips moved over the smooth rock to the right.

It looked like Eva's fingers came across an indent. It was ever so slight, but enough that Eva recognized it was there. She pushed at the indented spot and to Jace's amazement, a small amount of rock sunk in, and Eva pushed the wall like it was a door, swinging open to one side.

The scraping sound ended as Eva lifted the torch from the wall hanger and took a few steps into the exposed tunnel. The tunnel was long, but Jace couldn't tell how long, since it was pitch black beyond the reach of the light.

"Well, I stand corrected," Willow stepped up beside Eva. "I have a good feeling about this tunnel. Can it be closed after everyone is through?"

"Yes," Eva answered.

"I will think on this," she turned to Eva and Eva turned toward her. "I have a strong feeling that you are leading us on the correct path." They stood there for several seconds, probably assessing each other. "Very soon, we will be evacuating." Willow turned back toward where Jace was standing on the edge between the used tunnel and hidden tunnel. She walked out, passing him.

"I suggest you two also get your belongings together," Willow said over her shoulder. "Soon after the council meeting, we will be leaving." She continued down the hall without a backward glance.

Eva stepped up beside him. "So, what do you think?" she asked.

"I think this will be a very interesting journey."

"Yeah, it will be."

Chapter 3
Following a Ghost

Eva

"Are you serious? We're going in there?" Ruby said with a hint of disbelief in her voice. Eva didn't realize she was standing so close to the entrance of the hidden passageway.

Over the last hour there was a flurry of activity within the caves. Stressed and anxious feelings were expressed on the Rens' faces that Eva and Jace had passed. There was nothing between them to express in words, so they gathered their small belongings back in the room where Eva first woke and traversed back to the room with the stone table.

While waiting, Eva was lost in her thoughts, thinking about the situation they were in. The issue was there was a reason that she came here. She was specifically looking for the man in her vision. She had not seen his specific aura from the people that they passed. She wondered where this man was. He had to be here, right?

She didn't know how long she tumbled around in her thoughts, but the room started to fill with people once again. An hour had passed already. She turned to Jace who sat quietly by her. He turned his head and gave her an encouraging smile and squeezed her hand.

The meeting was short and to the point. Based on the Elites reports, even if they decided to leave through the main entrance, they would run into Brosch's cronies. A battle would most likely happen, and the Ren would be outnumbered. Willow made the decision to use the hidden tunnel.

Eva led the way to their hopeful escape route with Willow by her side and Jace slightly behind. Now they stood in front of the entrance, several torches were lit to continue into the darkness.

"Yes, the decision is final," Willow answered Ruby's question. "I would think, Ruby, that you would want to have a better option than to be slaughtered?"

"Yeah," Ruby grumbled.

"We will need to have someone close the entrance once everyone has made it through," Eva said to Willow. The older seer nodded her head and turned her gaze on Ruby.

"You heard Eva. Someone needs to close the entrance."

"What, you want me to do it?" Ruby's eyebrows shot up to her hairline.

"I trust that you will make sure everyone is safe and through."

"How in the world am I going to get this closed?"

"Simple," Eva said "Just push on the rock like you would a door. Once it is closed, the entrance is sealed."

Ruby didn't look so confident about it, but one look from Willow and she was conceding. "Fine," she made her way to her place next to the entrance and Eva took her place again next to Willow.

"Lead the way, Eva," Willow commanded. This was it. She wasn't one hundred percent sure this was going to work, but if she didn't try, it wasn't just her and Jace's life on the line, it was all the people standing behind her.

A soft but firm hand fell on her shoulder. Jace's feeling of confidence bleed through their link. He believed in her and her ability to lead them in the right direction. He leaned over and spoke softly in her ear, his breath a little ticklish. "You'll be fine. I'll be right here if you need me."

Okay. She can do this. With a torch in her hand and Jace by her side she started into the dark stone tunnel ahead.

It was eerily familiar to Eva. She would catch glimpses of a shadowy blond-haired figure leading the way. She knew it was Seraphim, the young woman she met at the Station. How was it possible that she could see her? Another mystery to add to the bucket.

After a short while, the tunnel opened to a large cavern. The cavern had items about, pickaxes, buckets, carts, and small tools. At the edge of the trail, it dropped off into what seemed like an endless pit. This area had wooden bridges and ropes and pulleys. There were also steps leading down into the cavern's depths. As more people entered behind, Eva could hear people gasping and murmuring. It was a glorious sight to behold.

"This must be where the Wedset people did their mining," Jace exclaimed from behind her. She could feel his awe and excitement.

"It was said that when they were attacked the resources for mining were destroyed by the enemy so no other people from this country could have this advantage again," Willow said in a sing-song voice.

"Well, apparently, that was incorrect. They just hid what they did from everybody," Jace stated matter-of-factly.

"It appears so," Willow agreed. "Eva, you said that you are a descendent of the Wedset people?"

"I did," Eva nodded slowly. She was also taking in the site of the mining cavern and making sure she watched her step as they traveled close to the edge.

"You are the first person I've met to have said these claims. How is it that no one knew that anyone survived?"

"Well, my ancestor who did survive, she escaped through this very passageway. There are other hidden passageways elsewhere. But this one, she used." It was an odd feeling to trust her visions. As she recalled, this mountain was filled with secret tunnels. Seraphim wasn't the only one who escaped. She was just the only one in her family line to escape using this passageway.

It did make Eva wonder what happened to the others that had escaped. There had to be more Wedset descendants.

"Are you saying, there are more?" Jace asked.

"I believe so. Why they never indulged their heritage, I have no idea." That would have to be another conversation topic she had with Seraphim. But that had to wait for another time. Right now, she had to get these people out of the mountains away from Brosch's cronies.

"Family secrets," Willow's faint whispery voice said to Eva's right. "It's as if everyone holds secrets in this world. Especially now when the Might are being hunted. I suppose at the time, no Wedset was safe, even outside the mountain at the strongholds."

"Willow, it sounds like you speak from experience," Jace surmised.

Willow exhaled and Eva caught a sad smile on her face amongst the torch light. "It wasn't so long ago that seers were revered and were celebrated for their gifts. My family grew-up in a small farming community. This gift was rare enough that when my sister and I started to see visions, my mother feared we would be taken to serve in the stronghold."

"Your sister was a seer as well?" Eva asked.

"Yes, another rarity to have two seers in the same generation from the same house. In the end, my mother kept our secret hidden. She loved us too much to see us go. However, we all make our own choices. I chose to keep my ability a secret. My sister, did not."

"Where is your sister now?" Jace asked.

"Who knows? We never shared the same visions. I knew that I was needed one day and that keeping my existence a secret was essential. My sister's path was not the same as mine. But, enough about me. I would like to learn more about you, Eva. You seem to be a Healer? I only ask from what I saw when you were out on the field after the battle."

Oh right. Jace was injured by a poisoned sword to his middle. It was pure agony feeling what he felt. Through their connection she knew exactly what he was feeling and how slowly the poison was taking effect. She didn't think, she just acted, healing Jace and taking his pain deep inside herself. Miraculously, she didn't poison herself in the process, but she did make herself very weak from the effort.

"I guess so. That was more instinct than anything. I needed to do it, so I did," Eva tried to explain. She didn't want to indulge her other abilities, so if Willow wanted to believe she was a Healer, then she was going to let her think that.

"Hmm," Willow's pale blue eyes narrowed slightly when Eva turned toward her. Her violet aura pulsed ever so slightly, but before reaching Eva, it was pulled back in.

"What is it?" Eva asked her, knowing the older woman had something on her mind.

"It's just a rarity to not project an aura. I would never have guessed you were a Healer."

"You can see auras?" Jace asked from behind us, obviously keeping up with the conversation.

"Any person with the Might that receives the correct training is able to see other Might auras. It does help tremendously, especially in these troubling times. I can certainly train you, Eva." Willow was just assuming that she was not able to see them, maybe because she was lacking one herself. Which was strange, it gave her a kind of flutter inside her. Eva only knew of one other person with no visible aura, and he was only steps away from her.

"We'll see," Eva said as they came up to a split in the path. She stopped and looked down the right one and then the left. No distinct markers were present to tell which possible way to go.

"And now for the first test. I hope those directions you were given were accurate. I would not want to send my people to be trapped inside the mountain with no exit," Willow softly said, but there was some power behind her words. Eva got the sense that she was trusted, but only so far.

Eva took a deep breath and exhaled, closing her eyes to focus. She needed to reconnect to Seraphim. She slowly opened her eyes with Seraphim in mind and her shadowy figure appeared in front of her. She had stopped, her back turned to Eva and then her head turned back, and a pair of hazel eyes met hers. It was like she knew we were there. She turned back around and drifted left and slowly faded. Left it was then.

"This way," Eva pointed toward the left tunnel and with confidence followed the blonde-haired apparition.

Chapter 4
Halted Escape

034

"Is this the last of us?" Ruby demanded of the Elite that stood beside him. Number 034 looked down at his bound hands and then at the Elite's hand that gripped his upper arm. It's not like he wanted to run away, where was he going to go at this point?

"Aye, it is," the brute of a man responded. As soon as they passed by her, she pushed the rock closed. It covered the pathway that they just passed through, sealing them in.

"Hopefully that'll hold the bastards," Ruby spat. She was never a happy person. Her red aura leaked from her.

"Hold it in," 034 quietly said. It wasn't quiet enough because she got right up in his face.

"Do you have something to say to me?" she growled. She was a very powerful Seeker and once her ability was set in motion, it was hard to lie, but it's not like he had any reason to lie.

"Don't use so much power, their hounds are trained to detect auras." She should have known that Brosch's cronies trained up dogs to detect a Might's ability use. The more potent the usage, the easier time the hounds had of detecting it.

Ruby narrowed her brown eyes at him, but in this light, it looked like staring into a bottomless pit. She slowly breathed in and out and, thankfully, her aura eased back. Hopefully by the time those hounds arrive, they won't be able to pick up any auras. Maybe lingering ones in the only known mountain caves. They must hope that they can't detect through thick stone walls.

"Let's just get something straight," she crossed her arms and gave her most menacing look. "We could have easily left you for Brosch's cronies to find. Don't forget that."

"I would rather kill myself if I could." That was the key. If he could. He still didn't know exactly how Brosch was able to do it, but he was blocked from anything closely related to the tyrant, plus, when 034 ever had the compulsion to put himself out of his misery, he was unable to do it, like he was blocked from taking his own life.

"We will extract the information we need from you one way or the other."

"I don't doubt that."

"Move him along," she said to the Elite with the tilt of head in the direction of the larger group. Thankfully they unbound his feet for this trek. He wondered when they found this hidden tunnel. The guard forcefully pushed 034 to get him moving.

"I can walk on my own." The Elite grunted in response, not caring about 034's discomfort.

Why did that crazy seer send him here? He was meant to meet the One. So far, all the people he's came across in this mountain, was nothing close to this proposed child prophesy. There had to be a distinctive marker the One had. Something special that would help him with figuring that out. Or maybe this wasn't where he was supposed to meet him. Only the Fates knew what they were doing, and now, 034 wanted in on their plans.

Jace

"This isn't good." Eva stopped, holding the light up in front of her. Jace stopped next to her, taking in the scene before him. Instead of the smooth tunnels that were purposely cut along the path, this area had rocks and boulders that looked to be blocking an opening. If Jace would guess, there was a cave in.

"What?" Willow asked on Eva's other side.

"The exit should be here, but it's not." Jace could feel how devastated she felt through the link. He was even getting hints of failure and fear. He gently smoothed his fingers down the underside of her arm. Her startling hazel eyes met his.

"I think at one point there was Eva. But it seems that there was a cave in," he gently pointed out. Having his hand touching her arm, skin to skin, the link seemed to be more pronounced. Along the link he tried to send her hopeful thoughts, that it's okay. "We can just turn around and try another path."

Her eyes never left his, but he could see the small panic. She whispered ever so quietly that only he heard, and maybe Willow, "But I don't know any other way." He gave her arm a reassuring squeeze before letting go and faced the rumble in their way.

"We'll just move them," he blurted out.

"We'll what?" Eva asked with a look of confusion on her beautiful features.

"I'm sure we have enough men here and use our strength to move these rocks."

Willow took a slight step forward with a look of interest, "Are you suggesting they 'use' their strength?" Jace had no idea what she was hinting at and Eva at first didn't, but then her eyes widened, and a small smile graced her lips.

"People with ability of strength," Eva tentatively said.

"Yes, they are all the men in my Elite. The correct designation for their ability is Warrior but it was such an old-fashioned term I chose another one," Willow explained.

"I will join in the efforts," Jace volunteered. He knew he was strong. He didn't know about using this strength ability like the Might, but at least he knew what he could handle.

Willow narrowed her eyes at him, looking like she was trying to assess him like she had with Eva earlier. She shook her head. "It would be pointless for you because you don't have the Might."

For some reason that irked him a little. Didn't she say only people with the Might can see auras if trained? It's only been a short time since Eva showed him that trick, but she said that everybody has an aura. Could Willow only see people with the Might and not everybody like Eva could? Well, he didn't fully understand all that stuff and the whole child prophesy weighed on his mind. If indeed he was this supposed child, shouldn't he have ability too?

Only one way to test it. "I guess we'll make camp here and we'll gather the Elite to form a plan on how to get this exit unblocked," Jace said, staring at the boulders challengingly.

"Very well," Willow bobbed her head. "I will go make the rounds." She stepped away and he could hear her voice starting to discuss the proposed plan.

"So, what do you really have in mind?" Eva stepped up to his side and asked for his ears alone.

"Do you remember when we were young, and you burst out a large force?"

"Why do you bring that up?"

"Because I think that you can help with this by concentrating that force to move these boulders." He could already see her shaking her head.

"No way. I am not going to use my other abilities if I don't have to. I want them to think I'm as normal as them."

"And what is normal to them?"

"Only one ability. Don't you see? I am not normal."

"Okay, don't really care because I still need you to help." He gave her his most pleading look he could. She was glaring at him, but he could see a small smile tug at the corner of her lips. She was trying not to laugh.

"I propose, you just make it look like I'm strong," he puffed up his chest and beat it lightly with his fist. He smiled at her slight chuckle at that. "What? You don't think I'm strong enough?"

"Jace, I've known you a long time, and strength you have in abundance. Your father was naturally strong, so I would expect you to be." Her eyes roamed slowly over his arms and chest. He could feel through the link her appreciation for his looks. When she saw his smirk, as in he knew exactly what she was thinking, her face turned red. Not that he wasn't feeling the same thing for her, and she had to have known, but now wasn't the time, even though he could feel his body temperature rising.

He coughed and turned back to the boulders to try and get his feelings under control.

"So," her voice drifted to him, "how do you suppose I use my ability?"

"I'll go to lift with the rest of the guys, and yes, I will be trying, and you just focus on lifting as well. If you want, you can just target the ability at me."

"Um, well, I don't want to push you over with it. I did do that last time in training, remember?"

"Don't worry I didn't forget. But I knew that I've taken some, what do I want to say, pressure from you before, so maybe I can do it with this and just redirect it?"

She was quiet for a while. He knew she was thinking about it. Would she go with his plan? If this was the only way out, they needed to get out before the chance that whoever Brosch is sending, might find the secret passageway. Let's just pray they didn't.

"Alright, I guess I could give it a try." Jace put a big grin on his face knowing he just got his way. She shoved him a little for it. "But just to be clear, I'm not going to be standing right next to you all. I'm going to make it look like I'm not helping. I don't want to expose anything to these people that I haven't already."

"I get it, Eva. I would never want to put you in that kind of situation. Plus," I leaned close to her ear, "you're my secret weapon. I'm not going to give that up for anything." His breath feathered her neck and he saw her shiver slightly in response. Or dear, they both were getting quite aroused. This was not the time.

She slowly stepped away with bright eyes. She had more will power then him. She just nodded and broke eye contact. He released the breath he was holding. Holy smokes. If he didn't get that under control, he was going to do something stupid.

"Jace," Willow stepped up as Eva walked away. "We'll follow the plan you put in place."

"Excellent. We'll all rest and eat. In an hour, all the Elite will gather in front of the boulders where I'll go over the plan to get this path cleared."

She slightly bowed her head and turned back to the rest of the Ren to update them. This was going to be one heck of a plan. He just hoped that he would make Eva proud and give her some confidence back. He didn't want her to feel like they led them wrong. He wanted to prove to her he would do anything to help her feel victorious.

Chapter 5
On the Trail

He waited outside the door of the decrepit looking cottage after knocking on the thick wooden door. He attuned his ears to hear the soft shuffling of feet inside. They came to a stop on the other side of the door. A latch was released, and a small opening appeared on the door where two violet-colored eyes peered out. He just raised an eyebrow in response.

The violet eyes narrowed, and the opening was shut forcibly followed by the multiple other latches being released. The door opened and he strode into the cramped space of the hut. He held a hand up to his guard that followed him here. He knew that the woman inside would bring him no harm. Although, it would be a surprise to him if she ever did, because he would never have expected it.

The door closed behind him, and the woman moved back to her table and took up her bowl where she was grinding down some type of plant in a fine powder.

"I have to ask, have you done something to your hair recently?" It wasn't like he didn't know already. She stilled in her work and turned her head in his direction. "Is this what you looked like years ago? I have to say that whatever you did was remarkable to your health."

"It would be pointless to state what you already know, Rudd." He really hated that name. It never inspired the fear he was looking for. No, people called him Brosch for a reason. He will not be intimated by an old woman.

"You are right. Before some of my Chasers went missing, they were reported going in this direction after my Healer. I could ask if you know anything about that, but I can clearly see that you know quite a bit." He didn't know how she did it, especially because she had no Might ability of her own, just her little tricks with her plants. Old magic was at work in her methods. Potions that are now only known in fairy tales.

Somehow, she extracted the Healer's ability, even though he blocked that Healer to only be used on himself.

"You forgot one little detail," she said not expanding on the detail he forgot.

"So, I have. Where did you send him?" He had the Healer for quite some time, it would have been impossible for him to know exactly what direction to take once he left the stronghold.

"Getting right to the point as usual."

"Do I have to remind you why I allow you to stay here? The only reason I allow you to stay? I'm sure you don't want to jeopardize this tiny bit of freedom I've given you." She set down her bowl carefully and turned fully toward him. She had a startling beauty about her. Her white-blonde hair cascaded down her back in thick curls and her violet eyes shined brighter than he'd ever seen them. Seers naturally lose their eye color over time. Her skin was smooth and free of wrinkles and aging spots.

"The Point of Aster."

"What?"

"I sent him in the direction of the Point of Aster." She crossed her arms in front of her.

"The spear in the Aster constellation?"

"Indeed." That spear pointed to the Wedset mountains. Interesting.

"I have already sent my best there to retrieve another one that went missing." He slowly walked closer to her, only leaving inches between them when he stopped. "You already knew that I would send my army there, what am I missing?"

"You believe that you are missing something?" How dare she! Challenging him like this. He narrowed his eyes at her.

"Your usefulness is almost up, unless you can give me something of value." Her eyes never wavered from his stare. She was never afraid of him. After a long pause, which he believed she might not actually know, she spoke.

"Your Tracker will not be successful."

"Why?"

"You know visions can be fleeting and not tell me explanations."

"But you always have a theory, or other visions that would help answer that question." She was a crafty one, but he knew better than anyone what seers can do.

"You will see her, but not see her. She will slip past on your way to Nertman Stronghold."

"I haven't planned a trip to that swamp. Why would I take such a journey?" That stronghold was surrounded by Kretz Swamp. There were many ways into the swamp, but there was only one safe route. It wasn't guaranteed that the journey was safe once you got past the outer trees. A man could be swallowed up if they took a wrong step. Also, the swamp gave off the worst smell. It wasn't a pleasing aroma if he remembered correctly.

"You will know when the time comes, and you will remember my words. Do not trust the people closest to you."

"I don't trust anyone." He wasn't lying about that. He killed many to get to where he was, and he wasn't going to change his ways. She gave him a sad smile and nodded her head in understanding. "Well, it seems that both my escapees found their way to the Ren. Now I have an excuse to wipe out those free Might. No Might should be free. They are much too valuable to roam around un-tethered. Maybe I will even get a chance to gather even more to my ranks." The possibilities were endless.

"Ambitious, like always." He smirked at her. She turned and lifted a small leather draw-string bag and held it out to him. "This will help." Ah yes, his issue. The only weakness of his and the reason he had a Healer in the first place. He took the bag from her. She continued, "Mix a pinch of that in drink of your choosing and it should last for a day. It won't stop it, but it will help with the symptoms."

"As soon as my Tracker captures my Healer, I will be right as rain. I really wish I could stay and chat," he really didn't, he was just saying it, "but I have things to do." He turned on his heel and yanked open the door. Before he stepped outside, he thought of one more thing to say.

"And, if I find any more dead Chasers by your cottage, you will join the pile with them. This is your warning."

"I understand," he heard her say. He didn't miss the other awful endearment that he hated with a passion as he closed the door behind him, "grandson."

Chapter 6
Sneaking Strength

Eva

She watched as the first group of Elites got in position around the first large boulder. Luckily, they had come into a large bowl-shaped cavern and so the plan was to move the large rocks to one side and the other side is where they made camp. Eva watched others without any ability clearing some smaller rumble out of the way. It seemed like the majority didn't want the chance of being trapped in the mountain with no way out if the enemy did find a way to this point. It felt highly unlikely, but things change. Nothing is ever absolute in this world.

Jace was a natural leader. He took charge and the men followed him without question. Eva wondered if he did have an aura, how bright would it be. Would it be like his other family members? She remembered the first time joining his family after being rescued from that awful tower. Their auras were in such contrast to Brosch's men.

Brosch's cronies' auras had this tint to it, like looking through a film. There was color, but it was muted behind something. Whatever they did or whoever they were associated with caused that. It had to be influenced since she has met many outside of Brosch's ranks that did not have that covering over their auras. Especially the Jebrows' auras, which could blind her they were so bright and full of light. She could imagine Jace's would do that too. If he had one that is.

"Alright, first group ready. Here we go," Jace gave orders for his group to step up to an exceptionally large boulder. It was slightly taller than Jace and at least four times as round. He had seven others taking up positions around this boulder. The men's faces looked determined and each person activated their ability. It was a beautiful site, full of blue hues wrapping around the boulder. Not one blue aura the same shade as the next, but mixed, it reminded her of the sky outside.

Then her gaze drifted to Jace, absent of any color, but still impressive to look at. His brownish-blonde hair was a mess and a little long, but it suited his rugged appearance, especially with the few days of scruff on his face. His muscles on his arms bunched as he found a grip on the boulder and his thigh muscles strained against his pants when he crouched down.

Eva swallowed and felt the tiniest bit of fluttering in her abdomen. What was wrong with her? Her gaze swept back up to Jace's strong features and his sea-colored eyes locked with hers with a smirk on his face. Oh, this darn link! Every time this happened to her, he got that look. For some reason it embarrassed her to know that he knew how she felt.

Her gaze didn't leave his when he tilted his head toward the large rock. Right, she was supposed to help with that. She gave him a quick nod back and he broke their staring contest to concentrate on lifting.

As she continued to look at Jace she concentrated on their link, this crazy thread that seemed to attach to them. They haven't tested the boundaries of this before. It started when they were young when they held hands or when their skin came in contact, it projected what the other was feeling. Before that night in Newly Stronghold, that was it. It wasn't like what it was now. This all the time, every minute of every day link to his feelings.

But, because of the link, he helped her not fall into the dark abyss of her mind. He was the shining light in an otherwise world of emptiness. If he could do that, then she could certainly try to boost his strength.

Eva thought about her training with that crazy force and knocking things over. She gathered that feeling that surfaced every time before she let one go into the middle of her chest. She let the feeling swirl there, and then she thought of a slow trickle moving down the connection she had with Jace. She couldn't see any of this, but she could feel the swirl change direction and felt like it was leaving her. She just hoped it was going where she sent it.

"Get ready," Jace's voice commanded of his team. "On three. One," his brow furrowed just a bit. "Two," his muscles started to quiver as Eva assumed he must be receiving what she sent to him. "Three!" he growled out. She watched and felt a small release of energy come from his direction. With the combined efforts of the other members, they were able to lift the bounder and shuffle several steps to the right.

"Stop and ease down," Jace's voice strained. A line of sweat beaded his brow. The men all in sync crouched down. "Release!" The men let go and the boulder thumped to the ground. Their auras lazily sucked back to their prospective man, and they seemed to all be smirking.

"That's one. I'm not going to stop until our group moves the most," Jace announced. The group of seven around him agreed with back slapping and large grins on their faces. Did Jace turn this into a competition with the other groups? Yes, he did. Men!

As they strategized on the next boulder to move, Eva swept her gaze amongst the other members of the Ren. The auras that could be seen the most were shades of yellow, green and this mix between blue and purple. There wasn't as many of that color, and she remembered Willow's was more violet than these other brighter auras. She wondered what the difference was. Maybe something to ask Willow later.

She saw the familiar red color of Ruby sitting off to the side sharpening some knives with always a serious look on her face. Eva wondered what she experienced in life to make her so serious. Yes, there were times in Eva's past that she did not want to remember. But there were moments that she would never forget, and those moments gave her hope. Hope that this world can be better than it was.

Maybe Ruby just didn't have any of that hope left. Eva could change that for her. As she went to turn back to the men moving boulders another color caught her eye. Wait a second. Was that? Eva slowly started in that direction, not believing what she was seeing. A faint orange-red aura emanated from the back corner of the group.

Her feet wove in and out of the Ren until she was able to see a clear path to the man with this specific aura. As if he felt her staring, his eyes rose to meet hers. Eva inhaled slightly. It was him! The man from her vision. His aura was unmistakable, and the red hair and green eyes were the exact shades she remembered seeing in her mind's eye.

She stopped a foot away from him, both refusing to break eye contact for a second. Eva eventually did look at the state he was in. His hands and feet were bound, and he was dirty and scruffy. It was obvious to her that he had not been treated with any kindness since he arrived. She knew her brow was raised in question when she locked eyes with him again.

His own brow wrinkled in confusion, but they smoothed out and a small smirk appeared on his face. It was like he had his own private joke and Eva didn't know what it was.

"Yes? Is there something I can help you with?" he asked.

"Why are your feet and hands tied? Did you do something wrong?"

"What's it to you if I did or not? I obviously deserve this, or I wouldn't have them on." She got a sense that he was being sarcastic. He didn't think this conversation was worth his time. She looked around her and saw that he was given a wide berth. Well, it looked like he was being outcasted, but for what?

He was sitting on the floor with his back leaned up against the stone wall. His bound hands sat in his lap where he managed to cross his legs, even with his feet bound at the ankles. Eva stepped closer and he visible shifted not knowing exactly what she was up to. She decided to sit down and cross her legs just in front of him, with maybe a half a foot of space in between.

She settled there and looked back at him. "I don't believe that," she tried for a kind smile.

"Well, you would be the only one here." He looked skeptical, not sure of her motives. Well, she didn't even know her own motives.

Before she spoke again, she felt a little tug down her link from Jace. She turned her head and glanced over her shoulder to see that they were in position to lift the next boulder. She did the same thing as before, filled up her ability in her chest and sent it down the link. It was easier to do than last time, so she was able to quickly get back to the orange-aura man.

"You were supposed to meet me, except you never showed."

"What?" He obviously was confused.

"You were supposed to come to the Jebrow Stronghold, yet you never arrived. I had to leave to come find you." His eyes widened at her statement.

"That's impossible. I only went in the direction I was told."

"With the stars?"

"How would you know that? I haven't told anyone that." He was shocked and was getting a bit defensive too.

"I wasn't told by anyone. Anyway, what was the purpose of you seeking me out?"

"I thought I was to meet a man," he mumbled to himself. "She didn't say specifically, I just assumed it was a man and she didn't correct me. Was I wrong? No, there must be a mistake."

Eva stayed still while he made up his own mind about it. She waited patiently. She felt her eyes close briefly as she thought about the situation she was in and what her true purpose was for meeting this man.

Chapter 7
Impossible Healer

034

Number 034 was never approached by people in this group. He was shocked that this bold female would just waltz right up to him. Also, she didn't look bad with raven-colored hair and hazel eyes that seemed to change depending on how the light hit it, brown one second and green the next. She was quite stunning, long lithe limbs but toned. She was graceful, but he could tell that was more deadly grace then anything. Don't get on her bad side those arms screamed.

The more surprising part was that she didn't seem to be afraid. She plopped herself down right in front of him and started asking him strange questions. He was here for the One. That was what his journey was about. The crazy seer lady told him to follow the Point of Aster toward this prophesized person. He always assumed it was a man.

Here this young woman sat, knowing that he followed the stars looking for someone. If she knew that, then it was a possibility that she was who he was looking for. He didn't want to believe it. He knew he was mumbling to himself trying to get his mind set straight and she just sat there waiting, like she knew his mind was in turmoil.

What he wasn't expecting was the words that she said next. Because as soon as she started speaking, it was undeniable what he was witnessing.

In a monotone voice she spoke, "Fifteen will come, all will flee. Fifteen will continue to march, but to no avail will he capture thirty-four or even one. Fifteen is close and one will need strength. Close the wall, trap fifteen to later free fifteen." The eyes that stared at him were pure white. When her voice stopped, those eyes of hers blinked and were back to their original hazel color.

She looked at 034 waiting like she was before she started speaking. But his mouth hung open and the look of shock on his face made her brow furrow in concern. "What is it?" she asked him.

"You're a seer," he breathed out. Her eyes widened and she looked around them. No one seemed to be paying attention anyways, but it looked like she didn't want that knowledge out.

She leaned forward and quietly asked, "How do you know?"

"You just prophesized."

"I what?"

"You just stated a prophesy. Your eyes turned white, and you spoke." Now it was her turn for her mouth to hang open.

"Is that a common thing among seers?" she eventually asked in a small unsure voice.

"No. I've only seen it happen twice. Yours was the third time." He could see that she was thinking about this information. "You do know about visions, right?"

She waved her hand dismissing that. "Yes, I do have those."

"Is that why you said I was searching for you? You saw me in one of your visions?" She nodded her head in confirmation. Then that settled it. He was completely wrong. Well, he still had reservations that this was the One because she didn't have an aura. But that isn't right, because if she was a seer, she had to have ability, right? That meant she had to have an aura. He must have missed something in his learning.

"And what is a prophesy?" she asked.

"It is when a seer goes in a type of trance like state and speaks. It's actually very rare like I said. Some seers don't even have prophesies. It's believed that the Fates speak through seers."

"I didn't know that was possible." She was being genuine. He could tell she didn't know much about her own seer abilities. He could tell that it was one thing she didn't want people to know about by the looks she kept darting out among the others.

"Don't worry, I'm not going to say anything."

"You are asking me to trust you, not even really knowing who I am."

"I could try to guess, but all I know is that you are a *seer*," he whispered the word, "and you possible are the One. That is the person I am looking for, prophesized to bring down that bloody tyrant." He had no warm feelings toward Brosch. All of it was hate. Lots of hatred for what he did to him, but also the others he has captured over the years. No child should be stripped from their family and forced into a servitude that they do not believe in.

"You are a Healer?" she asked, helping him come back from his dark thoughts.

"And how did you know that?"

"Your aura," she smiled sweetly. So, she knew how to read auras. This just gets better and better. "My name is Eva." He couldn't help but smile back.

"It's a pleasure to finally meet you, Eva."

"And your name?" Yes, the dreaded name that he was given. It reminded him of his imprisonment. He didn't want to tell her, but it would be rude since she just gave him her name.

"Number 034."

Her brow furrowed in confusion. "That can't be right."

"I'm a numbered branded by Brosch. My number is 034." He tried to state it matter-of-factly, but he knew there was a small amount of venom in his words.

"How," she started but stopped suddenly and turned her attention to where the Elite men were moving the boulders. At least they were using their abilities productively, instead of just standing around being intimidating. 034 noticed a man with the Elite absent of an aura. He was looking in their direction with concern, but then his brow smoothed out with a nod of his head. Eva nodded back and he turned back to lift another boulder.

It was an interesting exchange. He'd have to keep his eye on that person who thought he could lift rocks with the Elites repeatedly. He's going to collapse at some point, just wait.

Eva turned back toward him, starting her question, and finishing it this time. "How is that possible? Branding someone? It seems barbaric."

"It is, see," he pulled his sleeve away from the inside of his wrist were the number 034 was burned into his skin. Her sharp inhale of breath was enough to make him want to cover it back up. But her eyes never left it and for some reason, he wanted to see what she did next.

Her hands slowly made their way across what little space separated them and she took his wrist in one hand and skimmed the mark with her thumb with the other, sending a slight shiver along his skin.

"I can fix this," she said barely above a whisper. Before he could ask what she meant, a sudden cooling sensation raced across his skin where her hands were. Impossible.

Eva

She didn't want to believe Mayor Jebrow. That was the first time she heard about the branding. But even though she didn't want to believe him, she knew it to be true. To see the branding on another's skin was enough to drag back those painful memories.

Eva was branded several times because she would heal the brands every time they applied one to her. It must have been her rebellious behave, even at that young of an age. That was the only thing she could do to show that she would not give in, that the hope she saw in her visions as she spent her hours in a dark, dank pit would eventually come true.

If she could make anything right by the man sitting in front of her was erase this mark that brought reminders and shame for what he was. No one should feel ashamed of who they are. She wanted to give this green-eyed man a piece of himself back. The first step was erasing this mark.

She could tell that it happened long ago and that the scarring was old. She remembered the sickening smell of burning flesh and the searing pain. She always healed hers and never seen what it looked like if she ever left it.

It was an ugly mark to be sure. They must have made sure there was ink that soaked into the skin to permanently show the mark black. She didn't know if she could heal an old wound, but she certainly could give it a try.

She felt the soft tendrils of her healing ability bubble up within her. This wound she had done before, but she knew she had to put a little more effort in because of the age of the wound and the ink. Once she started, she knew she couldn't stop until she was done, even when that familiar pain etched along her skin.

That was the price a Healer paid. Taking the pain inside oneself. Thankfully, this pain she remembered, not like Mayor Jebrow's pain. She'd think twice before attempting to cure the incurable again.

She felt the slight stinging in her own wrist, and she concentrated on removing the scarring and ink. She could feel the inky tendrils gravitate off his wrist and through her fingers that were held there. It was like the ink settled in her own wrist and the stinging was quite intense.

Eva released his hands and instinctively looked down at her own wrist. She never thought she'd see it again. That dreaded number. The ink from the man made its way to her own mark, but she wrapped her hand around her wrist with the mark and began to extract what seemed to be impossible to extract. Eventually, she was able to move the ink away from her wrist and inside that weird little hole that she locked the pain behind in. The number slowly faded until her wrist was smooth once again.

She inhaled and exhaled slowly as the door shut inside her on that pain. Stupid memories. She looked down at the man's wrist and she smiled. She did it. His mark was healed by her.

"There. Now you don't ever have to identify with that number again," she said and looked up into the man's wide eyes. His mouth was open again in shock. "Is something wrong?" Maybe he wanted it there. Some people liked reminders of their past to see what they overcame. She should have asked before she just assumed he didn't want to keep it.

"You were branded." Ah, he would have seen that. She thought it was only there for a second, but he must have been so intent on what she was doing to him that he caught it.

"A long time ago, but it's not something I talk about." He blinked his eyes, and he was muttering to himself again. He must do that a lot. Then a startling laugh escaped him, and a smile spread on his face.

"That's what she meant? Holy smokes this is unreal."

"What?" Eva was lost. He obviously was talking about something she didn't understand.

"She said that thirty-four would meet one. I thought she was talking about the One, mentioned in the prophesy, but she was talking about the Numbered 1. I didn't even know you existed."

"Seriously, what are you going on about?" She was lost.

"Brosch branded the Might children he took with a number. He branded us in order that we were taken. I was the 34th child he took. So, based on your brand, or the brand you had, you were the first." The first? She was the first one Brosch ever took? Her mind started to drift but the man in front of her kept talking.

"I heard that Number 1 was dead. No one ever saw who it was. They were kept in a secret place. It was assumed that because of Number 1, that's why he started collecting all the children. There was something about that first one that gave him the idea. With what I've seen with this healing, he wouldn't have used me the way he did."

Everything came rushing at her, the familiar smells of the tower, the long ride with a bag over her head, the rough hands holding her down branding her skin repeatedly and finally two dark eyes staring at her with a small snarl on his face while her mother lay dead at her feet with her eyes staring at nothing.

Anger, fear, sadness assailed her senses, and she grabbed her head. It was too much. The memories were too much, she didn't want to see it. She didn't want to see those beaded eyes again. He was the reason her life changed. He made her do it. He sent in guards, and they surrounded her. They were going to hurt her if she didn't hurt them first. It was the only way to survive.

She felt rough hands on her arms, and it sounded like listening through water as an angry, "What did you do?" made its way into her head.

"Nothing, I swear!" she heard a voice squeak out, probably fearful for his life.

"Eva," the muffled voice said soothingly. Those hands wrapped her up and her forehead touched the shoulder of a person. A familiar smell drifted into her nostrils, calming her scattered nerves. The memories were slowly receding.

She started to feel grounded. The fuzziness left her, and she began to relax into the only person she would trust with her life.

"Rest. I got you," Jace's rich voice floated into her and settled there. She could feel his strength and he was taking that emotional scarring into himself. She didn't want to burden him, but at that moment, when the last of those awful memories floated away, she was too tired to do anything. She succumbed to sleep, knowing she was safe cradled into the arms of her love.

Chapter 8
Mayor's Son

Jace

He was absolutely terrified over what he felt. Jace looked down at the now peaceful features of Eva. Her breathing was even, and her limbs were relaxed, unlike what he witnessed moments ago.

He was just getting ready to lift another rock with the Elite when a little speck of pain came down the link, but it was so faint and when he looked back toward Eva, she seemed fine, still talking with that strange red-haired man. Shaking off the feeling he approached the boulder, but then it assailed him like a horse and carriage running him over and dropped him to his knees.

He felt all this emotional turmoil down the link, and it almost broke him in half. When he did get his feet under him, he immediately made his way through the crowd of people that were staring at his weird antics, but he didn't care. He needed to get to Eva, she was hurting.

He was angry at first with the man, but he knew he would just have to deal with him later because Eva needed him. It took a few minutes but finally she let him take her pain. Such deep emotional scarring that he winced at it. What caused this? What was Eva thinking about?

Jace had so many questions, but in the end, it was best to just leave them for later. She needed his comfort and strength. That's what he gave her, just like she had been lending him her ability to lift the boulders.

He brushed her hair off her forehead, and he pressed a soft kiss there. He wasn't going to let her go right now. It didn't matter that people were now staring at them and he saw that crazy maroon-haired woman storm away, probably to go find Willow. It seemed like anything unusual that happened, they had to get the old seer involved.

Now that Eva was settled, he lifted his gaze from her face and up at the man she was just talking to. His eyes narrowed at him. He needed to stay calm for Eva, but he wanted to know what set her off. He would be the only one that saw it.

"What were you talking about?"

"Nothing, I swear," his gaze darted from Jace's face down to Eva's. "Just known facts about Brosch's stupid branding tactics. That's all." That couldn't have been all. Eva wasn't branded, so that couldn't have been it.

"Maybe that was part of it, but you had to have said something that had her lost in pain." The red-haired man shook his head side to side, not knowing what he possibly said that would start this.

The maroon-haired lady, what was her name, Ruby, led Willow through the now formed circle of people around them. The older lady looked at the scene with a frown, but she turned to the others and asked, "Isn't there work to be done? Nothing to see here. Get back to your posts." The people started to slowly peel away back to their respective areas, a few still glancing back maybe to not miss anything.

Willow knelt next to Jace and peered down into Eva's sleeping face. "Is she alright?" she asked.

"For now," Jace answered.

"I'm a little confused what she was doing over here though," her gaze drifted to the disheveled man with his wrists and ankles bound.

"What? You think it was my fault?" His eyes darted from hers to Ruby's where Jace could see a hint of red spread down closer to the man.

Ruby's stern expression and crossed arms made her slightly menacing. Her eyes narrowed at the man as she said, "I've been watching, and she wasn't around anyone else." A dark purple color mixed with the red and Jace realized it came from Willow while the red came from Ruby. Her gaze was on the red-haired man. His mouth formed in a grim line and his own orange pulsed against theirs. It was interesting to see and with Eva snuggled against him, he was probably seeing what she normally did. It was fascinating in a way.

"Tell us why she came over here," Willow's voice said with authority. The man winced like it was painful for him to stay quiet. It was like Willow was compelling him to speak. Interesting.

"To introduce herself." The man's face relaxed somewhat.

"Why would she do that?" His face twisted in pain again at Willow's question.

"Because she was the one I was seeking," he said through clenched teeth but his face relaxed. Both the red and purple colors receded, and Willow turned and looked back down at Eva with a little awe in her look.

"Eva?" Ruby said skeptically. "You believe that she's the One? From the prophesy?" That peaked Jace's interest.

"What prophesy?" Jace asked, looking between the three of them and finally settling his gaze on Willow who answered his question.

"Only the prophesy that has been told over and over for the last twenty years."

"Not quite twenty," he grumbled, knowing the exact date the prophesy was spoken. They must not have heard him because Willow continued.

"The prophesy speaks of a child of the Might that will save us all. The prophesy speaks about the One." He remembered what it said. It didn't quite word it like that and as a prophesy goes, it was lacking in detail.

"Yes, I assumed the seer said that I would meet the One, I thought she meant the One in the prophesy, but I think she was speaking about two different people," the bound man said thoughtful.

Willow narrowed her eyes at him. "Explain."

"Not going to force it out of me?"

"Would you like me to?" she asked in a wickedly sweet voice.

"Not particularly," he grumbled and continued before Willow could make him talk again. Is that what her ability was? Some sort of persuasion or something? "She was just introducing herself to me, like I said earlier and when it came to the subject of my name, well I answer

034 and that's when the whole branding conversation came up," he gestured toward me as a way of explanation to the state she was now in. But that didn't explain anything at all.

"That doesn't make sense," Jace said with narrowing eyes. He visibly saw this man gulp.

"Hold up, not finished. I showed her my branding because I think she didn't want to believe it, but as soon as she saw it," he lifted his sleeve and showed us his wrist. There was no mark of any kind on it. "She healed it."

Ruby stepped forward and grabbed his wrist roughly making him wince. She stared in shock at the empty skin. "Impossible," she muttered. "I've never heard of these marks being removable."

"They aren't," the man said. "Trust me, I've tried several times with my own ability and wasn't able to do what she did within seconds." He took his wrist back and rubbed the spot where Ruby grabbed him.

"Still doesn't explain why she ended up in this state," Jace growled out. His impatience was wearing thin.

"Okay, so in the process of this miraculous healing she was doing, she got a small side effect as most Healers get when they heal." Jace knew that. He felt her take his pain when he was cut. It drained her of most of her energy. That explains just the tiny amount of pain he felt a bit earlier from their link. "Apparently, her own brand came to the surface." What?

Jace gently lifted her wrist, not seeing anything, he checked the other and nothing was there either. What was he going on about? He raised his hands in a sign for them to wait for his explanation.

"She probably healed her mark from years ago and only she and the people that gave it to her ever saw it. But I saw a remnant of it. She was a Numbered." Jace remembered his father telling him how she was found close to Brosch's land. They were all confused because she wasn't branded, but that's the thing. She had been branded and because of her ability she was able to erase that mark from her skin.

"Which you might not find this significant, but I do," the man continued, "she is number one. The first child with Might he took. Hence, maybe the prophesy I was told was talking about the Numbered 1 and not the One or maybe she was talking about both, I don't know. No prophesy ever makes sense."

"Yes, the prophesy you heard was a bit strange," Willow agreed with him. "It seemed like the One and the Child were two separate people, but that the Child would become One."

"You see? I'm glad I'm not the only person confused by that."

"What is the significance of being the first child taken by Brosch?" Jace asked.

"It's not widely known what started Brosch's crazy jaunt around the country to snatch up children with the Might," the orange-aura man continued to explain. "We Numbered heard bits and pieces, and one rumor was because the first child he took was so special that he had to take the others."

"And you're saying that Eva was the first? She is somehow special," Jace could hear in Ruby's voice that she didn't believe a word this man said.

"I'm just telling you the rumors," he shrugged. "I also heard that Number 1 also died, so you can see that rumor was wrong."

Willow stood and looked between the man and Eva considering his words. Her gaze rose to Jace's. Her light blue eyes studied him before she asked, "What is your relationship with Eva?"

"Um," that wasn't what he was expecting. They weren't in a relationship, not that he didn't want one with Eva, he just hasn't really asked if she feels the same, even though sometimes he thinks she does with the way he can tell through the link.

Willow's smirk suggested she knew where his mind wandered to. "How do you know Eva?" she suggested instead.

"Oh, well, she was adopted into our family."

"So, like a sister?" she suggested.

"Um, maybe to some of my family members, but no, not a sister." He was pretty sure he never felt for his sisters the way he felt for Eva.

"How did she end up with your family?" He didn't know how Eva would feel about this, but if it cleared up who she really was, then maybe he could finally take her back to her family.

"A few good men found her in an old watch tower in Obern Forest."

"That's the one near Brosch Stronghold?" Ruby asked from behind Willow.

"Yes. The men were on a scouting mission. I believe you know one of the men. Mayor Newly." Willow nodded her head in acknowledgment. "Well, Newly and Mayor Holds rescued her from the tower. Both men were young and didn't know exactly what to do with a little girl, so they asked if my father could take care of her."

"Who's your father?" Willow asked.

"Mayor Jebrow."

"Wait," Ruby stepped up beside Willow with a startling look on her face, "Are you saying you're a mayor's son?"

"I am. I'm Jace Jebrow," he confirmed.

"Interesting to find a future mayor roaming around the country," Willow commented.

"My father is a good man, and he knew I had to leave to find out the truth with this prophesy. It was driving him and my mother with worry. Eva was just tagging along. I didn't think that her history would be brought up in all of this."

"Well, at least one piece of the puzzle is solved on who she is and why Brosch found her so special," Willow mentioned.

"Really Willow, what is so special about a Healer?" Ruby asked with a little venom behind her words and a sharp glare toward the other man listening in.

"It's not the fact that she is a Healer, it's that no one would know because she doesn't project her aura. That's something I've only heard of one man who could do it and he's not around anymore to really ask what he did. Of course, we all knew what his ability was, just like we know Eva's, but no one that was close to her would know." What they all didn't know was that she wasn't just a Healer. But Jace wasn't going to offer up that knowledge.

Jace felt the eyes of the man on him, studying him like he was some interesting looking bug that needed to be dissected. It was quite unnerving.

"Some specialty," Ruby mumbled.

"Now, we will leave you and go set up a spot for you to settle Eva in while she rests," Willow suggested. "Ruby and I will be right back." Before Ruby could respond she was yanked away. That left Jace, Eva and the other man.

"So," he began, "a mayor's son." Jace could see a little bit of hatred shine out of the man's eyes. It wasn't something he hadn't seen before. People believed he was entitled and Jace understood he had it better than others. He wasn't going to lord that knowledge over people though.

"You got a problem with that?"

"No, no. Not at all." Jace didn't believe that of him. "I am assuming you and Eva are close though."

"Why do you ask?"

"Well, if your family raised her, then you had to have noticed her, other attributes?"

"Meaning?"

The man leaned forward and, in a voice barely audible said, "A seer."

"She told you this?" Why would Eva say something to this man? Who was he to gain her trust?

"I don't think she could help it. Especially since she had no control over the prophesy she uttered."

"Another one?"

"Huh? What do you mean by another one?" Now his eyes sparkled with interest rather than hate. Jace would have to figure that out later.

"What did she say?"

"Oh, something about fifteen will come but we'll all get out," the man shrugged it off.

"That couldn't have been all of it."

"Fine, if I remember it was something like fifteen will come, all will escape. And then, fifteen won't even capture thirty-four or even one, person," he paused and was thinking. He looked down for a second and then back up. "Fifteen is coming, not are coming. That is what she said. She wasn't talking about how many people; she was talking about who."

"What are you going on about?" Jace didn't know what this man was blabbing.

"When she said Fifteen, she meant Number 15. Oh, this is not good," the man groaned.

"What's not good?"

"If Brosch sent 15, we are in for some trouble."

Chapter 9
Heritage

Eva

She opened her eyes slowly and looked around herself. Oh great, she was back at the Station. Eva was so not in the mood for this place right now.

She sat up slowly from the bench and looked around in the white abyss, if that can be an abyss color. Maybe only here at the Station was that a thing.

"Oh," someone exclaimed next to her which made her jump a little, until she recognized who it was.

"Seraphim?" The blonde woman lifted her gaze and then a smile broke over her face.

"Eva, so good to see you."

"Yes, it hasn't been long though, has it?"

"Maybe not for you, but it has for me."

"What do you mean?" Eva asked.

"When was the last, yes, I think it was three years ago now? Yes, that's about right."

"How is that possible?" It was weird just seeing Seraphim not even twenty-four hours ago and it's been three years for her? I guess that is possible, but still.

"You should have learned anything is possible, as long as you believe," her smile was so sweet, like she knew exactly what she was talking about.

"Okay, well how has been the last three years then?"

"Oh, same old same old. Settled in a small farming community. They love having me around, ever since I saved that boy's leg last year."

"What do you do there?"

"I'm the community Healer now. I tried to keep that a little secret, but I couldn't help it! I can't sit by and watch when I can truly be helpful, you know?" That was fascinating to learn that she was a Healer.

It made a kind of sense though. Eva felt that she related to this woman in more ways than just being related by blood. Eva had so many questions.

"You do look a little older," Eva commented.

"Really?" her eyebrow rose.

"I mean, not that it's a bad thing. I just can tell that you are more, I don't know, you just don't feel as young."

"I shouldn't be shocked by that. Of course, I am older, but you hardly look different from the last time I saw you. You are even wearing the same outfit I think."

"It's not even been a day."

"Oh," her expression grew serious.

"Is that bad?"

"No," she waved it off. "It's just a little surprising that you are seeing me so soon. That shouldn't happen like that usually. Unless you are under a great deal of stress." She looked at her in concern.

"Yes, a little. We are still in the mountains. I followed you all the way up where you exited, but it looks like there was a cave in at some point and now we are stuck there moving large rocks around. Everyone is on edge because they think the enemy will still find the passageway and get through."

"Oh dear. I am so sorry about the cave in. I really didn't know it was there."

"It's not your fault. You did help though, and I do appreciate it."

"I'm glad."

"I know our last encounter was brief, but do you know why I am able to connect with you?"

"That is an easy answer for me." She was in a lovely yellow dress that made her sparkle like sunshine. Her hazel eyes seemed to match in whatever shade they were in against the dress' flowery design. She moved closer and gathered Eva's hands in hers. "We are seers. And not only seers but relatives. Only another seer can speak like this with another relative. The last time you saw me was the first time for me, but since then I've gotten used to this Station and now know exactly what it is."

"Wait, I still don't get it."

"It doesn't matter where we are in history right now. Relative seers can speak across time. Just two weeks ago I spoke with a young version of my grandmother. She was so adorable when she was twelve."

"That's, amazing." Eva never heard of this, but then again, she didn't know much in the ways of seers. "And having prophesies is a thing seers do too, right?"

"Yes, but not every seer. I haven't had one, at least that I know of. I live alone and someone would have to be there to hear my prophesy. I don't think the Fates would be that cruel."

"But, why can't I remember saying it? I only remember the visions I have."

"You know, I have no idea why it's like that, it's just always been that way."

"Do you know a lot about seers?"

"Are you kidding? I am descended from the greatest seer couple in all of history."

"Wait, did you just say couple?" Eva couldn't have heard her right. If she said couple, then that means there was a man that was a seer. That can't be right, all seers are woman.

"My grandmother used to tell me the story. It seems almost like a fairy tale, but if you really thought about it, it made a lot of sense. Think about the Fates. Gods that decide for us what our lives will be like on this world."

"That doesn't sound like fun." Eva didn't want anyone telling her what she was going to do, let along map out her whole life. Didn't she have a say in it? Seraphim continued.

"Well, the Fates realized that they were having a terrible time communicating with the people in this world. It was tedious for them to drag them to the Station every time. So, the Fates thought on it and they gifted the world seers. They were to speak for the Fates."

"That's crazy."

"I know! When I first heard it, I thought that a Fate would inhabit my body or something, but grandmother reassured me that when a seer is speaking a prophesy, that is one of the Fates speaking." That was hard for Eva to wrap her head around, but I guess it made a little sense since Fate already knew what would happen in the world.

"And visions?"

"Also from the Fates, but those are more to see what the people will choose when presented with what the possible future could hold."

"I hate them sometimes. To have to make the choice." Seraphim nodded her head in understanding.

"Yes, sometimes it's tough to make that decision. But, back to the story." Seraphim wasn't easily waylaid. Eva smiled about that. "One special girl and one special boy were gifted this ability. Of course, they didn't know this, but they were born on the same exact day and the same exact time. Only that one was born in the northern country and one in the southern country. They didn't know the other existed, not until much later when rumors started to develop. Like all rumors, sometimes you're curious as to see if it is real."

"I just try to ignore them."

"But something led you to be where you are today, right?"

"I guess you're right." Jace was chasing after the rumor of this prophesy. Not that it didn't happen, just that he needed answers, which Eva realized she didn't know what Jace's questions regarding the prophesy were.

"So, the young boy, now is a man, and heard about this young woman who could tell what will happen and see people's lives far in the future."

"Seers can see in the past too, right?"

"More in the future than the past. It's only up to the Fates whether the past is relevant or not to be seen."

"Makes sense." That's why they sent a vision of the mountains to Eva. To show her that there was another way out and that the mountains were thriving at one point in history.

"So, after hearing this, he was curious and went searching for this young woman. He traveled all the way up through the land to find this woman that supposedly had similar abilities to him. Of course, you could guess what happened next."

"He found her?"

"Yep. And he instantly fell in love with her at first sight. Since they were the only two of their kind, it was only natural that they were together."

"That's such a beautiful story." True love. Eva wasn't romantic, but it was a very good story.

"I'm not even finished yet," Seraphim laughed. "Well, of course they found out all about each other, even sharing a day of birth. And yes, they married and had ten beautiful daughters, each of them gifted with the ability of a seer."

"Well yeah, both parents were seers, which makes sense. Wait, they had no sons?"

"Nope. I don't know why that was, but that is the only male seer that I have heard of was from the fairy tale. Do you have any in your time?"

"No, not that I know of. Most anyone that does have any ability has been snatched up or is in hiding."

"That's so sad to hear. We were revered once for the powers we held as the Fates' speakers."

"So, what happened to the two seers?"

"Like any one stuck on this world, they eventually died. Probably in each other's arms. But the point is, that each family in the Wedset mountains can trace their heritage back to one of the ten daughters."

"And in turn back to the original seers?"

"Yes. So, you can say all seers are related in a way, but after being diluted down so much, only close relatives are able to speak as we are speaking."

"But I don't remember my family and I've never met you before."

"Yes, that is such a mystery. But I just attributed it to the Fates. Who else could make this possible?" She was a little right. They were talking at the Station, and it seemed that they were the ones who created this place. Well, it is nice to know at least one person from her family, even though that person must be long gone. Eva wasn't going to think about that right now.

Seraphim let go of her hands and stood and stretched. "As lovely as it was to see you, I had fallen asleep in a field on a short nap, but there were clouds on the horizon. I feel if I don't return soon, I'll probably end up in a rain shower."

"Do you think we will meet again?"

"I'm counting on it Eva. Whenever I see you, it reminds me of what is in store for my future."

"Really. What's that?"

"Well, you are of my blood. So, I won't be alone forever now, will I? The only way you can be of my blood, is if I have a child. I hope that I can tell you when next we meet if the child I am meant to have is as lovely as I imagine she will be."

"I didn't know I gave you that hope."

"If there is no hope, then what do we have left? We cannot live without it or we will just be lost to the darkness." Eva knew exactly what that feeling was. "Until we meet again. Goodbye Eva." Seraphim turned and walked off into the whiteness, fading away.

"Bye Seraphim," Eva called after her. It probably was time that she got back as well. She knew a certain someone was waiting for her.

Chapter 10
Found Out

015

"Sir, we've checked every hall and cavern in this place. It seems like there is a lingering of Might use, but there has not been a single person found."

"Recheck all locations that had stronger readings of Might use. They couldn't have gone far."

"Right away sir," the man dressed in a standard black tunic and pants with Brosch's symbol blazoned on the left breast bowed sharply and turned in the other direction away from him.

Number 015 stood surveying once again the space around him. His sole purpose in life was to be the best Tracker for his master. He knew of no other in the country with this ability.

If he failed now, he was sure death would await him. Master would see to it that he would perish, just like all the others. 015 didn't want to die, yet.

His ability allowed him to see like the hounds they trained, only better, since the Chasers didn't know what the hounds were sensing. 015 could see the little wisps of ability in the air. He could see the paths they took. Only issue here was the group that was here, the Ren, had been here awhile, so a lot of the paths intersected and were mixed up. He needed to hone in on the paths that were brighter, hoping those would lead him to where they had gone. There was something else in this mountain, he was sure of it.

His blonde-white hair hung low in his eyes. He knew others shrank away from him because of his eyes. Pitch black, like a spark-less pit. It was what endeared him to his master. He had no other memories before knowing him. He was raised in close corridors of people that were somewhat like him, but none of them really were. They did not understand what he was capable of.

015 caught onto a particular group of auras that seemed to have traveled together toward a similar location. Based on the direction, it seemed unlikely that many would go in this seemingly useless tunnel leading to nowhere. He was curious, nonetheless.

He traveled from the magnificent hall of pillars to the hallway that was determined by some Chasers earlier that it only led to small rooms. He moved along this path, still taking in the stone walls around him and the hard ground beneath his feet. Such a marvel that man had carved rock to create these tunnels and rooms.

He continued in the dark, not really needing light to see. That was his anomaly, more than any other Tracker recorded in history. Day or night, he had clear vision. This allowed him to sneak up to groups of people in the dark without their knowledge. It was helping him right now because shadows can offer details that are missed in the light.

The Chasers were correct, that the hall did lead to just a few small rooms. This hall ended with no room on the end. 015 found that strange. Over the last half hour, he walked other halls and tunnels that had a room on the end. There were only two others that did not. Design flaws? He didn't think so.

The aura signatures seemed to end abruptly at the wall. He stopped and placed a hand on the wall, wondering what was so special about this one that several people came to. His gaze took in the dark spaces, and he looked above him and below. There, he almost missed it.

There was a faint red signature coming from the ground. He knelt where the red was and skimmed the ground lightly. He realized it was a seam that the red was on the other side of the wall. Which meant, this was a false wall and he just found where they all went. Now he had to figure out how to move this wall. He let his fingers trail over the surface of the wall and down the sides of it. He didn't know what, if anything, he would find.

A Chaser approached with a torch. Idiot Chaser. He didn't know how much the light changed everything for 015. This could cause him to have to start his whole process over.

"Sir, our search is almost complete. What are our next orders?"
015 glared at the guard while silently thinking. What will they do next? As
he was going to look back at the blocked passage, his gaze landed on
something. He would have missed it, if he were anyone else, but there
was a slight indenture in the wall. Strange, since most all the walls were
very well crafted and smoothed stone. Why would someone deliberately
put a divot in an otherwise flawless wall?

He reached out and touched the area. He put a slight amount of
pressure and the stone moved under his touch. The depression caused
the wall to move and the path that was so clearly blocked before was
now open to him. He stepped up to the opening, and there as a blaring
light to him, was the signature of a red aura.

"Gather the men in the great hall of pillars. We will soon be
heading into the bowels of the mountain, to retrieve and destroy."

Jace

He brushed a small strand of dark hair off her forehead as she was
dreaming. Jace could tell that Eva left again. It was the weirdest feeling,
one minute feeling her relaxed state, and then nothing the next. The only
indication at this point that he knew she was alive was because she was
still breathing.

They were getting close. Just a few more large boulders and there
will be a clear path out of the mountain. Crazy red-haired guy believed
we'd make it, maybe. He kept ranting on about this legendary Tracker
that Brosch had. He never disobeyed Brosch's orders, and that meant he
had no sympathy for his fellow Might people.

Jace never met a Tracker before and at this point, being in a
mountain that had the best on his heels, he didn't want to meet him.
Someday, but not today.

Jace moved another six boulders, but without the boosts from Eva, he was done. The Elite weren't expecting him to do so many in the first place, so at least he earned a little respect from the guys.

He shouldn't be enjoying his time, but, when around Eva, especially with her in his arms, how could he not? It was like everything else just drifted away and it was just her and him. His fingers traced her brow and down her cheek to the soft curve of her jaw. Her skin was so warm and soft. He couldn't help that his eyes drifted to the pair of pink lips slightly parted in sleep.

Jace had to admit he was hungry to taste her again. The first time really wasn't a real kiss, especially since it was more panic-based, and she wasn't breathing. And, that whole episode led to this connection they had now. Not that he didn't want the connection, it just didn't feel as solid as it should be. Well, that was something else to explore later, for now he just wanted to look at this peacefully sleeping beauty.

He then felt joy and relief flood into him from the link. Eva was back from wherever she went. He had to prod her a little more about that. That was the second time that had happened recently, and he wasn't too excited about it. He waited and very soon her lush lashes opened, and hazel eyes stared into his blue-green ones.

A small smile tugged at the corner of her mouth, and she sighed and snuggled in closer. Well then. He could get used to this.

"How long was I out?" her soft voice asked him. His one arm was under her where he was able to stroke that long hair of hers down her back and the other rested on her hip.

"Oh, about four hours or so."

Her eyes widened, "Four hours? How could I have slept so much?"

"It wasn't that much Eva. You needed it," he cupped her face to make sure her eyes stayed on his. "Did you go somewhere again?" His hand dropped down to play with some loose threads on her shoulder.

"You can tell?"

"Of course, I can tell. It's like this void in the link. You never explained to me earlier. I do remember you saying it wasn't a dream."

"I was at the Station," she said softly, with a hint of awe in her voice.

"Never heard of it."

"Supposedly it's where sparks meet? I don't know how it works or if other people can use it. With me being a, you know, I don't know if it's just because of that or if others can as well."

"It sounds like a very interesting place."

"It's all white anywhere you look and other people, well, technically sparks, just pop up out of nowhere. I don't know if you'd like it. It really is devoid of all color." He chuckled, making her move with his laugh which in turn had her smirking. He would do anything to keep that smile on her face.

Jace's eyes zeroed in on that smirk, noticing those lips of hers again. Why did he have to be so fascinated with them? His thumb grazed the soft curve of her bottom lip and her eyelids fluttered in response. He could feel her need start to grow through the link. This searing heat that scorched its way straight into his own need. He leaned in to finally lay claim to the only woman he wanted for a long time.

"They're coming!" a frantic voice dragged his attention away at just that moment. What the heck was going on? Eva also turned toward the person with a questioning look on her face. Great, he lost the moment.

He let Eva get up, even though he just wanted her to stay in his arms. He decided to drag himself up too and followed her over to where the frantic Elite was talking with Willow.

He caught the tail end of the conversation as he and Eva approached.

"It won't be long, and they'll be upon us."

"Are you certain?" Willow asked.

"Yes," the Elite answered sternly.

"What's happening?" Eva asked as they approached. Willow held up a finger to indicate to wait a moment and turned back to the Elite.

"Tell the Elites at the exit to get those last couple boulders moved. Then notify Ruby to plan to evacuate immediately. We need to get ready for a battle." The Elite nodded and moved off doing Willow's bidding. She slowly turned to them with a tired expression on her face.

"My scouts confirmed that there is a group of Brosch's cronies headed in this direction. Somehow, they found the secret passage."

"How can that be?" Eva asked, not believing that it was possible.

"I don't know, but what I do know is that we got to get out of here. I suggest you make a move for your things and help others as well," Willow moved off, looking every bit the leader the Ren's thought she was.

Jace didn't understand. Didn't that red-haired guy say that in Eva's prophesy they would escape? Well, he did say something about this extremely good Tracker, so maybe this was the trouble he was talking about. He needed to go find him.

Jace grabbed Eva's hand, "Come on. We need to get information." He stomped toward the bound man. At first Eva was a bit confused, but then understanding bled down the link.

He stopped in front of him and as the man looked up, he startled a bit, probably because Jace had a very determined look on his face. It was probably the 'I'm going to kill you' face. He never looked good when he was angry. He let go of Eva's hand and hauled the man to his feet and demanded, "Tell me everything of Eva's prophesy."

"Okay, okay," he choked out. Jace didn't realize he was practically cutting off his air supply until a gentle hand landed on his arm. He looked over into hazel eyes and her look of, be calm there big man, that's when he relaxed his grip on the man's shirt and eventually released him.

He shrugged his shoulders and stepped as far away as he could get, which at this point was right up against the wall. "She said that we will escape."

"What else? There must be more to it."

"Yes, yes there was." He was panicky, but he continued with his hands up pleading for Jace to wait. "She said something about one using strength, yes that was it. Using strength to close the wall. Yep, close the wall and trap fifteen, which I assume is Number 15, a formative Tracker. The only known one in the country."

What the heck did that mean? Why did prophesies have to be so confusing? Can't they ever be straight forward?

Eva grabbed Jace's upper arm, which caused him to sharply look over at her. She thought of something, and he could feel her un-sureness through the link.

"You've thought of something?" he asked.

"What if I do my thing? You know that force thing?"

"You think you can?" That was a lot to move at once. A lot. She couldn't do it on her own.

That's it. She needed strength and because of the link, he could probably send his to her to use to move that many boulders all at once. Yeah, he was not liking what he was figuring out in his head.

"It's the only way," she said with determination in her voice. "I feel like I led those cronies here and I can't let anything happen to these people." She would sacrifice herself. He could feel it.

He held her head softly in his hands, "Don't do anything stupid. Like, without me. Got it?" She smiled that smirk of hers and an eye roll.

"Got it, bossy." She batted his hands away. "I'll go get our stuff and start helping others outside. I'll be waiting just on the other side of the exit." He nodded and she was off to do just what she said she would.

Jace turned his attention back to the man, who flinched as Jace's gaze took in his appearance. This man couldn't escape like that. He released the small dagger behind his back and approached the man.

"Please no," the man pleaded as soon as he saw the weapon. Without warning he grabbed the man's bound wrists and a startled squeak sounded out of the man as Jace brought his dagger down and cut the ropes.

The man had his eyes closed and was confused for a second. Jace bent down and did the same to his bound feet. As he stood the man looked down at his wrists in shock and back up to Jace.

"There's only one thing you will do." Jace's commanding voice washed over the terrified man. "If either I or Eva need healing, you will heal." The man's eyes got large, and he tried to say something, but Jace just wanted confirmation that he would do it, "Understood?"

"Yes," the man nodded vigorously.

"Go, help some others along the way and be close by." The man didn't need to respond, he immediately went to it.

Jace moved toward the exit, helping people as he went, urging them to hurry out of the exit. He saw the last boulder being moved out of the way and as soon as the path was clear, a stream of people, as quickly as they could, made their way out. They were able to clear a small path out, so at the most two at a time could leave. He just hoped that everyone would make it out, just like Eva said in her prophesy.

As he made his own way to the exit, he heard plans from the Elites about the formation they would take once outside. It was ideal for them since this was a small opening so that the enemy could only come at them two at a time.

He made it out in the bright sunlight. He shielded his eyes with his big arm to let his eyes adjust. He guessed by the sun's position it was already past mid-day. He looked around him and watched as the Elite took their positions and the others moving beyond them to some semblance of safety.

Jace looked and searched until his gaze locked with the tall dark-haired beauty. Eva looked all warrior and grace. Not many women would break the norm and wear slacks, but hers melded to her like a second skin. Her hands were on her hips as she continued to stare at the hole in the mountain that the Ren were currently leaving through.

As he made his way to her, Willow also came from the left to them.

"I take it there is some other plan in that head of yours Eva," Willow surmised. Not at all angry, she could just tell there was something brewing in that mind of hers.

"I do. I know it's hard to believe this, but, I'm going to close the exit."

"What?" Willow's disbelief was evident.

"I don't expect you to understand it right not Willow. But you will. Trust me, us," Eva indicated toward Jace, "to keep you safe. We fought with you once against Brosch's men. Let us do this."

"Alright." Jace was a little shocked that Willow would step down and let us do this. She must have heard something in Eva's voice to know that this was it. She nodded toward Jace and moved back amongst her troops where he heard her shouting orders.

"I need to know when the last person is through," Eva said as he sided up beside her.

"Not many more. Two Elites stayed until the end. Once they come through, we will know we can start."

"I'll need some of that strength of yours. Think you can handle that?"

"Of course, I can. You doubt me?" he raised an eyebrow at her.

"Never," she said with such trust, he was so close to just pulling her toward him and making her not look serious, like she was right now. He reached down and linked their fingers, getting ready to send her his strength.

"Um, Jace."

"Yes?"

"One small hand contact is not going to do it."

"Okay, what are you needing?" It confused him what exactly she was going to try and do.

"I need a lot all at once, and I don't think just one skin to skin contact is going to do it."

"Oh. So, how do you suggest I, um, touch you?" He didn't know if that was the right wording, but there was no other way to put it.

"Stand behind me." He released her hand and took up his spot behind her. Luckily, he had almost half a foot on her so he could see over her head toward the hole in the mountain. "I'd like to make sure my hands are free. I can concentrate the energy or whatever out of my two appendages since that's usually how I've done it in the past."

"Alright, so if I can't hold your hands, where exactly do I hold you?"

"My hips?" she shrugged. Or, for all that is sacred! She wanted his hands on her *bare* hips. She did say skin to skin, so it had to be under her clothes.

"They'll be watching," he murmured, indicating the Ren crowd around them.

"I don't care right now," she snapped. "All I care about is helping them, so unless you think I can do it on my own," she let the sentence hang.

"Absolutely not. You could kill yourself trying this. I'm *not* losing you."

"Then do it already." Jace placed his hands on her hips and felt where her tunic hung over the waistband. He raised it slightly until he felt her smooth skin underneath. Well, instead of her hips, his hands ended up around her waist, but it should work.

"You might as well just embrace me Jace. Your arms on my stomach will help." He stepped closer, her bottom pressing into him as his arms wrapped around her front under her top. He couldn't help it. He let his lips touch the side of her head above the ear and gave her a small kiss.

"Jace, don't distract me," she groaned.

"Me distract you? I'm blaming you this time because it was your idea." As he tried calming his racing nerves, he glanced at the mountain exit and saw the two Elites step out. This was it. Time to get that closed.

"That's your cue Eva. Get it done."

"So bossy," she mumbled. It just made him smile.

He felt the link that she was in complete focus. Her hands were held at her sides, palms facing out. He could imagine her eyes were closed while she was concentrating. With their skin to skin contact he could feel this draw toward the center of her, like she was building and storing up a massive energy ball.

"I need more Jace," she softly said. He concentrated, trying to imagine gathering up his strength like she did, but it was hard for him to visualize it.

"I don't know if I'm doing it correctly," he admitted.

"You're fine," she gritted her teeth, "Just think about giving me strength. Think about moving the boulders like before. Visualize that." So, he did. He thought about how it felt to lift those rocks with his own ability. That was all Jace, and no one helped him accomplish that.

He saw a flash of movement inside the mountain. They were coming. "Any time now Eva," he encouraged.

"Just another second," she said breathlessly. "Concentrate." He did, but he was still worried about it. It seemed like they were going to come through.

"Concentrate!" she grumbled. Fine, okay, back on task. He closed his eyes. *Strength. Strength for Eva. Eva needs this. Take it Eva.* He chanted in his head.

"Eva!" Willow shouted from the side causing Jace to open his eyes to see a glimpse of a figure start to emerge. But then his sight wavered as a massive tug took his breath away. He held onto Eva in front of him as he felt the pull of his strength. As one big, massive energy released, it felt like someone yanked the life out of his body. It physically hurt. He didn't recognize the loud deep scream that escaped him. He collapsed to his knees breathing heavily.

As he was trying to get back to what he was doing, he looked down to see who he had a hold of. What was he doing just a moment ago? It's like that energy sucked away his thoughts too. Eva was there, slumped against his chest, limp.

That made him panic a little. Still out of breath, he gently placed his fingers on the pulse in her neck. He waited and tried to even his breathing so he could feel it. There it was. Eva's pulse. She was still alive. He looked in front of him at the mountain. Nothing indicated that a hole was even there. She did it. Eva closed it.

He wasn't paying attention to anything other than getting back to his feet. It was hard and he was a little wobbly. He did feel like a thousand pairs of eyes were boring into the back of his skull.

Willow stepped up to him. He could tell she was in shock. It was like she didn't know what to say. He decided to put everyone at ease because he figured everyone was listening at this point.

"She's fine. Let's get out of here while we can." Willow blinked and nodded. She turned away and started making orders for the group to start moving west.

Jace tried steadying himself and finally looked behind him, seeing many awed expressions. They probably hadn't seen anything like that before. But now Eva was exposed. She knew it would happen if she did this. She wasn't just a Healer as they suspected. The Elites and others slowly peeled away from their staring and started moving to the west, just like Willow said.

Jace started that way too, carrying Eva. Of course, she was passed out, which he figured would happen with the amount of her own energy as well as his that she used. He staggered a few times, even landing on his knee to catch his breath. Was he even going to make it?

A hand landed on his left shoulder and a warmth spread down into him. His breathing lightened up and he felt a small amount of energy seep back into his muscles. The hand receded and he stood again, stronger this time.

He looked and saw the red-haired man, still looking deathly afraid of him, but a small glow of deep orange surrounded him. He healed Jace just enough for him to be able to care for Eva. He was grateful to the frightened man, who just nodded and moved past him to indicate his job was done.

Oh, it was far from over for that man.

Chapter 11
Using the Numbered

Brosch

He looked out at the expanse of yard where his men trained. They were all pathetic. All the trainers were Warriors and a few of the fighters, but most of the fighters were just regular men. Nothing special about them. Maybe that's why Brosch saw them as incompetent.

The sun glared down on the yard, making it hot and sticky. Just being close to the Hassin Desert made everything hotter in the summer months, even though his stronghold was technically in the forest. Well, at least it's only hot during mid-day. Blessedly, the evening will be cool.

As he watched the pitiful training routine, thinking on what he could do to motivate them, a messenger arrived though the yard in a straight line toward him. It didn't take a genius to know who the message was for. The bedraggled man stopped a couple feet away from Brosch and bowed to one knee waiting for Brosch to acknowledge his presence.

"What is it messenger?" he asked in a bored voice.

The man stood shakily to his feet. Brosch snorted at the man's lack of confidence. "A message was just received by crow." The man held the bound scroll outstretched. Brosch took the scroll. He waved at the messenger to dismiss him, and the man bowed once more and took off the direction he came.

Brosch was curious. He had several spies that were trained and the fastest way to get a message to Brosch was by bird. Each spy chose which bird, and he had a few that chose crows. He unbound the scroll and read its contents.

It was from his spy in Craggs Stronghold. Apparently, a large group of people passed south in the open fields through the night and have settled in the southern portion of Kretz Swamp. The spy supposes they are the Ren and the evidence that his Tracker, 015, arrived at Craggs Stronghold late this morning only collaborates his suspicions.

Interesting. What did that old witch say again? That's right, she said something about seeing *her* on his way to Nertman Stronghold. Looking back at the spy's information, he now had an excuse to visit Mayor Nertman. If he remembered correctly, the current mayor just ascended not too long ago. Well, letting renegades into his territory and not doing anything about it was a perfect opportunity for Brosch to set the young mayor straight.

"Onyx!" he called to his mountain of a guard while tucking the scroll into his vest jacket.

"Yes sir?" Onyx strode over and lowered his eyes in respect. Even though his guard could certainly beat Brosch by sheer strength, the man was loyal only to him, and because of that was his personal one-man guard. No one got through Onyx.

"Get my escort ready. I will leave in two hours for Nertman Stronghold." His guard nodded curtly and walked off to do his bidding. Brosch continued to stand there, watching his men train and thinking about seeing that girl again.

Of course, it's been years since he's seen her. How old was she now? A young woman. His brow scrunched as he tried to remember what she looked like. Shoot! That was a problem. Unless…

He turned from the training yard and into his keep. It was one of the oldest strongholds in the country and was built to withstand any attack. Unlike some strongholds where there were many windows and openness to their keeps or homes, his was nothing like that. The keep was dark, and the stone walls were thick. Natural light only filtered through tiny cross-holes, which were present for various archers to shoot though if the keep were under attack.

Who would attack him? It was a death sentence to be sure. He reached the main hall that boasted a large fireplace opposite the entrance with spiral stairs on either side leading up and down. Off to the left was a raised dais where a large chair sat behind a wide table. Below the dais were two long tables with benches.

He could still remember when he was young sitting at the end of the dais table looking at his father in the large ornate chair, drinking and laughing with his people. Fool that he was, not taking the country for himself when he had the chance. He was too drunk most of the time to see the potential this country had. Why have several separate groups, these strongholds, and not have one person above them all?

The hall sat empty, as was usual. When Brosch ascended to mayor, there were no longer large gatherings of people in his keep, if the layer of dust on the tables and benches were any indication. He passed by the dilapidated surroundings and entered the stairwell that led down into the depths of his keep.

Some would call him sinister, and it didn't bother him. His dark wild hair and sharp features helped accentuate his ruthlessness. His dark brown eyes could be mistaken as black at times. Apparently, it reflected his spark, well, if that was the case, then he was all right with that.

He reached the bottom and looked out among the large, dank area. This is where his precious Numbered slept. Most had access to the stronghold and were given tasks to complete. Yes, he had some attempt to escape but they were either dragged back or slaughtered. Well, until recently, he never had a problem with anyone getting passed his Chasers. It was just a fluke that 034 was able to get off his land. That will not be an issue soon with his best Tracker after him.

He walked toward the end, past the straw mats strewn about the floor to where a few cells sat. It was originally a dungeon after all. It wouldn't be called one if he didn't have cells and those cells had people in them. These housed the Numbered who stepped out of line. Many have died in these cells. If they died, to him that meant they were nothing and the ones that lived, well, even though he constantly had issues with them, they were meant to live for a reason.

Brosch stopped outside the second cell and there sitting cross-legged on the straw mat was 027. She was a little older when she was taken, much too old for his liking. He almost killed her when she was found. But he couldn't deny her unique ability. She was nothing like 1. Yes, 1 was in a class all by herself.

He knew that 027 didn't like to cooperate and she ended up in these cells more than any other Numbered. And yet, she still lived. At least it was easy to bargain with one who hasn't ate in weeks.

"What do you want?" she asked harshly from her mat, her eyes still closed, trying to be stubborn as much as possible.

"What I want, should matter to you. But every time I offer you a chance out of this cell," his gloved fingers stroked down the cell's bars, "you refuse to comply."

"And you think it will be different this time?"

"Perhaps. I give my Numbered all the chances to prove their loyalty to me. You only have to do what I ask, and you will be free of this cell."

"Free to leave the stronghold?"

His eyes narrowed at her. "Don't push your luck. I could just let you rot in here. Die among the rats and in your own filth. It seems to me you like it so much in these cells, there is no point to even offer it to you."

"I'd rather die," she said through gritted teeth.

"Come," Brosch commanded, sending his ability into the woman. He could see her jerkily rise, and she cussed under her breath because she had no control. She took the few steps to the bars and there she stood. Dirty blonde hair tangled and matted. Her angry dark green eyes bored into his.

"Now, now. I offered you a chance to do this willingly. You know that if there is something I want, I'll get it. And, if you do cooperate, maybe I'll make sure you get some food, hum?"

"Not a chance in hell!" she spat, and it cling to the lapel of his jacket. Disgusting woman. He commanded her hands to reach up to her neck. He watched as they slowly raised, the woman looking at her hands but unable to stop them. They reached her neck, and her eyes grew wide. As her fingers tightened over her jugular, her eyes grew panicky.

"It would be a shame if you were to commit suicide, never to see your brother again."

"Aright," she whispered past her closing windpipe.

"What was that again?"

"I said I'll do what you ask." He released her from her own grip and once she had control of her hands, they fell to her sides, and she coughed and sputtered in a breath.

"Good. For your services, I'll make sure you receive a large ration of food this week. It seems my guards have been neglectful in the past weeks. Hopefully they won't be so forgetful." She looked back up at him, seeing hatred in her gaze. But there was nothing she could do to hurt him, not when her brother's life was in his hands.

"Who do you seek?" she reluctantly asked.

"Number 1."

"She is dead."

"Rumors," he waved his hand at the ridiculousness. "She escaped many years ago from the Tower. I am told that I will see her again. But it turns out, I have no recollection of what she looks like, other than dark hair and eyes that changed colors. I need more facts about her to be able to identify her if I do see her. And that, is why I need you."

She tensed as he stepped closer, but that's only because he pushed his ability to not have her do anything rash. He particularly liked this vest and didn't want more of her filthy saliva on it. He put his finger under the woman's chin and lifted her gaze to his.

"Tell me what 1 looks like today."

Chapter 12
Evan

Eva

All around her were colorful leaves that fell from an oak that stood on the top of a grassy knoll littered with brightly colored flowers. The sun was bright, and the wind picked up her hair. She looked down and she was wearing a white dress. She felt relaxed in this world and breathed in the fresh scents of the earth. Peaceful. As the earth should be. The people one with nature and living in harmony with each other.

As she took in the scenery, on the distant horizon a storm rolled in, faster than she had ever seen. The peaceful world darkened as the clouds blocked the sun. Thunder rolled and it seemed like the wind stopped. A feeling of intense doom crashed down from above. The feeling pressed her into the grass, which was soft just a moment ago, but she watched as the grass turned brown and brittle and the flowers withered and died under her touch.

It was difficult to lift her head, but as she did, she saw a shadowy figure in front of her. She wasn't sure she should look. But, if she didn't, she wouldn't know who was responsible for killing this wonderful, beautiful world. She was able to push through, and her gaze finally landed on the dark figure's face with pitch black eyes and his mouth in a cruel sneer. The man who killed her family, come to claim her.

Eva awoke with a start from the intense feeling of hurt, fear, and lastly, anger. Anger for the man who destroyed her life. She took calming breaths to ease her discomfort. He's not here right now. He wouldn't hurt her. She had to remind herself that he was not in her life any longer. Her life was good and peaceful.

An arm that she hadn't realized was already snaked around her middle tightened slightly. She scrubbed her face and looked down to see Jace sleeping beside her. The last of her discomforts left her with the knowledge of Jace's comforting touch. It had been a long time since she had any sort of nightmare, especially of *him*. She could only guess the reason he crept into her thoughts, and that's because of the mystery

Healer. Yes, the man that was one of Brosch's Numbered. Their last conversation must have been on her mind.

Eva looked around her but could not determine exactly where she was. She remembered being outside the mountains and then nothing after. She needed to stop passing out. It was early morning, the sun barely showing above the horizon, but it seemed to be in a haze. The world around her was in a fog. She saw around her other people, the Ren, among the dense trees and foliage. She placed a hand on the ground, and it seemed to be spongy. What an interesting place.

She carefully extracted Jace's arm from her middle and laid it at his side. He grunted in his sleep but otherwise didn't wake. She felt that he needed a little more rest. She was done resting and needed to get a bearing on where she was and what was the next step for them.

Eva carefully made her way among the other sleeping forms and was able to find a water source. She took several large gulps and washed her face with the clean water. The next time they made it to an establishment, she was going to take a long, deep bath. She attempted to put her hair in order, finger brushing and getting some tangles out and pleating a loose braid down her back. That at least will keep it mostly out of her way.

As she made her way back to Jace, others were stirring and some, if they caught her eye, turned away abruptly like she did something wrong. Did she do something wrong? The last thing she remembered doing was closing the exit in the Wedset mountains. It had to have worked because it didn't look like they were on a battlefield being slaughtered by Brosch's cronies.

One pair of eyes she could feel watching her. She turned toward the feeling and there the orange-aura man sat. Of course, he was being shunned as well, but only because the Ren didn't readily trust people. She didn't blame them for acting that way. Why he was watching her like he was trying to figure her out, she did not know, but it did make her curious.

Eva decided to get a few more answers from the Healer if possible. Since they shared an unfortunate bond of being a former Numbered, she hoped that it would help him open up. As she made her way over, his eyes didn't leave her. Those sparkling greens reminded her of morning dew on the grass back at the old run-down cottage just outside Jebrow Stronghold. Many good memories in her life were with the Jebrow family. She would give anything not to have been put in that tower. But without it, she would never have met the Jebrows and one person she needed in her life, Jace.

She stopped in front of the man with her arms crossed. She wasn't sure what to say, but fortunately he spoke first. "I see you are finally awake."

"Concerned I wouldn't?" she lifted her eyebrow.

"A wee bit. I was more concerned about my life than anything."

"How would I waking, or sleeping be tied to your life?"

"As a Healer, people expect things, like positive results." She tilted her head not really understanding what he was talking about. He sighed and indicated with his hand for her to sit. He continued as she made herself comfortable on the squishy ground. "Your man there was not happy with me when I said I could do nothing for you. He's been given me death glares and I felt, well, like I probably should at least try something, but you have healing ability, I think that messed with what I could do."

"My man? You mean Jace?" He nodded his head vigorously. She had rarely seen him angry. The one time, that idiot Devon attacked her, and he got angry then. But that just reflected what she was feeling about that whole event anyway, so she was glad to have his anger, because, well, it wasn't directed at her.

"People who are not healers don't understand that we can't heal everything. Depending on the ability, it limits us. Some have, special things they can do that no one else can. Most can do the basics, heal cuts, set bones, whatever. But to rejuvenate someone's spark? Yeah, that's not something I can do."

"Did I damage it somehow? I didn't think that could be done." She still wasn't too familiar with sparks, but she believed they were tied to a person's aura. That's really all she knew about them, other than the spark is what makes a person a person.

"No, you didn't damage it," he reassured her with a small smile. "You just depleted your spark energy, which is hard to do. Most people don't get it that low to notice. When it is low, they just need to sleep, and it refills. Of course, telling Jace that still didn't make him happy. So impatient."

She chuckled a little at thinking of Jace impatient and demanding. Very much a mayor's son in that instance. She needed to get back to some of her questions though. The first one, hopefully, will be the easiest out of all of them.

"I hope it is okay to ask, but, what's your name?" He tilted his head thinking, looking off stroking the stubble on his chin.

"To be completely honest," his gaze reconnected with hers and he shrugged with a sad smile, "I don't remember."

"Well, I can't just call you Healer or Red-haired Guy."

"Why not? I'd probably answer to those." She just shook her head. There had to be something she could do. Maybe this wasn't going to be so easy after all. She slid a little closer to the man. He didn't move, just had a curious look on his face. She was thankful he didn't cringe away from her.

Eva didn't know how she knew. It was just something she had a feeling about. It was like when Mayor Jebrow was ill, she knew she could help heal him. Well, she didn't give her life for him, but she at least did what she could. And that's what she was going to do with this man.

She slowly reached up with her left hand and gently touched the side of his temple. His eyes grew wide, but he stayed where he was. She closed her eyes and eased into his mind. That was the best way she could describe it. Imagines appeared of his memories in her mind's eye. It was interesting seeing and feeling his perspective of just the recent past. Being in the mountain, being found by the Ren, meeting with a strange lady in a cottage, being hunted down by Chasers, hearing a prophesy, and –

She met a block. There was this big wall she hit. It was like these memories were off limits. Well, that was certainly interesting, but she wasn't in his mind for that right now. She was in search of his name. The block took up much in his memory. Little bits of his time in Brosch Stronghold would surface, but lots of it was not accessible.

For now, it wasn't important, but she had a feeling that she would be able to see them one day. She finally made it to a memory, an old memory, of him running in the grass and falling and scraping his knee. He cried and a tall woman approached and lifted him up. She realized this was a memory from when he was a child. She zoned in on the memory and concentrated. It wasn't as strong as some of his memories, but it still lingered in his mind, somewhat forgotten, but not entirely.

The blonde-haired woman kissed his knee, and she said some soft words. Eva pushed a little more to hear the words. Very faintly they came, *"There, there my sweet Evan."*

Eva opened her eyes and slowly retracted her hand from his temple. She smiled at him to defuse any tension that happened between them. She had no idea if she had hurt him or not with her little display.

"Your name is Evan," she said. He blinked a few times and a slow smile crept onto his face.

"Now that name, I have not heard in a long time."

"Well, it's about time it was used again."

"Agreed. But I am slightly curious about what just happened and I'm trying to piece together a very complicated puzzle."

"About what?" He leaned in close so as to not have anyone overhear his next words.

"What you are. You are an anomaly Eva," he said and dipped his voice lower that she had to even lean in herself to hear. "I have no idea what your aura is because you are not projecting one. And you have healed a poisoned wound, used strength to move several rocks without even touching them, and you were able to deeply see into someone else's memories. All feats that should be impossible. And, on top of all that, you are a seer."

"And that's not normal?" She was pretty sure she knew the answer. Everyone has an aura, even people who do not have ability. She only knew one person that didn't project one, but she didn't know that she didn't project one herself. She didn't know if people could see their own auras, so she just assumed she had one. The multiple abilities she's displayed, yeah, she was pretty sure from the beginning that was not something anyone else could do.

"Normal," he snorted. "What is normal? It's all perspective. What I perceive, is someone that can block anyone from seeing their aura, which only one man in recorded history could do, is a powerful seer who has multiple prophesies and visions, which most seers are lucky to even have one prophesy, and with all those other factors I mentioned, not only are you Number 1 to Brosch, I believe you are the One in the prophesy."

"You believe that of me? I'm nobody. I don't remember who I even was."

"But you know your name? It's Eva."

"No," she slowly shook her head. "I was given that name by Mayor Jebrow. I didn't remember it when I was rescued. So, the Mayor just gave me a name." Evan's eyes widened with the news.

"I'm sure some day, you will remember. Just like you helped me remember mine." She just slowly nodded. Maybe she will brave her memories from before that dreadful day. It was painful the last time her mind traveled in the past. It wasn't by her choice. The vision she had of the mountains thriving with people was given to her by the Fates. Maybe they had other reasons she didn't know for her to relive the pain all over again. But today was not that day to do it.

"So, no aura for me. I didn't even know that was possible."

"Everyone has an aura," Evan corrected. "Yours, is just hiding and the color would be helpful in determining what ability you have. But, with the different ones you've shown, I would have no idea what the color would be."

"You are familiar with the aura colors?" She always wanted to learn more about them. She can guess which colors led to which abilities, but it would be good to know of any other colors, like supposedly her absent one.

"To an extent. I've taught myself how to pick up on them. Not so easy of a task, but it's very useful."

"I agree that it's useful. You have a deep orange color, and that color is more specific to a healer and those men over there on look-out are blue in color, which means they are strong and are good fighters." When she said this, his eyes sparkled with intrigue.

"I'm guessing you weren't taught how to read auras." She just shook her head, because as far back as she could remember, she's always seen auras. "Interesting. Something we have in common then. So, why do you put so much trust in someone that doesn't have ability?"

"What do you mean?"

"Your man of course. The one that would probably kill me some day and is way overprotective of you."

"Why do you say he doesn't have ability?"

"We were just talking about auras and clearly, he doesn't project one like all people with the Might. Just like those two over there," he pointed at two women that looked to be sorting through some herbs. "No aura is being projected so they do not have ability."

"But they have auras." Eva saw them. The two women had light orange auras, which meant that they probably were very good at knowing about healing and how to make a person comfortable, but she knew by the brightness and projection that it was not an ability, just their natural aura.

"I'm not saying they don't." Eva was still very confused. He didn't see everyone's aura, like even people without ability. She decided it was best to keep that information to herself for now, along with the fact that Jace technically did have ability. Jace didn't know it and Evan certainly couldn't see an aura, so, maybe Jace and her did share something other than just their weird connection.

"Oh crap," Evan exclaimed. "He's here to murder me." Eva turned to see who was coming up behind her. She should have known it was Jace. Now that she was paying attention, she could feel his emotions through the link. Was that jealousy she was feeling?

Jace stopped just behind her and glared over at Evan. Such a typical male stance, with legs spread at shoulder length and arms crossed to accentuate his arm muscles. She appreciated him more than anyone else. Maybe others like Evan saw a mayor's son, spoiled, and pampered, but she *knew* Jace. He dealt with much in his beginning years when the country was at war. He was kind and cared deeply for the people he loved. He was strong and she would always want him fighting by her side. He was everything to her.

Jace blinked down at her, probably getting a sense of what she was feeling. His blue-green eyes softened when they met her gaze. A small smile slowly graced his lips. He had to know that she liked seeing him smile. It made her smile in return every time.

"What are you doing?" he asked her with an eyebrow raised.

Chapter 13
Second Guessing

Jace

"Talking to Evan," Eva said in a sweet voice and her hazel eyes sparkled with mirth. It was like she had her own private joke going on and if Jace were honest with himself, had no idea what it was.

"Who?" he asked. She looked back toward the supposed Healer and then looked right back at him with that same smile on her face. "That guy?" he skeptically asked.

"Yes. And we are taking him with us," she stood and brushed off her pants.

"Whoa, slow down there princess, you just woke up."

"The more reason to get going. I'm well rested and don't want to doddle."

"Still doesn't mean to make decisions on the fly, like taking him with us," he indicated Evan with a small flick of his wrist. "Why would you even come to this conclusion anyway?"

Eva's brow furrowed as she thought about this. As she was lost in thought for a second, he scooted up to her and placed his hands on her upper arms. He slowly rubbed up and down, from shoulder to elbow. Fates, he loved touching her. He thought she'd be snuggled in his arms this morning, but that wasn't the case. At first, he thought to himself, typical Eva, but then he remembered that she had passed out and it had been more than a full day since she was awake. That's when he went looking for her and found her here, talking with this idiot.

"I just, have a feeling that he has more information in him that we need," she said in a small voice for his ears only. Her eyes bored into his, showing little hints of indigo and sparkles of white. "We can't stay here with the Ren."

"I know. That," he almost said 'bastard Healer' but thought better of it, "Evan, said something about one of the best Trackers Brosch has under his thumb is looking for you. And whoever is with you, will be caught up in Brosch's schemes if you are found. Which I don't intend for us to be."

"Do you think the Ren will be safe here? Wherever here is."

"Kretz Swamp. And no, they won't be. They've already had plans to move to another safe location. But I wasn't privy to that information, so I have no idea what direction they are heading."

"We'll head in the opposite direction. We need to draw this Tracker away from them. I've brought too much on them already with the battle and closing the opening." Eva placed her hands on his chest and slid them up to his shoulders. He didn't know if she really was aware of what she was doing to him. He instinctively pulled her closer, enclosing her in his arms with only a hair's breadth away from devouring those luscious lips of hers.

"Don't even think this was your fault, Eva. I would do anything for you, even if that means my death." Her eyes widened but softened and her hand played with his light brown hair at the nape of his neck.

"Yes, you would. And I would do the same for you, but would anyone wish to give their life for a stranger?" Jace so wanted to comfort Eva right now. He was just relieved that she woke, even though Evan told him she would eventually and that she would be fine, he had to see it for himself. His forehead touched hers and he breathed in deeply, content that she was currently in his protective arms. It felt like nothing could happen to her if he held her close.

A throat was cleared next to them and Jace turned his head ever so slightly to see that Healer standing there. He started to speak even with Jace glaring at the interruption, "Hate to intrude, but don't I get a say in who I travel with?" Eva pulled away from him to speak to the man. He really was starting to hate the guy.

"You want to stay with the Ren?" she asked him.

"Well, no."

"So, your only other options are to travel with us or head out alone, and that's if the Ren do actually let you go," she ended with that mocking smile of hers, like she knew she was going to get her way. Classic Eva.

"It seems like the choice has been made for me. I guess I'll be traveling with you two," Evan forced a smile.

"Excellent," Eva said cheerfully and continued turning to Jace, "And you will go find which direction the Ren are going from Willow. Also explain we are not coming with and we're taking Evan. I'll go pack our stuff." She bounded off toward their bedrolls and supplies and left him with the Healer.

"Get you stuff together Healer. We leave as soon as possible." He noticed a slight twinge in Evan's expression, but he gave Jace a curt nod and began gathering his things, what little there was.

Jace walked off shaking his head. Eva seemed to be dictating their next move. Wasn't Jace in charge of this trip? In any case, she was right. He had to see what direction Willow and the Ren were heading. It was also an opportunity for him to ask his questions. He was seeking a seer to interpret the prophesy that was written in his Nanna's journal.

He wound his way through the Ren, who were now mostly awake and packing. They will be moving out soon. This fog cover will help them in the swamp. It wasn't really smart to traverse through places like this. Lots of areas to get sucked right down in the muck and you were gone just like that. Supposedly they are used to traversing places such as these, because they found a way in, and they were confident that they would find a way out. Maybe it was an ability of someone's that was helping with that.

He found Willow easily. She was a small older woman and easy to spot as she gave directions to various people. Jace used what Eva taught him and concentrated around her and was able to pick up on a violet aura. The color suited her, just like Ruby's deep red aura. That woman didn't leave Willow's side often and sure enough, she stood next to her as Jace approached.

"Ah, the Mayor's son. Just what do you want?" Ruby asked with her customary scowl.

"Ruby. There's no need to be hostile," Willow said to the maroon-haired hot head. "Go speak with Willis to secure the transfer." Ruby continued to glare at Jace. Of course, he didn't back down from that and just smugly waited. For whatever reason, Ruby had something against who he was. It wasn't like he could change that if he wanted. He was born where he was, whether for the best or the worst. If she didn't like where she came from, that was her issue not his.

She did eventually break eye contact with a humph and stormed off. He watched the woman go and could see people part away from her in her wake.

"Don't mind her. She's considerably better than she has been in the past," Willow explained.

"That, I can believe."

"Please, sit a moment," she indicated to a stump as she settled on a down log. She was very graceful, and she did remind him of his Nanna. It's been years since she died, but it seems like the hurt from her passing never left.

"You have some questions for me?"

"Yes. How would you know that?"

"I am a seer after all. If I didn't know some things, then my credibility as a seer would greatly diminish." He could imagine that of someone who commands such a large group of people like the Ren.

"I was in search of a seer to help me with a certain prophesy," Jace began, seating himself on the stump. "It seems that it is one everyone knows."

"The Child Prophesy I assume. That's the only one anyone ever talks about. Among seers, it seems to come out in bits and pieces. Who knows when it started? Some say before the war, others say much later. I do believe that it was prophesized, but it's more about hope currently. Something to cling to. Do we as a people cling to this purposed individual who will save us all? When will this occur? No one has those answers. It seems the Fates don't see time the way we do. They truly are the only ones who know."

"And you have prophesized?"

"No. I have not. It's not all that common for a seer. It is a rare gift from the Fates. I have been blessed with visions and those have been needed in my walk on this earth. But a prophesy, rare indeed." Jace thought of Eva and the prophesies she had. More than one and in a short period of time. He was also sure she had several visions, one leading them right to the Ren. It sounded like Eva was not a typical seer. That worried him a little.

"What if I told you that I might have the original Child Prophesy?"

"I would be very interested. But you do know how prophesies work? Some aspects get lost in translation."

"I do understand that. I'm positive that what was recorded was the direct words that were said, since three people heard it and can collaborate. Well, I mean, technically four people were present, but one didn't remember."

"Three? It is usually better when there is more than one. Four is good. But why didn't the fourth remember?" Jace reached into his vest pocket and pulled his Nanna's journal out. This was it, the first time this knowledge was ever shared outside of his family. What would Nanna think of him?

He held the small leather-bound journal out to Willow. She took it from him with a raised eyebrow in question. Jace spoke, "I trust that some family secrets, stay family secrets. The seer who said the prophesy is gone, so I don't think her reputation would be ruined now. But I don't know if the remainder of her family would be safe."

Willow took the book and started to look through the pages. A slow smile formed on her lips. "A seer's journal," she whispered. "She kept track of her visions. Incredible." Jace leaned forward and flipped to the page in question.

"This is what I wanted to ask about." He waited while Willow read the prophesy written in the journal on that very day in history. The light grey-haired woman's expression changed, mostly a mix between confusion and awe. She slowly lifted her head and her light blue eyes locked with his. "Was my grandmother, right?" Willow had to have read the comment written in his Nanna's scrawl just after the prophesy.

By all accounts, this prophesy is about the very child I witnessed being born. Just moments after he appeared into the world, I spoke these words. Words that were witnessed by three individuals. It is my belief that my beautiful grandson is a part of this prophesy. He is destined for great things in his life. What that is, I have yet to know, but I bless the Fates for their information. I pray he becomes a strong, powerful man, who will complete all the tasks the prophesy asks of him. I swear to protect you little one.

"Please tell me that my Nanna didn't die believing in something that wasn't right." She gave her life to save his. At the time of the war, his mother went into hiding with him and Nanna. She was also pregnant and as they waited for the threat to their lives to pass, his sisters were born and grew up away from the stronghold. Jace couldn't remember exactly where they were, but they did stay safe.

Until one day, his Nanna had a vision and forced his mother to leave with the children and she stayed and told them she would not survive. That was the last time he ever saw Nanna. They eventually made their way to Newly Stronghold and from there were safely reunited with his father.

"From what I know, events happening at the time, strongly relate to the prophesy," Willow said gently. "I think she had sufficient reason to believe what she did," she closed the journal and held it out to him. He took it and she continued, "I am to assume that the fourth individual, was you?"

He nodded his head tucking the journal safely back in his vest pocket. "Do you think that I could be the One?"

"I'm sure you hear this a lot, but prophesies can be confusing. This could be taken several ways. Are you this fated child come to save us all? Is there only one child? What is this about the Mighty? All subjective. But I do know one thing. I agree with your grandmother that you are a part of this prophesy. I don't know what part but be sure that you will have front row to these events. If not a spectator, then definitely a participant."

"Thank you. I don't know if this puts me at ease or not. Just hearing that her sacrifice was warranted, eases my pain somewhat." It didn't erase the fact that she still died, but at least it was to save not just him, but save them all.

"And, you wish to know where we are heading," Willow stated. Jace should have been surprised, but he wasn't. His Nanna used to do things like that all the time. He just smiled and nodded in agreement. "I can't tell you exactly, but we will be heading south."

"Good. We'll be traveling a different direction than that."

"I figured as much. Not that I wouldn't appreciate Eva's, uniqueness, but most of the people are still a little shaken up from the mountain incident," her gaze settled beyond his shoulder. He turned his head and saw Eva making her way toward him with the Healer on her heels.

That's right, he was coming too. He turned back to Willow and stated, "Evan will be coming with us."

"Evan?" Willow asked.

"The Healer. Since he brought you all this trouble, we feel like taking him off your hands."

"How thoughtful of you." She knew exactly what he was trying to do. But at this point, if Eva wanted Evan to come along, then he'd make sure it happened. "Well," Willow slowly stood, "Best of luck to you three. I'm confident our paths will meet again one day."

Jace stood and nodded, "May the Fates guide you." The older woman smiled and nodded and moved off toward a large group of Elite that had gathered.

"All set Jace?" Eva asked from behind him. He turned, meeting her gaze.

"We head north."

Chapter 14
Where To

Eva

They decided to make their way in sight of the main road, picking their way through trees and brush. Thanks to Willow, they were given a guide that led them to the edge of Kretz Swamp. Eva was very thankful for that because she could see herself stepping in the wrong spot, but at the same time, she had never travelled the country before so she could have been fine. Best not to chance it.

The guide left them once they reached the edge of the swamp. They did eventually reach an inn, but unfortunately there were no horses for sale. She hoped the ones that Jace and her had to leave before entering the Wedset Mountains made it back to the stronghold. One can hope.

Judging by the position of the sun it had reached just after noon, but clouds lingered on the horizon, predicting rain soon. Jace decided a rest was good and they found a decent spot next to a small spring and in the shade. The best part is that it looked slightly down on the main road, so they were likely good from being spotted and were in prime position to scope out anyone that walked by.

Eva was leaning against a tree taking a sip of the fresh water she just gathered and dug into her pack for some of her meat preserves. As she fished out food and started in on it, Jace came over and sat next to her. He also had with him his water skin and a piece of dried meat.

They sat in silence for a bit looking off toward the main road. Off to the right Evan was leaning against his own tree and soft snores filled the silence. She felt sorry for pushing him so hard, but it was necessary if they were going to get to a good traveling inn. Some you just don't venture in, no matter how convenient it is.

"Hopefully we can make it as far as the crossroads between Nertman and Tatter. Since this is the main road heading north and south, it should have more than one inn to choose from," Jace stated.

"That would be good. I fear Evan won't make it if we push too hard." Jace snorted. Eva turned sharply to him giving him her 'what the heck' look.

"As much as I should feel sympathy for his previous situations, I don't. He's a man and should toughen up. If you can make it with no issues than he can too."

"What do you take me for? A delicate flower or something? I would think you would know by now that I'm not a typical girl. I do spar with you on occasion, and win. Did you think I couldn't do hard travel?"

"What? I didn't mean anything by that. Of course, I knew you would do fine."

"Then why are you comparing him to me?"

"I didn't mean it like that."

"Then what did you mean?" Jace got that nervous look in his eye, and she could tell that he had no idea what to say to make it better. She wasn't mad or anything. It was just funny to make him sweat a little when he was in an uncomfortable position.

Eva chuckled and lightly punched his arm. He playfully rubbed the spot and said, "Ow," but she knew he wasn't really hurt.

"Eva. I'm an idiot sometimes and don't think before I say stuff."

"Yeah?"

"I'm sorry," he took her hand in his and threaded their fingers together. "You should know that there is no other person I could compare you to. I've never stopped thinking about you when I was away at school. I'll admit that you seemed to be annoying at first following me around and such."

"Hey!" She tried to pull her hand away in mock anger, but he held on and brought her hand to his lips and kissed the tender skin on the back of her hand. It sent chills racing down her arm. She had to have been blushing.

"But you really did become someone I wanted to see and hang out with every day. It was torture when I left and seeing you running toward me when I came home," he gave that half smile of his that made a small dimple appear and his eyes dropped to her lips. Please, yes. She really wanted to kiss him right now. He continued in a whisper, "was one of the best days of my life. It was like a part of me was now complete with you beside me. I'll admit I didn't want you to come along on this trip, but right now, I'm glad you talked me into it because I would be miserable without you."

"You would?" she asked on a breathy exhale. His sea-colored eyes sparkled as he seemed to look into her soul.

"Too miserable to do the basic necessities of living."

"I think, I'd feel the same way. I mean, when you left for school, I didn't eat for a week."

"Really? You missed me that much?"

"Of course, I did! You left me with your sisters and parents for company. Do you think I talk to them about the weird stuff that happened? You were, and still are, everything to me."

"This is what I felt back in Kretz Swamp," his hand lifted a stray strand of hair away and tucked it behind her ear. His fingers lingered by her neck and his gaze dipped back down to her lips. He slowly pulled closer and as her eyes fluttered closed and her lips prepared for the sweetest of touches…

"So, where are we going exactly?" Evan's voice cut into the moment and her eyes snapped open to see Jace just as startled. Jace sighed, dropped his hand away, and turned his exasperated expression toward Evan. They were so close that time. It always left her flustered and wanting. She hoped her face wasn't red because it certainly felt like it.

"First an inn at the next crossroads. I figure a few horses would be better for traveling since it would be faster and better for us than walking," Jace answered as he stood up and started closing his pack back up.

"That's good," Evan nodded. "And then, where to after that?"

"Well, let's see," Jace tapped his chin. "I fulfilled my original objective, even though I think I have more questions with the answers I got. I would certainly love to travel home, but we sort of have a problem, don't we?"

"What problem?" Evan asked.

"The Tracker you moron!"

"Oh right. *That* problem."

"I don't want to lead this crazy guy to my family. So, we must go somewhere else in the meantime." Eva listened to their exchange and agreed with Jace. They couldn't go home. That would be putting others in danger. The whole reason they left the Ren was to get them out of the situation they were in now. But where could they go?

As an answer, a vision appeared to her. There was a massive bridge suspended over a fast-moving river. It was familiar looking, but she couldn't place it. The vision showed a large stronghold tucked away at the base of large mountains that disappeared into the sky. As she neared the stronghold, a battle raged below. Men wearing black with a crest emblazoned on the left breast were fighting against a group of old and young alike who were not wearing anything specific.

It was like she was seeing the battle from above, watching it as a bird would, gaze darting this way and that. The gaze then landed on, her. Yes, that had to be her. She stood tall with her sword in her hand and her long hair whipping around her, which must have come loose from her braid. Her eyes were black as midnight as she shouted something. Did she really look like that? Off to her right, Jace fought with all his strength and to her left, a face appeared that she had not seen in several years. One of the men that had saved her from hell was fighting by her side.

The next moment she was blinking and was back leaning against a tree with two pairs of eyes looking at her.

"Care to tell us what you saw?" Jace asked.

"We don't know that she had a vision," Evan countered.

"She did. You noticed her eyes, right? Classic indicator for a seer."

"Guys," she raised her hands to stop their squabbling. She did not want it to turn into drama fest. She had enough of that at the stronghold. "Yes, I did have a vision."

"Told you," Jace said out the side of his mouth.

"And I know where we need to be."

"Did you like, see the future or something?" Evan asked. She started putting her pack together.

"Dude! Do you not know what a seer can do?" Jace scoffed. "That's the whole point of their existence. They are the recipients of the Fate's knowledge of future events."

"All events in time Jace," Eva softly said.

"What?"

"I'll explain later. What is important is what I saw. And it was us at Holds Stronghold," she finished with her pack and stood, swinging it up to settle the straps on her shoulders. She now remembered that the bridge was the only way onto Holds land. The river was too fast moving and dangerous to cross. She remembered crossing the bridge as a child.

"Wait, Holds Stronghold? Isn't that the farthest north you can go in this country?" Evan looked sick to his stomach. It seemed he didn't like the prospect of traveling that far.

"Yes," Jace answered. "Have you been there before?"

"No, I haven't," Evan's eyes narrowed at him. "You do know where I've been the last thirteen years of my life don't you?"

Jace narrowed his eyes right back, "You could be from there. How would I know?"

"By asking me. And no, for your information, I was not from the north."

"Before you both start a shouting match," Eva stepped in between the two men. It looked like they were both sizing each other up. She had to hand it to Evan for standing his ground against Jace, but she would most definitely bet on Jace to win a fight between the two of them. "Let's get going. We need to reach the crossroads as soon as possible. Jace is right. Horses will help, but I also want a bath and the sooner we get there, the better I'll feel."

Jace laughed at her reference to a bath. He gave her a pat on the shoulder and then slung his pack on his shoulder and said with that laughing twinkle in his eye, "You don't smell that bad." He walked off before she could retort.

Chapter 15
Tracker

He couldn't fail. It was not an option. 015 rolled his head trying to relax the kinks in his neck. He was so close the last time, until the entrance closed. He remembered the tingly feeling on his skin just before the large boulders flew from their spots on the cavern's floor and jammed themselves in the hole. He'd never seen or felt anything like it. It had to have been a Might, but when he searched for the aura signature, there was none.

Who was this mystery person that could move the earth in such a way? They must be just as powerful as Number 1 supposedly was. If he could bring her back, along with this powerful individual, maybe it would take away from his apparent lack of already capturing them.

He could blame it on something else like others did, graveling and sniveling his excuses to Brosch, and for what? The guy didn't tolerate that stuff and he would just end your life. 015 never failed before, and he didn't intend to fail. Yes, momentarily he was set back, and it was taking him longer than it should have, but he'll eventually find his mark. He was the best at what he did.

His black eyes roamed the edge of Kretz Swamp, where the physical evidence of the Ren was not as clear as it was leading to the swamp. If he didn't have to back out of the mountain and go around then he wouldn't be in this predicament in the first place.

Brosch's cronies and some Chasers searched the edge and ventured in the swamp slightly to get a feel for what went on. 015 was using his ability, seeing each trail of Might. Although, as soon as they hit the swamp, they vanished. It was like the swamp itself erased their existence. That was a good call on their part. There were natural occurrences in this world that disrupts Might auras and one does happen to be fog.

He could understand how the Ren had been under the radar for a long time. He hoped to change that though. All he needed was to find a trail that led out of the swamp. It does delay him yet again, but he will not yield until he finds Number 1.

He knew Brosch wanted Number 034 as well, and he would be a bonus find, but that was not the objective he was given. He knew the Healer was in no danger of sharing anything about Brosch. And it did make him harder to find due to the restrictions that Brosch had placed on the man. Might binding was tricky and Brosch had years perfecting it with his Numbered.

Did he, 015, like being classified as a Numbered? He could tell from the looks Brosch's cronies and Chasers were giving him that they feared and respected him. Not sure at times to fear what he could do or be awed by it. They knew his loyalty ran deep and no one could outrun 015, no one.

Some little trollop was not going to stop him. Well, he didn't think she would. Number 1 he had no information on. Never meeting her, he couldn't track her by aura signature. He just hoped that they still traveled with the vibrant red aura that he had been tracking. What carelessness on that Might's part. Even as all other streams faded, hers glowed like a beacon, just like the first time he picked up on it deep in the mountains. Unfortunately for him, it did vanish at the edge of the swamp.

They had already been at it since mid-morning and it was approaching on evening, when a Chaser came up to him, jogging him out of his musing thoughts about the red-aura person.

"Sir," he nodded sharply and continued. "It's faint, but I'm certain the hound picked up a scent on the northeast corner of the swamp. We did a sweeping search of the area and there are tracks showing a few men leaving on foot."

"Show me," he directed the man to lead. The sky was currently cloudy, blocking out the harsh sun. This close to stagnant water, the air was hot and humid. On the precipice of rain, it was becoming unbearable breathing in warm, sticky air. As he walked his clothes clung to him like a second skin. It'll probably rain by the end of the day, he was sure.

It was quite a distance from where he stood at the Ren's entry point from the supposed exit the Chaser found. Once they reached the spot, 015 used his ability to search for traces of Might aura. Unlike the hounds, who can only pick up hints of ability being used, he could pick up on the aura of a Might if they used or not. It was why he was so successful as a Tracker.

The Chaser's hound sniffed a soft boot print in the soil. 015 bent down and touched the spot, breathing in the scents around him, calming himself and opening up to see if this was truly a footprint of a Might. After several minutes of grounding, he opened his eyes to see the undertones of the world.

This print didn't have an aura, but a faint one caught the corner of his eye. He rose and walked over to it. He would possibly have overlooked it if the sun was shining. It was his lucky day that it was cloudy. A familiar hue of orange barely shone a line leading out and turned north. 034.

What is he doing going that direction? He wasn't alone. After looking closer he was traveling at least with two others. It was a smaller group to be sure, but they weren't people with Might aura. Now that was interesting.

It would take several more hours to search to the south, and he had a feeling at first that was the direction they would have taken. It was so obvious. Of course, they might have used 034 as a decoy. He didn't think the Ren could leave a Healer to his own whims, without protection.

015 thought on it and he decided to take the risk. He could go after 034 and once he easily captured him, then he would go south. Because that was the only logical place Number 1 would be.

"Chaser. Take a message to your patrol. Take two Chasers and five cronies and travel south. Check the edges of the swamp for any signs of an exit. If the hounds pick up on anything, give chase. Send a report directly to me of anything that could be Might-related. I will take the rest and travel north. Understood?"

"Right away sir," the Chaser strode away with his hound. 015's gaze shifted back to the trail of orange. A sly smirk appeared on his lips. The Healer was no match for a Tracker.

Chapter 16
Crossroads

Jace

The clouds that seemed to appear slowly throughout the day decided to finally release the rain they've been holding. Jace, Eva and Evan continued along next to the main road. It was a drizzly sort of rain for the last two hours, but now as dusk appeared, the rain was a heavy downpour. Jace didn't want to admit it, but a bath did sound nice.

It was well into night when the three of them reached the main crossroads. Trading is very common at the crossroads and since many travelers pass and need rest, inns were available. They joined back up on the main path, not many traveling in this kind of weather, especially on foot. At least when they were slightly covered by the trees on the roadside, they didn't soak through as fast.

Jace led them unto the main stretch and looked about. He spotted two stables that looked decent, and they might be able to pick up a few horses. This crossroad also had several inns, some not so well-kept as others. Jace knew Eva really wanted that bath and if he didn't find an inn with that accommodation, well, she would probably beat him up. He smiled at the thought. Eva beating him. She would put up a good fight. Her swordsmanship was top notch. But when it came to brute strength, Jace had her beat.

Each of them had their hoods up, trying to keep the rain from their faces. Jace spotted an inn sign saying *Tillman Crossroad Inn.* The building was one of the largest inns, and the wood on the outside looked to be kept well and painted often. The stables attached also looked well-tended, or at least that's what he guessed, since it was slightly obscured by the rain.

He ambled over with the others following and pulled open the door. Warm air hit his face as he stepped into the common area. A fire was roaring to keep the chill of the rainy night away. He shook as much rain from his shoulders as he could and tipped his hood off his head. He glanced around the room where patrons were having a merry time drinking and dining.

Jace got a good vibe from the place and knew that he picked a decent one. As he made his way to the bar, he looked over his shoulder to see Eva put a hand on Evan's arm to stop him from pulling his hood back. Jace wasn't sure exactly what that was about, but Eva's instincts were usually spot on so if she didn't want or wanted you to do something, you better well do what she asked. She also left her hood in place.

Jace leaned against the bar and tapped his knuckles roughly on the counter to get the barman's attention. A rather large fellow wearing a stained apron ambled over his way. He was just as tall as Jace and although he could tell the barman was friendly, he had the strength to throw anyone out of his establishment, literally.

"What can I do ya?" the barman asked around his thick mustache.

"Two rooms please."

"Two ya say? I'm sorry lad, I just have one available." Jace glanced around and even though there were people in the inn, there didn't seem to be enough to justify only one available room.

He met Eva's eyes through her hood, and she shrugged, obviously leaving the decision up to him. He turned back to the barman. "I guess we'll take the one room please."

"That'll be 20 sir."

"20? Seems a bit high," Jace mumbled as he pulled out two shiny coins and placed them on the counter.

"It's nothing against ya lad. If you want cheap, you can go find another inn, but I guarantee that it won't be this nice."

"I can indulge every once in a while, as long as a bath can be brought up to the room," Jace placed another shiny coin on top of his other two, "And food and drink delivered as well."

The barman's mustache twitched at the corner, and he put his hand on top of the coins and slid them his way. He picked them up and pocketed them and immediately turned to shout in the back room to have a bath sent to room 11.

When he turned back around, he had a key held out to Jace. "For ya room," he explained. "Bath will be up shortly along with some food. Anything else lad?"

"That'll do for now. Thanks." Jace took the key and turned toward the staircase. He looked behind him and indicated with his head that Eva and Evan follow. He knew they would and didn't look back until he ascended the staircase and stopped at the door with a number 11 on the outside. He fit the key in the slot and with a click it was unlocked. He removed the key, opened the door wide and stepped in.

The room wasn't bad, well, compared to the last inn he stayed in when he traveled home after leaving school. The bed could at least fit two people comfortably, there was a small table with two chairs, a comfy couch with table in front of a fireplace, and a desk and chair which looked to have supplies for writing. Fancy.

He stepped in and went over to the fireplace to start it, since he still had a chill from the outside. He heard Evan sigh and plop down in a chair at the table and Eva was the last in shutting the door behind her and locking it. As Jace continued to use the striker to light the fire, she strode over the window and looked out it into the stormy night.

It didn't take long until the fire was blazing and once a soft light filled the room Eva closed the curtains on the window and dropped her hood so that her black hair cascaded down her back. It came loose from her braid and little wispy tendrils framed her face. Evan also threw back his hood and was shrugging out of his coat.

"Man, what a relief," Evan began as he started to shake out his coat and drape it across the other chair. "I am glad we got here before the weather turned on us. I couldn't take another minute walking around in this soggy footwear." He sat again and started tugging off boots that looked well-worn and obviously not in a good state. Jace noticed Eva also looking at Evan's boots with a slight frown. She didn't approve of their state either.

"Don't get too comfy over there. We'll only be here a night," Jace said while adding a few more logs and standing. He heard the strike of a flint and turned to see Eva lighting a few of the lamps in the room, making it possible for them to see the furniture and other items in the room.

"Do we really need to get to Holds Stronghold that quickly? We don't have to get there as soon as possible, right?" He turned this question on Eva, since she was the one that said that was where they needed to go.

"I'll only feel safe once I'm in the stronghold with thick walls around me," Eva gave her answer and pulled off her coat.

"But it's so far," Evan whined a little. He was such a wuss.

"I'll be going out once we've eaten and see about procuring some horses," Jace commented, taking off his coat as well, "unless you prefer to walk all the way there." Evan glowered at him. For some reason Jace liked goading the guy. It was just easy on someone like him.

"Don't start that," Eva scolded him, but he could feel her amusement through their link. A small smirk appeared on his lips, and he could tell she was trying to hold down a smile.

A small knock sounded on the door. Eva immediately indicated to Jace to get the door and she strode over to the privacy screen and snuck around it. Interesting, he wondered what that was all about. Not wanting to keep the person on the other side of the door waiting, he strode over and unlocked and opened it. As expected, there were people with a tub and several with buckets of water.

Jace directed them inside and they set up the bath. For a few minutes a stream of people continued until the bath was full and then two maids appeared carrying trays laden with food. They came in and set the food on the table, curtsied, and left. Seeing as there was no one else that needed to drop off anything, he went to the door and shut it, locking it once more.

Evan was already eyeing the food and looked to be contemplating what to eat first. Jace called out, "Eva. You take the bath first, you're the one that wanted it." She came out from behind the screen, and it took him only a moment to realize that she was already stripped down and was wrapped in a robe. Jace's mouth dropped open at the sight and he probably could guess Evan's was too.

She dipped her fingers in the water and let out a sigh. "Oh, it's just the point past warm, which is perfect. You sure I can take it first?"

"Yes," Jace struggled to say. She wasn't going to just get in right there was she? As much as he would have loved to see Eva in all her glory, he did not want Evan to see her. He was acting possessive, but he would punch anyone that laid eyes on his woman.

Eva must have sensed his emotions because she lifted an eyebrow at him. "What is it, Jace?" She began to move her hands to the robe's tie, loosening it and started to grab the edges of the material to slip it off her shoulders when he shot towards her and stopped her by grabbing her wrists.

"What are you doing?" he asked through gritted teeth. He was really on edge, and he could swear that Evan's eyes were just as wide as his.

"Oh, I was just playing," she took her hands out of his grasp and lightly swatted him on the arm. She promptly tied the robe and stood there with hands on her hips, looking at him with that small little smirk on her face and twinkling hazel eyes.

"Right, sure you were." He was close enough to her that one small movement and he could have her body pressed to his as he greedily took her mouth. Why he thought that he didn't know. Well, maybe deep down he did know. He's been craving a taste of her ever since Newly Stronghold when he this whole connection thing started.

Her breathing hitched and her eyes widened. He felt a flutter of desire from her, which only fueled his own. But they weren't alone in the room and the obvious throat clearing at the table lifted any sort of trance that Jace was in.

"I can just move the screen," she turned and started pulling the screen toward the tub. Jace was still frozen to his spot for some reason watching her. As she blocked off the tub from the food table, she started to step around it and stopped glancing over her shoulder. "Get some food Jace. Try not to think too much to what's going on behind the screen," and she gave him a wicked smile.

He gulped and started toward the table, sitting down he still stared at the screen. He caught the vague outline of her form lower into the tub.

"Really dude? You can't be any more obvious," the annoying voice next to him spoke around a mouthful of food. That dropped Jace's mood as quickly as the possibility to see Eva naked would raise it.

"Watch it, pal." He grabbed a chicken leg off the tray and began to devour it with a snarl. Evan raised his hands in a playful surrendering gesture, even with a chunk of bread still in his hand.

"Just joking there big guy. Trust me, there is no time or place do I want to be in a tousle with you." He lowered his hands and continued to eat his hunk of bread. He caught his eye wondering over to the screen momentarily, but as soon as Jace narrowed his eyes to a death glare, Evan's eyes would snap back to the food, or the ceiling, pretending he wasn't just caught looking.

Once they reach the safety of Holds Stronghold, he was going to be glad to get rid of the guy. It's not like he had anything against him being a Numbered, because technically Eva was one and she didn't do anything for Brosch. Which begs the question, what did Evan do?

Chapter 17
Searching

Brosch

Brosch dismounted and his boots splattered the mud. He strode purposely up to *Tillman Crossroad Inn.* He had a few of his people ride ahead and reserve rooms for the night. The rain had come down harder in the last hour and he was relieved to be out of this nasty weather. He was planning on making it all the way to Nertman's, but the rain slowed down their progress.

No matter. It was an advantage being who he was. He had leverage when it came to business owners. If they didn't cooperate, family members died. Plain and simple.

He pushed his way into the inn and took stock. It wasn't terrible and looked to be large enough for the men he brought with him. He made his way up to the counter where a large man with a dirty apron stood. Brosch was flanked by his one-man brute, Onyx. No one messed with him because that meant messing with his guard.

A scrawny errand boy greeted him before reaching the bar. It was always the pathetically weak that had these jobs, hoping to not see death day in and day out. The boy in a bow spoke, "The rooms have been prepared as requested."

"Very good," he tried to wave the boy away, but he just stood there still staring at him as Brosch took a seat at the bar. He narrowed his eyes at the boy. "What?"

"Also, there was a lookout to the south that spotted 015 moving this way. Estimates he'll be here in about 2 hours."

"Is that so? Thank you, now leave me." The boy this time did go. He scurried away like the scared little mouse that he looked like.

Brosch shrugged out of his coat and handed it to Onyx who took it from him. So, 015 was headed toward the crossroads. Was he on those retched Rens trail? Doubtful. He sent many ahead of him and there were no reports of a large group coming through this area.

"Barkeep! A plate of food and ale." The man made a slight nod and strode in the back, presumably to get Brosch what he asked for. He continued to think about why 015 was coming here. Was it hopeful to think that the witch was right? She had said he would cross paths with 1 on his way to Nertman's. Did 015 have her trail?

That's impossible. She didn't leave trails. But she could be with others that did, and the Ren had plenty that could lead someone with 015's ability straight to them. The bar keep came back and placed a steaming pile of food with utensils and a large tankard of ale in front of him.

"Excellent, and bar keep. Make sure my men are also fed."

"That's a lot of food, sir."

"I expect you do have enough."

"Of course, sir. All I'm saying is food cost money." Ah.

"And I'm sure your daughter's life cannot be replaced, can it?" He was used to making threats. Because everyone knew that he meant every one of them.

"Your men will be fed," the man said through clenched teeth and moved away to make sure it happened. Brosch never gave anyone his money. They knew even to ask was sure to illicit a death sentence. Brosch was feeling generous, and technically the barkeep didn't ask for money, he was just making a statement. He let it slide, for now.

As he sat eating his food, he thought about the information 027 gave him about *her*. The way she described 1 was to say the least surprising. He remembered what her mother looked like, all softness with beautiful golden locks. Her blue eyes could pull you in and it seemed like she could heal you with just her look. Brosch was infatuated with her the moment he met her. The only problem was he wasn't the only one that noticed her.

No matter. That man and the only woman he fell for were now gone from this world. It was their punishment for loving each other.

And, to get his revenge, he slaughtered their children too, except for *her*. Even at a young age, he could see how much she looked like her mother, except for the hair and eyes. Her mother looked like an angel, whereas her daughter looked like a dark angel. Especially right after her little stunt when her eyes were completely black. Never, even in his wildest dreams, would he believe he would witness this fierceness in someone so young. He had to have her, and he was willing to wait.

027 confirmed that she had black hair and her eyes hazel. She was tall for a woman, which didn't surprise him either since her father was massive and her mother was above average. She wore her hair in a braid and her skin was described as kissed by the sun. He was pretty sure with that description and his memory of what her mother looked like; he could spot her.

"Onyx. Have each building searched in this area and ask if a woman arrived or passed through that had long black hair. She should be traveling with others as well."

"Yes, sir." He moved off to a table where some of his cronies sat scarfing down food to get the job done. Brosch sipped his ale and thought how he would feel when he found her. He didn't know. She was his and no one else's. He didn't know how she found her way to safety or even how she escaped out of a locked cell. But she did leave carnage behind. His men where all dead when her weekly torturers arrived. He wasn't very happy with the news of losing his prized possession.

He spun in his chair and leaned up against the bar looking out in the common area. Wouldn't it be something if she was sitting in this very room? It gave him a thrill to think that she could be this close. But he was determined to find her, no matter what that stupid crone said to him.

First off, his Tracker never failed. And secondly, he will see her and recognize her. He moved his gaze over the patrons that weren't his men as he sipped on his beer. Travelers all of them, some still in their cloaks. He only spotted two women and they were nothing like her description. One was blonde with a turned-up nose and the other had brown hair and was a small thing. When she stood, she didn't look taller than a child.

There were darker areas of the tavern, where lone travelers sat. Unlike him who didn't mind people knowing that he was looking at them. Some looked like shady characters, which helped him out a lot. He used many low lifers to do his dirty work. Maybe he'll see if placing a few coins in their hands will loosen their lips.

He put down his empty tankard and stood. He moved his gaze to the darkened tables and spotted a lone travel tucked away in the corner. The perfect first target.

Chapter 18
New Ability

Eva

This couldn't be happening. When Eva decided to scope out the patrons down below while the boys cleaned up, she didn't expect *him* to show up. She had a mixture of hatred and fear mixing within her. She had to keep her feelings under control. Jace didn't need to know why she was feeling this way. She took calming breaths and reminded herself that in no way did he know she was here.

She'd have Evan come down and confirm, but he was recognizable, and she couldn't risk losing him. He was safe, tucked away upstairs. He offered to go down with her. She refused and told him to stay and clean up, which she was now glad she did.

She watched him from her shadowed seat in the corner. He walked in like he owned the place and when he took off his cloak, she almost choked on the ale she was drinking. He was the one that would haunt her dreams, showing up unannounced and always emitting darkness. Just like he was right now. She had never seen an aura so black.

It was like that with all the men that came in with him. That's where her hatred came from. She could smite them. It would be easy, and she wouldn't even feel remorse. But she knew how taxing it was to her strength, so she reluctantly decided not to.

Interesting enough, the man standing next to him was not like the others. Yes, he had a strong blue aura, but not enough to be considered one with ability. No doubt he was strong by the way he was built. She wondered how his aura still had the soft white inner glow, untainted, yet still be will *him*?

Eva sat there observing him, making his threat to the nice man behind the bar. He was scum, and she wanted to hurt him. The trouble was, she knew she couldn't. She had tried once before, that night so long ago that she tried to forget. Somehow there was a block around him. Probably because of his ability, which was a contradiction.

He hated people with Might, yet he had it himself? He exploited these special people and used them like cattle. Milking them of their ability and reaping all the glory. Well, she vowed that it would end. And soon.

She knew that she sat too long and that it was bad if she was spotted, expect, did he remember what she looked like? No, she never saw him at the Tower, and she looked different now that she was older. She still didn't want to take the chance.

His eyes started to scan the place and when they landed on her, a shiver ran down her spine. She sat very still, her eyes locked to his, expect she knew that he couldn't see her, as her hood covered her. What if he decided to make his way over here? It would look suspicious if she got up now and headed back to her room.

They couldn't stay. As soon as Jace and Evan were done, they had to leave. She watched him set his tankard down and he stood, again glancing around the shadowed section of the place until his eyes again landed on her.

No, this can't be happening. He was not coming over to her just now. What was she to do? Help me, Fates!

A brief image flashed in her mind's eye of this vile man talking with another young man, who sat in the same exact spot as she was sitting now, wearing the exact same clothes, except, the man had fine blonde hair and green eyes with a nose much too large for his face.

She blinked and he was still on path toward her. No wait. The image. He wasn't going to sit with her, but was it possible? Of course, it was, it had to be if the Fates sent her the answer.

She closed her eyes concentrating. What did she need? It was inside her, wasn't it? She had to concentrate. She let the image of the young man rise in her mind, the blonde hair, green eyes and slightly too large of nose. Where is it? What did she need? She searched her inner self until she snagged on something tucked away in there, hidden behind most, but still there just waiting to be used.

She grabbed and let the sensation take over her body, feeling a slight tingling run along her arms and legs. She had to be a different person. He couldn't recognize her, not now.

"Greetings," his oily voice reached her ears. "Is this seat occupied?"

Keeping her cool, she opened her eyes. He was there, looking down at her with that smirk on his face. She really wanted to punch him. She shrugged and gestured toward the empty seat across from her, even though she really didn't want him to sit down, but she didn't want to draw negative attention.

He took the seat and a maid appeared almost instantly with a full tankard. It was placed in front of him, where he took it and drank a long pull. She didn't know if she could bear it, so she sat stone-faced, trying to calm her emotions.

"I have a proposition for you. One that I believe you would be interested in."

"Why would you think that?" she asked but was startled a little to find that she didn't sound like herself. She sounded a little deep and huskier than usual.

He chuckled. It was grating to her ears. "You do know who I am, don't you? It would be in your benefit that you cooperate."

"Or what?" She couldn't help herself, could she? Poking at the man who didn't tolerate anyone.

"Let's just say, you won't see the next sunrise." A death threat.

"I don't work for free." She really didn't want to do anything for this man.

"That's fair. I pay for valuable information." He produced a large purse from his side, and he jingled it. He wasn't lacking in funds. "But I only pay when the job is done." He replaced his purse back to his side.

"What makes you think I have it?"

"I don't. That's the fun of the hunt. Not knowing. But," he leaned in making sure that she heard the next part, "if I'm misled and I find out, you would be good as dead." She didn't say anything, she didn't have to.

"Now, remove that hood and let's talk," he said, and she recognized that feeling that she got from Jace. Was he trying to compel her to take it off? She knew she could resist it, and she most definitely did, but she knew what he was expecting. He was expecting the *man* in front of him to do as he asked.

She lowered her hood and prayed that she was what she believed herself to look like. He didn't look at all phased, almost bored. It worked. She really did change how she looked.

"Now, I'm looking for someone and want to know if she has been spotted."

"What does she look like?"

"She'd be tall for a woman, not your average height. Long black hair, presumably in a braid and hazel eyes." What the crap? How did he know that? It wasn't possible, and yet, it was. He had a resource that knew.

"What's she wearing?"

"That is a good question. I would think she would be dressed like any other young lady, but maybe not. She was with a group that their woman didn't do conventional clothing, so." She could see he was thinking on this. "More than likely, she's trying to blend in dressed as a man, which how could someone with long hair and probably all curvy blend in. She probably would stick out." She does indeed, but not right now she didn't.

"I haven't seen anyone by that description," *other than myself* she added in her head.

"Well, if you do, you will report it," his ability tried to compel her, but he was wrong that it would work. It didn't even faze her.

"Of course, sir." She smirked, knowing that statement was far from the truth.

"Excellent. Your name?" That stupid prickly feeling of his ability again. Thank the Fates that she knew how to repel that.

"Sam." It was the first name she thought of.

"Sam. It was nice talking with you." He emptied his tankard and left the table, off to another dark alcove. Eva just talked with the devil himself and she survived. But, for her and her two companions to survive the night, they needed to leave. As nonchalantly as possible, she placed a coin down for her drink and she rose and headed up the stairs to the room. She took out the key and unlocked the door.

She stepped in and shut and locked the door. "You wouldn't believe who I saw," she said and turned around. She met a very hostile stare and a demanding voice.

"Who the heck are you?"

Chapter 19
Auras

Jace

Jace had just finished his bath, which he would admit felt good and just covered himself with his pants when the door lock clicked. Eva was back already. Of course, she was, he could feel the whole time he was in the bath that she was uncomfortable and had a whole slew of emotions boiling inside her. He finished as quickly as possible to go see what was going on.

He thought to see her beautiful face as the door opened and closed, but the person who stepped in and shut the door thinking he was in the right room, was in the wrong room. How in the world did this jerk get a key? He couldn't have been the help since they knock.

When Jace asked who he was he just stood there with a confused look on his face.

"What?" the idiot asked. Did he not hear him? He was pretty sure he spoke clearly.

"How'd you get a key?" he demanded. The blonde idiot looked down to the key in his hand and back up to him.

"I took it with me," he spoke slowly and arched an eyebrow. Jace continued to glare at him. "Why are you looking at me like that Jace?"

"How do you know my name?" He menacingly took a step toward the man. The guy didn't even cower, just looked amused. What was up with this guy? And how did he know who he was?

"Because I grew-up in your home." Excuse me? Did he hear that right?

"I've never seen you in my life." The man's eyebrows bunched together as Jace took another step forward. Then it was like a revelation occurred and the man slapped a hand to his forehead.

"I totally forgot! I must look like a complete fool right now." Yes, Jace would agree. "Um, give me a second." The man placed the key on the table and had turned his back to Jace.

"I don't know what you're doing, but you need to leave," Jace strode over to him and grabbed him by the shoulder and turned him around, only to find Eva's hazel eyes staring into his.

What just happened? He stumbled away, blinking rapidly like he wasn't seeing this.

"I'm sorry. I forgot to change myself back. It worked, didn't it?" Her eyes sparkled with mirth as she reached up to her head and pulled her hair to her shoulder. "Yep, it did," she gave herself a self-satisfying smirk.

"Who you talking with Jace," Evan called over the screen.

"It's just me, Eva. Don't be thinking about coming around that screen in all your naked glory because I am not interested."

"Yeah, yeah."

"Eva," he spoke softly, still trying to figure out what he saw. "Did that just happen?"

"Um, a guess so," she shrugged. "I don't know how, I just did it, like with all the other stuff I've done."

"Okay, but I've never heard of someone doing that, change their appearance."

"It was a necessity. Trust me, I had to," her tone turned serious. She stepped closer and placed her hand on his arm. It was her. He felt the familiar pull that they shared together. It was still a little creepy that she was able to change like that, even her voice was different when she first walked in.

"And why was it?"

"I saw him. Brosch. He's downstairs." This wasn't good. He was after two out of three people in this room. Jace rubbed a hand down his face. How are they going to get out of this one? "Let's just say, I really didn't want him to recognize me, so I made sure he didn't."

"And he didn't, right?"

"Not how you just saw me when I walked in the door he didn't." Thank the Fates for that. "But we can't stay Jace. We must leave." He agreed with her.

"Who's talking about leaving?" Evan rounded the corner of the screen as he was buttoning his shirt. When Jace glanced over he was not expecting to see the multiple scars lining the man's body, plus he was emaciated. No wonder he looked like it was the first decent meal he had in a decade, because it probably was.

He felt Eva's sadness through the link. She didn't like what he looked like either, because they both knew it was because of Brosch that he looked like that. Even though he didn't like the guy, he still shouldn't have been treated like that.

"Brosch is here Evan," Eva said, which a hint of anger surged through their link. He felt the same way she did. He not only hurt Evan, but a lot of other people, including Eva.

"That's not good," his eyes got wide.

"We can't risk staying here if they decide to check all the rooms. He is looking for me and knows what I look like. And since he already knows what you look like Evan, if you were also spotted, we are screwed."

Jace sat on the arm of couch and grabbed Eva's hips and pulled her to him. She was cocooned in between his legs, and she had a surprised expression on her face. "I will not let him hurt you again Eva. You're mine to protect and if he even tries to do you harm, he will meet death."

She laid her hands on his shoulders looking right into his eyes with a warm smile on her face. "I know you would. But I can protect myself and I would hate to see anyone else hurt." He didn't want to let her go. He wasn't wrong when he finally caved in to let her come with him. To be separated from her felt like a piece of him was lost. That whole time away at school and even when she went downstairs. He was afraid for her.

Her eyes traveled hungrily over his naked torso, and he could feel her arousal through the link. It was nice to know she was appreciative, but reluctantly, now was not the time.

"We need to make a plan then." Jace continued, "We need to leave undetected, and we need horses. That's the only way we can get to Holds in a decent time."

Eva sighed, taking her lust filled eyes away from his chest. She stepped out between his legs and moved toward the table, snagging a piece of bread and nibbling on it.

"And how would we do that?" Evan asked, his shirt now buttoned. "He will have others looking. I'm sure he also will pay people for the right information."

"He will," Eva confirmed. "He just offered me money when I was downstairs."

"What?" Evan asked, looking thoroughly confused.

"Yes, Eva, please explain," Jace narrowed his eyes. Did something happen down there that he should know about?

"Well, as you know Jace, I didn't look myself, and he came up to me and offered money if I spotted me," she snorted. Jace smiled too because it was slightly funny. The guy is looking for her and asked the very person he is looking for to find herself.

"I'm lost," Evan said with a scrunched brow.

"I can change my appearance," Eva explained.

"Really?" Evan was skeptical, but a smirk graced his lips. "Show me."

"I think it's hardly the time to ask her to do that. We are supposed to be working on a plan to get out of here, preferably without getting caught."

"No, Jace, it's fine," Eva waved me off. "It would be interesting to see if I could do it again." Both Jace and Evan stared at her in anticipation. "Just, don't say anything and let me concentrate." She closed her eyes and looked so peaceful. It was interesting to be tied to her emotions and feeling the awe and wonder that is Eva, because he also felt that too.

In a blink, her features turned. This time she had brown hair and a little goatee. She had a strong jaw and when her eyes opened, they were a light blue.

"Whoa!" Evan exclaimed beside him. "That. Is. Awesome!" He really did look like it was the coolest thing he ever saw.

"Not just the looks either boys," her voice was an octave too low for her and Jace even had to admit that it was a pretty neat ability. She closed her eyes again and just like last time, she was back to herself in a blink.

"I can't believe it, it's too much," Evan shook his head.

"Believe it," Jace said beside him.

"That is the most powerful manifestation of the yellow aura," Evan stated.

"Really? I've seen yellow before but didn't know what the ability attached to it was," Eva was deeply interested in auras. Truth be told, it was a bit interesting, and it would help in knowing what everyone was, especially if Jace had to fight them.

"They are good at growing things and making them beautiful," Evan continued like an information booklet. "Most with this aura are beautiful in looks and are natural gardeners, seeing as anything they touch grows and looks the best."

"So, how is what I just did a manifestation of that?"

"It's not very common of the Might to reach the height of their ability. It has a wide range as well. I just know that I read a private journal from my grandfather's library when I was young and in it the man talked about meeting a crippled man on the side of the rode and he helped the man, took him to his home and fed him, only to find out later, the man was a beautiful young woman who ran away from an abusive husband."

"That's a weird story," Jace had never heard of anything like that.

"I thought it was too and mentioned it to my grandfather. But he told me that he met the woman himself when he was a boy. My grandfather said she had the Might and he remembered seeing a yellow aura. Because the woman was still beautiful even in old age."

"Okay, so what?" Jace asked.

"I have seen Eva do some interesting things. Heal, move some large rocks, read my memories, and now change her appearance. Let's not forget she is also a seer."

"Yes, I know all this," and much more, but he wasn't going to tell Evan what else.

"That means she is exhibiting orange, blue, indigo, and yellow auras. There's only been a few rare cases, mind you, rare, of a dual aura but never have I heard of any individual that had more than that. Which is probably why she doesn't have a specific aura color."

They stood there thinking about this. Jace knew Evan was right. Eva did exhibit all those abilities and more. It was even possible that she could have ability from all the auras. What did that make her?

To him, she was still Eva, but the whole no aura color was throwing him off. He guessed he didn't see it before, and didn't want to think about it, but Evan was right. When he really looked, he did see Evan's orange aura, but nothing surrounded Eva.

"Well, boys, that is some heavy stuff to think about," Eva went and sat on the bed. "As much as I want to learn more about myself, we have bigger problems. Like, getting out of here."

"Yes, we do," Jace agreed.

"Then let's get going with a plan."

Chapter 20
Trapped Again

Eva

The plan had been quite simple. Since no one knew Jace was tied with either of them, he was the one to go and get horses. The second step was to make sure that neither Eva nor Evan was seen, which Eva was good with her newfound ability, but that still left Evan.

They needed eyes and ears in the inn, so Eva changed her appearance, back to the blonde hair, green eyed man with the large nose, and went down to linger in the shadows once again. Most of Brosch's cronies that he brought with him were there, drinking and talking. They were practically enjoying their downtime while the storm passed, and they moved out in the morning.

From the snippets of conversation she heard, they were headed to Nertman's Stronghold. No one seemed to talk about why they were headed there, which made her believe that they truly didn't know. Just like, why did Brosch take the Might children? Only one person knew and that was Brosch himself.

A few cronies left to do checks, which could only mean that they were asking questions to the various shop owners. Not long after, Jace arrived back and he was not a man to be missed, especially with his height and build. Some of Brosch's cronies eyed him suspiciously and the few women that were there sat up and fluttered their lashes at him.

Yeah, like that was going to get his attention. He made his way over to her and leaned back up against the same wall, arms crossed with a brooding air about him.

"So, I secured some horses. Of course, the guy I talked to advised that it would be suicide to leave tonight. But with a few extra coins he started getting them ready right then. We'll be good to leave in 15."

"Great," in her low voice, which still sounded weird to her. "All we need to do is get Evan past without being noticed."

"Remind me again why you wanted to bring him along in the first place?"

"He's a wealth of information. Not only about what I'm going through but more. It's blocked or whatever currently, but if I can get that out of the way, what he knows will turn the tide."

"I hope you're right." She hoped so too. She had a vision of Evan looking for her back in Jebrow Stronghold. Whenever someone is looking for her, she knows. Maybe that's why she kept seeing Brosch's face in her nightmares? Or maybe that was the reason she never slept because he would always appear?

"Time to leave," she said. Eva felt that it was right. It was like confidence seeping into her giving her the decision that what they were doing at that exact moment was the correct thing to do. Jace nodded once toward her in agreement. She also felt his assurance about the plan through their link.

Jace again made his way out into the night and Eva made her way back to the room. Evan was waiting inside putting the last of the remaining food in the sacks. He was just finishing and moving them to the window, where the curtains were drawn.

Eva went around and extinguished the candles that were burning, and she took some bath water with a cup from the table and doused the fire, blanketing the room in darkness. Her eyes took a second to adjust and then she moved over to the window.

Evan drew the curtains back and the rain slashed at the windows. They both lifted their hoods in place and opened the window. It was inevitable that rain would make its way in, and they hoped to be long gone before anyone would make any connections to them if any.

Evan climbed out first, finding some hand and foot holds in the wall. Once he made it to the bottom, Eva leaned out the window with the first sack to drop. Once all their packs were through the window, now it was her turn. She'd never done this before, all this sneaking around, but it gave her this adrenaline rush.

Once she was on the window ledge, as best as possible, she closed the window. There was just a slight crack where it didn't close all the way. She also made her way down the wall without any issues, using similar foot and hand holds Evan used.

She reached the ground and took her pack from Evan. She could see a figure approaching with three horses. It was Jace and it was perfect timing.

They all mounted on their newly purchased steeds and slowly made it out of town, making sure that their faces were covered, but in the rain, it would be hard for anyone to really see who they were anyway. The weather turned out to be the perfect cover to leave town.

Eva was slightly disappointed that they weren't taking a break, but it wasn't safe for them. She didn't know where these feelings and urges came from, but one thing she knew was that it was not a smart idea to stay in the very place of the person who is trying to recapture you.

They trudged along through the night. The rain didn't let up and the road was starting to get a little treacherous to travel on. Jace was in the lead and moved the horses just slightly off the road to travel in the grass, which was more solid. They didn't see any other travelers, which was to be expected. Who would travel in this weather?

Oh yeah, they did.

To avoid any other complications, they decided to go across the open plains bypassing Tatter Stronghold. This also would cut their journey down significantly. The rain finally did let up and when the sun peaked over the horizon, it was amazing. Eva had seen many sunrises, but never had she witnessed it with the backdrop of nothing. Just openness, once the sun was out, there was no place to hide from its glaring heat. The farther north they went, it was cooler, which would help as they traveled throughout the day.

Eva was ambling along behind Evan and noticed that his head kept bobbing. She was fine, but she didn't sleep, so she knew if Evan was almost about to pass out, then Jace had to be close too. She felt that they were in the clear and steered her horse alongside Jace's to mention they should stop.

Jace was very alert on his horse and had a scowl on his face like he was not at all happy. Yeah, it was a bit uncomfortable. She was getting chaffed from the saddle because she was soaked through.

"I think a short break from riding will be good," she quietly said and motioned her head behind him where Evan was fighting to stay awake. Jace turned toward her, and his features smoothed out in a more relaxed position and when he looked back as well and saw Evan, he let out a huff of a laugh and now a smirk appeared on his face briefly before going back to stern.

"Good idea. Looks like there's a small group of trees up on the left, so we'll stop there," Jace indicated with an outstretched arm toward the tall pines. "I'd rather not sit out in the open. Evan would be easy pickings."

"Just Evan?"

"Yes. Since I know you can defend yourself, I'm not worried about you, or me. But him," he hooked his thumb behind him toward the man in question, "I'm thinking he didn't get the extensive combat training at Brosch Stronghold."

"I'm getting a weird feeling from you," Eva said. "It's like I can't tell if you are joking or not." His feelings were all over the place, a little bit of playfulness mixed with stress. It was a tough journey in the rain so it's understandable. Thanks to the Fates they didn't have to do it walking.

"I don't know if I am, to be honest. Maybe I just find it weird that I'm still talking to you when you look that ugly."

"Excuse me?" She moved her hand up to her face and that's when she realized she still had that ridiculously large nose. She forgot about changing her appearance. She quickly pulled what she needed inside her and let it sweep over her body. She touched her hair and felt the long braid. She smiled brightly back at Jace and in her normal sweet voice she asked, "Better?"

"Absolutely," his eyes raked over her. Her checks became heated from his stare. It was becoming increasingly more difficult to understand her feelings. With Jace's sneaking in through the link, it was like she didn't know if that was her or if it was him. In any case, one of them was lustful. Maybe it was Jace, but she couldn't deny that she didn't feel the same when she made the same perusal of his chiseled features. And those blue-green eyes stared into hers. It felt like falling into the water's depth and once there, she would never be able to get out.

She looked away from him and tried to compose herself, but she couldn't help sneaking glances at him. He looked so natural on a horse. His well-muscled leg clenched at the horse's side, moving him easily and all she could think about was her legs tangled up with his.

Geez, she really needed to reign in her thought pattern.

They made it into the woods without any hitches but that didn't mean they were out of the clear. She had an uneasy feeling when they passed into the grouping of trees. They traveled a little deeper in when Jace decided it was good to take a break and stopped.

Jace dropped down and so did Eva. Evan was in and out on top of his horse, but thankfully his horse followed suit and stopped with the other two. Eva reached up and patted Evan's leg. He blinked several times before focusing on her.

"We're taking a break," she stated. "Why don't you find a nice tree to sleep against?"

"Oh, thank goodness," he sighed. He slid down off the saddle and stumbled a little when his feet touched the ground. Since Eva was right there, she reached out to steady him.

Her hand grabbed his and upon contact an image flashed into her mind.

A large opposing wall stood in front with elegantly carved winged creatures adorning the tops. The entrance, flanked by two large open wooden doors carved meticulously, was clogged with people and once inside the wall a towering palace stood in the middle in the distance with smaller buildings surrounding. A hand was holding the smaller one when she looked down, knowing it wasn't really her hand. When she looked up, she saw a reassuring smile of a man with the same flame-red hair as Evan. The man squeezed the hand in reassurance.

Her vision snapped back into focus as soon as her hand released Evan's. His brow raised and he asked, "You alright?" She nodded slowly, looking at Evan and seeing the similarities of the man in the vision.

"You look just like your father." She knew that's what she saw in the vision, Evan's father. There was no doubt in her mind.

"Really?" He turned and started pulling down his pack off the back of the saddle. "I don't remember him all that much," he mumbled. When he turned back, she could see the sadness in his eyes. She wanted to ask about his father, but she held back. She didn't want to hurt him, even his feelings, by bringing up painful memories. She knew how painful it was. Forgetting was just easier.

He was moving off toward a tree when Jace appeared next to him and put a hand on his shoulder, stopping him.

"What do you-" Evan started but stopped when Jace put a finger to his lips. The sign to be quiet. Jace's gaze turned back toward his left and that's when Eva heard it. A soft rustling of brush and slight crunch of dry needles.

Something was moving out there towards them. She heard the noise again but behind her this time. Jace noticed to and when their eyes met, they both knew they had the same thought.

They were trapped.

Chapter 21
Missed Her

Brosch

"What?!" Brosch growled at the man in front of him. He did not tolerate failure and what he heard out of this supposed person wearing his seal is that no such woman by the description given entered. That was not possible. The old seer told him he would meet her on his way to Nertman's. She didn't lie to him, he was sure.

"It's the truth sir," the man squeaked and started shrinking from Brosch's intense stare. He was done with this man and obviously he had no use for him. Before he could dispatch him, like he normally did, Onyx stepped into his peripheral.

He turned his head to his guard and raised a questioning eyebrow. "Do you have something to add, Onyx?"

"015 just arrived in the crossroads."

"Did he now?" Brosch was interested to hear exactly what his best tracker had to say. Especially if he happened to be on someone's trail. He didn't forget the cowering man with the bad report. He narrowed his eyes at him and growled, "I'll deal with you later."

He followed Onyx out the inn door into the morning sun. The ground was still mush from the amount of rain that fell the night before, so he knew he'd have mud later that needed to be scraped off his shoes. He approached the white-haired tracker with the black eyes. Such a formidable looking man to everyone, except Brosch.

"I would say it was a coincidence meeting you here, but you and I know that's not the case." He already was informed that 015 was heading this direction which is why Brosch was so eager to know why. He had a gut feeling that 1 was here. She had to be, even though that stupid idiot inside said that all places were looked through in the crossroads.

015's gaze drifted toward the inn door behind him. Then looked back at him with those cold looking eyes. "I know this seems out of character for me. I did have Chasers travel south with the hounds to locate the Rens trail. I'll have word soon as to their location. They won't be able to go into hiding again. Now that I know exactly what to look for."

"That's all well and good. But you aren't tracking the Rens right now, are you?"

"No, sir." The tracker's eyes narrowed again at the inn's door. "It's the escapee. 034."

Brosch's face twisted into a sneer. His prized Healer. How that idiot hasn't been captured yet is still a mystery, but he was betting on 015 knowing why that was.

"I'm gathering since you are standing here that he came this direction." 015 nodded swiftly confirming his statement. "And where exactly is the trail leading to?" He could already guess since 015's eyes kept moving there throughout their conversation.

"The inn sir."

"I've had the inn checked and have been in it since last night. There is no possible way he was there. I would have known."

"I believe your word sir. But I still need to check."

"Is he traveling alone?"

"He looks to be traveling with two other individuals. By what I have, and haven't picked up, they are not people of Might." That was very interesting news. Brosch was positive the Ren did have people among them that didn't have ability, just like he did, but that didn't explain why they would just give a very powerful Healer up. Well, he did know 034 was useless to them and only used his ability on him, but that didn't mean he couldn't be held as leverage.

The question was, who was holding him as leverage now? "Check away 015. I will watch your progress." And so, he did. 015 continued the lead inside the inn with Brosch watching his movements. He never had many chances of watching 015 work, but he wasn't called the best for nothing. They eventually found their way to a room on the second floor, room 11. It was unlocked and when they entered the room was empty, just as it was reported to him earlier.

"He was here," 015 stated. He moved about the room in a way, picking up on things Brosch couldn't see. He hated to rely on people like 015. Why couldn't he just have all the abilities? It would be easier to take over if he had that much control. Instead of years, and still getting opposition from a few rebel groups, he probably could have taken over the country in a matter of months. No one would oppose him, and truthfully, once he had 1 back, no one would.

015's brow scrunched in confusion. "He didn't exit back out through the door, and he was here with someone."

"Find out where he left from this room while I go talk to the owner of this fine establishment." Brosch made his way back down the stairs and flagged down the owner, the towering mustached man in a dirty apron.

"Who was in room 11?"

"Didn't catch his name, sir."

"You surely remember what he looks like."

"Of course, of course." The man he described was very much not 034.

"Was he traveling with others?"

"I believe so sir. He asked for two rooms originally, but I could only give him the one."

"Two?" That was curious. Many couldn't afford the prices of one room in an inn like this one,
let along two.

"Did he look affluent? Someone who looked to have a lot of money." The barman fidgeted uncomfortably. Brosch knew the man didn't want to tell him, but the man also knew if he didn't, there will be blood on his hands, either his or his family's.

"He paid generously. He wore traveling clothes, but they still were in decent condition, sir." This was a very good development.

"And his companions?"

"Had their hoods up sir. One had similar attire to his and the other looked, well opposite them. You could tell his clothes didn't fit and they were worn through." So, the little Healer found some deep pocketed friends.

015 came down the stairs and when Brosch lifted his brow in question the man stated, "He left out the window. Guessing last night."

What was wrong with his cronies? Did they not know how to do their job? How can that sniveling Healer slip by once again?

He had help. Brosch knew this now. Two individuals, one very influential man and means and the other… he turned back to the bar man. "The other well-dressed one. Was it a man or woman?" He saw the barman scratch his head, thinking about it.

"I can't recall sir."

"You can't recall, or you won't tell?" He was getting nowhere, which meant he wasn't being threatening enough.

"I swear sir," the barman started pleading. "I couldn't tell. The person was tall but not as muscled as the man I talked to. That's all I remember."

Could it be possible? Was she here? *You will see her, but not see her.*

"No!" Brosch roared. He saw her just like that seer said, but he didn't. He would have recognized her. Unless…he received the wrong description.

Don't trust anyone. He should never have trusted her. No matter. He'll deal with the traitor when he gets back. For now, he was on a mission. He had a feeling that 015 was on the right trail, and that trail could lead not only to his Healer, but 1.

He turned to his tracker with a very deep frown on his face. "Keep tracking him. I think his companions are more then they seem, since they escaped under my whole army. I have business in Nertman. I will be immediately heading back to my stronghold to get some answers on exactly who we are dealing with. I want a report of where they're headed."

"Understood," 015 nodded and strode out the inn. He didn't need any other direction. He was that good.

"Move out, Onyx," he barked at his guard. The man took a step to hover in Brosch's shadow. They were going to deal with one traitor after another, until no one in this country resisted his rule. No one.

Chapter 22
He Lived

Evan

"Well, well. Who do we have here?" A large man wearing what looked to be animal furs of some kind stepped out from behind a pine to the left. Evan was still too hopeful and optimistic. He should have known something like this would happen. First the Chasers were after him, then he was essentially a prisoner with the Ren and now that he was with these two, whoever they were, they were getting ambushed. Can he not just visit somewhere peaceful? His life never seemed to be just that.

"I don't know Zeke, but they sure look tasty," a voice called from behind them. When Evan glanced over his shoulder, another man, smaller looking but still with the same furs and a few teeth missing by the look of it, was ambling slowly forward. He only looked scary because of his crazy eyes.

And then what do you know, they were surrounded as eight other men emerged around him, Eva and Jace. Three on ten? No wait, he shouldn't count himself because he didn't know anything about fighting, so two on ten. Did Eva fight? Oh crap! What if she didn't? Then it would just be one on ten! The odds were just getting smaller and smaller.

"Did he just say tasty?" Jace asked him out the side of his mouth.

"Yeah, I think he did."

"Okay then. Just didn't want to think I heard wrong." No, he heard what Evan heard. The larger man, called Zeke by his cannibalistic friend chuckled at the comment. Evan saw that he had a large club in his hand. The other men closing in all had different weapons, but one thing was clear. It didn't seem like they were getting out of this with a friendly chat.

"Looks to me like some rich little boys and their servant got lost. Maybe we should relieve them of their belongings."

He dared a look at Eva, but he had to blink several times because in her spot stood, well, what he would imagine a male version of Eva would look like. Did she mean to change her appearance? He'd have to ask her *if* they got out of this alive.

"Lost?" Jace called out to the man. Oh please, no. Don't antagonize him. "I think you are mistaken sir. I know exactly where I am."

"You hear that Gabe? He said he knows where he is," the man yelled across to his wily friend.

"Nope. He don't Zeke. He can't know, because no one ever leaves here alive," he snickered like it was a dirty secret. Evan just gulped knowing that it was probably true. Considering the now ten pairs of eyes looking at them like meat snacks.

"Maybe we can settle this with words." Jace said confidently. They just laughed at him, the whole lot of them.

"I don't think that's happening, Jace," Evan hissed at him. Jace shrugged his shoulders, looking at Evan with a smirk. No, that wasn't a look of terror like his insides were feeling now. He looked pleased. Was Jace sane?

"Let the record show Evan, I did ask nicely." And as if that was the cue, everyone started moving at once. Some of the men charged and Jace's arm flung out with a knife leaving his fingertips and burrowing into one of the wild men's leg. He howled and dropped clutching his leg.

He spun around to make sure Eva was okay, but she seemed to already have a sword unsheathed and already taken several steps toward the crazy men. He felt a large hand on his shoulder and a knife handle was shoved into his hand. "If they get close, just stab the pointy end in," Jace winked and went to clash with the oncoming foe.

His head swiveled left and right watching between Jace and Eva as they blocked and moved flawlessly, deflecting blows, and delivering their own. It was happening all so fast. The howls and grunts of men and horses stamping their hooves in disapproval of what was happening around them.

Evan wasn't prepared as the crazy eyed wily man came at him with a knife raised above his head. He knocked over Evan. His breath rushed out of him as he landed on his back. And as the man leapt, it was the fear of death that came over Evan, that once familiar feeling every day he was in Brosch's Stronghold.

No more. He was sick and tired of being afraid. His grip tightened on the knife handle, and he did what Jace told him. The knife sunk into the man's thigh and stopped him in his tracks. That gave Evan enough time to jump up out of the way, leaving the knife stuck in the man's leg.

The guy was still half crazed and charged at him again. Crap! He didn't have another weapon. He was doomed. Throwing up his arms to shield himself as much as possible and awaiting the impact, it never came. He didn't realize he had closed his eyes and when he opened them, the crazy man was withering on the ground with Eva standing over him, her sword to his throat.

And yes, when he meant Eva, he meant in all her glory. Long braided black hair, skin that looked as smooth as silk and her penetrating hazel eyes. However, she was looking at the man now though, he cringed and tried crawling away, with the knife still in his leg.

"I suggest you all go crawl back in the hole you came out of and leave us alone," Jace's voice was raised for all of them to hear. "Otherwise, we'll take your life next time."

Evan looked around and saw that every one of them, cut or stabbed, were not fatally wounded. He knew this because of his ability that every one of them would live. Well, except for one man, Zeke. It wasn't anything to do with his current wounds. The man had a large spot on his lung. He was dying and probably wouldn't last the winter. It seemed to be Evan's curse to find these incurable diseases. He never asked to be that type of Healer, he didn't. It was kind of like knowing a person's fate, and he was a nobody. That wasn't a responsibility he wanted.

"Tell them to forget about us," Eva said softly, not moving her gaze from the crazy eyed man. Jace must have known she was talking to him because he continued.

"One more thing. Speak about this or tell anyone about us, and I will personally hunt you down." It was weird seeing these men, now broken and bleeding making their way back among the trees, leaving marks of only their blood on the ground as the only evidence of an altercation.

Once the last man shuffled out of view did Jace relax. He turned toward Eva with a cocky grin. Eva, eyes still fixed on the trees, didn't see him. His grin faded as he walked up to her, now concern written on his face.

"Eva," he said her name softly touching her elbow. Always with the touching and looks with these two. There had to be something going on between them, even though he's sure they would openly deny it if asked.

Her head turned slowly to meet his gaze and Evan saw that her eyes were glazed black. He stumbled back a little from shock. But, with just a few blinks of her eyes and they were back to hazel once more. Did he just imagine that?

"He's not a good person," she said softly to Jace.

"But you are," he said back brushing one of her raven locks out of her face. "You also looked pretty good wielding that sword, sort of."

"Sort of?" Now her face softened, and a small smile appeared on her lips.

"You were a little slow. I think that's because we haven't kept up with our training with all this traveling. We'll have to rectify that."

She pushed him slightly, but Evan could tell it was in a playful manner and she mumbled, "Jerk."

"So, Evan," Jace's gaze landed on his, "you're alive!"

"It appears so." Jace chuckled and came over and clapped him on the back.

"You did good. You just forgot to keep the knife. You let yourself become vulnerable. We'll have to work on that." He sauntered off to pull his pack off his horse.

"What do you mean by that?" Evan asked.

"He means, you need some training," Eva looked at him and shrugged. "You have fight in you, so there's no reason not to."

"Can I ask you something?"

"Sure," she moved toward her horse and was also removing her pack. Evan followed her so his question wasn't overheard.

"Is there something between you and Jace?" He knew he'd get the response that he did. She shook her head and huffed out a laugh.

"And why would you think that?"

"Don't think I don't know how the two of you look at each other? Like you're the only two people there. And I think you know what I'm talking about." She blushed but she kept her mouth in a thin line. Evan continued, "That's not all either. You were on the brink just then. You were somewhere else, and he brought you back. You can't deny that."

Her eyes fixed on his studying Evan for a few moments. He wasn't sure how she would react to that. Again, he was taken by surprise at her reaction, like he always was with her.

"You know so much, and I hardly know anything about me. I don't really know what we have," she turned her head to look at Jace who was now moving around, picking up large logs, apparently to build a fire. "And I'm afraid that if I let it out, then it won't be our secret anymore."

"What's the worst that can happen by telling me?"

He saw that little flicker of black again. So, he didn't just imagine that.

"I can think of a lot of things. Mainly, if someone pries you for information against your control, well, that's a big deal."

"There is a way for you to bind that information, so I don't tell anyone else."

"Is that what Brosch did to you?" He opened his mouth to answer, but he couldn't. Of course, he was bound by the very man she asked about to not ever answer questions about him. It hurt like hell if he pushed against it or gave any indication. "I'll just take that as a yes."

She walked toward where the firewood was being piled up and rolled a log onto its end and she perched on top of it.

"I'm not going to bind you Evan. That isn't right. Maybe I'll tell you eventually, but we have more pressing matters at hand."

"Like?" he inquired.

"Breaking the bind Brosch put on your mind."

Chapter 23
Squabbles

Jace

He continued to gather loose twigs around him while Evan quietly talked with Eva. Jace wondered why the conversation had to be hushed up. Shouldn't Jace be privileged to that conversation too? He shot Evan a death glare, but of course he wasn't looking his way, so it went unnoticed.

This activity reminded him of all the logs he split up at school. They weren't far from the school. It was back south a little way, but he really should forget that place. It took him away from his family and away from Eva.

His arms were full of small kindling, so he turned to go back to the other two. Eva looked, well, like Eva always looked. Her long black hair made Jace want to wrap it around his wrist and pull her towards him and crush his lips down to hers. Whoa, where did that come from?

Jace shook his head and dropped the wood next to the logs he had already collected. "What'd I miss?" he tried to ask nonchalantly.

"I'm going to invade Evan's mind. He doesn't seem so happy with the idea." What was she going on about?

"Woman, I hope you have a more detailed explanation." He worked to build a fire as quickly as possible. Their clothes were soaked and the only way the rest of this journey could be bearable is if they were dry. She continued with her explanation as he worked.

"His mind is blocked. For some reason he thinks I might have this same ability as Brosch, since he mentioned about me binding him to information."

"What information?" he narrowed his eyes at Evan, seeing the man visible gulp. That's right, be weary.

"Nothing," Eva waved it off, "it wasn't important. I just don't think any of us knows what I'm capable of." Oh, did she forget all the times in training that she knocked him on his ass with some crazy weird wind and that she says prophesies all the time like they're the most common thing? She had a lot more crazy in her than sane. He knew there was something dark in her. He didn't know exactly how it got in there, but he's seen it more and more as their time together wore on.

In his heart, he knew that there was something he had to do to help her with that darkness. Fates, he pulled her from those very scary depths only a little over a week ago at Newly's. He couldn't lose her to it and whatever this binding business she was talking about was too risky.

"No," Jace said sternly from his crouched position. He was using his striking kit from his pack to ignite the kindling that was now neatly stacked at his feet.

"Um, did you just say no?" he could hear the hint of disbelief in her voice.

"Well, someone has to say no to this crazy plan. Since Evan here thinks it's all fine and dandy to poke around in his brain, I'm going to be his conscious and say it's not a good idea."

"I've already did before and he's fine." What did she mean by that? When did this happen?

"What? Why would you do that?"

"He didn't remember his name, Jace," now there was that fight he was waiting for in her voice. "What was I supposed to do, call him that stupid number? I wasn't going to lower him to that status."

He looked up and his and Eva's gazes locked. They stared at each other, determined not to blink before the other.

"Hate to interrupt," Evan's voice rung in his ears, but he was only half listening to what he said next. "I get Jace's point, it's risky poking around in my brain. And Eva, you've only glimpsed in my memories which isn't as evasive, and I just realized reading memories and mind control are different abilities." Wait, what was he saying? Jace blinked and turned toward Evan.

"Did you say mind control?" and at the same time Eva asked him, "Reading memories and binding are separate?" Evan threw up his hands to try and get them not to talk at once.

"It's a fine line, but yeah essentially it is different. Your typical Scholar, great at learning and memories, is common and it's more of an indigo aura. However, violet, which can have varying shades, is the aura for someone with ability of mind control. Yes, Eva's read my memories and she could possibly have control of mind, but I'm just speculating."

"So," Jace began, "you would take the chance, even though you don't know if she can or not?"

"Yeah, I would." Evan must have had something slipped into his water and made him crazy because there was no way that logic made sense. Jace just shook his head and finished lighting the fire and feeding it with wood.

"Jace, listen to me," Eva crouched right down next to him, probably trying to draw his attention away from the fire, but didn't work. "We have a better chance against Brosch if we knew more about him. What if we learn a weakness of his? I'd rather have an advantage then just sit around in the dark and be surprised."

He finally turned and looked at Eva. Even though she seemed to be stern in her decision, her eyes said what she was really feeling. She looked scared. That feeling of not knowing, not being able to prepare. Yes, she was a seer, but that wasn't always reliable. She needed information to form a plan.

Jace did believe Evan knew some things, like all the aura and ability stuff, but he hadn't heard him say a peep about Brosch, even though he'd been in his stronghold for years. Deep down, he knew this had to be done, but was he willing to risk Eva's or Evan's lives trying?

Eva reached out and put a hand on his cheek. She probably felt his feelings on the subject change, but he still wasn't saying it aloud. He sighed and went back to making sure the fire was big enough for all of them to dry their clothes.

He saw Eva out of the corner of his eye stand and say to Evan, "We're going to try it."

"I don't know if I should feel grateful or relieved at that," Evan continued. "And why are you building a fire?" The last was obviously aimed at Jace.

"We need to dry our clothes. Unless you want to chafe and possibly contract some cold or flu from the cooler air we're entering." He stood and started taking off his cloak. He grabbed two sturdy sticks and shoved the points in the ground and strung up the cloak between the two so the fire could warm it.

"Well, those seem to be two things I would like to avoid," Evan agreed. His gaze drifted over to where Eva stood, and his eyes widened. Jace looked that way too and a large smirk appeared on his face. Eva had already done the same as he with her cloak and was unbuttoning her top.

Her fingers stilled at what she was doing and looked up at the pair of them with an eyebrow raised. "What?"

"Are you really going to…" Evan waved his hand about, probably tongue-tied at the prospect of Eva taking off her clothes. Jace probably should help her to stay modest, but if he were honest with himself, he'd love to see her anyway he could, and without clothes was at the top of his list.

"We need to dry our clothes," she stated. "How else are my clothes going to dry?" She shrugged and continued with the buttons.

"Well, I, umm," Evan stumbled over his words. "You're a woman!" he finally squeaked out.

"So, I should do something different because I'm a woman?" By now her top was off and her breasts, sadly for Jace, were contained in a binding. Jace was working on his pants as Evan's head swiveled to him quickly.

"You're not going to do anything?"

As an answer Jace smiled and winked. Of course, he wasn't. No way was he going to stop his tempting vixen. But he also paused in removing his pants, because, well, he realized that right now, he'd be sporting a visual of what he was feeling. So, he made the decision to leave the pants on.

"Oh fine, Evan. You're more of a prude than an old woman," Eva dug in her pack and removed a blanket. She wrapped it around her shoulders, and it covered her. Jace groaned and sat on a stump that he moved over close to the fire.

"Way to go Evan, I was enjoying the show."

"Of course, you would. Look at you! You've probably had hundreds of women throw themselves at you. What's one more?" Evan thought that of him? That had never happened to Jace. Oh sure, the last birthday party there were some of the village girls who came up and talked with him, tried to even flirt with him, but he only wanted one woman to flirt with him.

Eva's eyes sought his out and two things blazed inside, which wasn't good for him now. Anger and sadness. He could even feel her tumultuous feelings which were making his lust-filled feelings disappear and be replaced by hers. It was an odd feeling, but yes, he was angry at what Evan thought of him and how the comment effected Eva, but he also was, well, not sad but worried that anything he said, she wouldn't believe him and in turn does not want him, which that made him sad.

"Is that true?" she asked in a small voice. He didn't look away, he wanted her to know that it had always ever been her.

"No, love. No one's ever thrown themselves at me," he used Evan's wording. "And besides, if they did, I wouldn't know because I never paid attention to them. I've only ever wanted your attention."

"Mine?" Maybe she felt his sincerity, because she wasn't feeling as angry, and she was more confused than sad now.

"Oh, for Fate's sake!" Evan threw up his hands and got to his feet. "I don't get you two. How can you not know how you each feel for each other? Are you two that dense? Eva, of course he wants you. That man would probably lie in front of stampeding horses for you."

"Then why did you say that he'd been with other woman?" she asked.

"Well, because that's the obvious thing, isn't it?" he started to be unsure. Which he should be because he was wrong.

"Eva," Jace started, "I think he's made his mind up about me being a mayor's son and what mayor's sons are typical of. Or am I overstepping my assumption, Evan?" At the look Evan was given him, he knew he was spot on in that assessment.

"I don't follow," Eva admitted.

"He thinks that because of my position, and I would assume also how I look, because I know I don't look like the underbelly of a toad, that woman want to be with me and if I let myself, I could be showered in affections and could easily take my pick. And women would be willing to remove their clothes and much more with me." He wasn't the least bit amused.

"That's not right," Eva stood and moved toward Evan with her eyes narrowed. He looked about ready to bolt but stood his ground. "You'd say things about him without even knowing him?"

"They are all the same," Evan seethed. He obviously had someone in his life that made him view mayor's sons in this light. Eva stopped inches away from him. With her height, she was able to stare straight at him and her face was hard as stone.

"If that's how you feel about Jace, then what about me? Jace's father practically adopted me, which makes me a mayor's daughter. What do you think of that?"

"Uh, what?" Jace could tell Evan was caught off guard with that bit of information.

"If you so abhor mayors' sons, then you must abhor their daughters as well. Come on then, don't hold back, I want to know what you think about the daughters."

He didn't know what Evan saw in Eva's eyes, but it was enough for him to concede. He saw her fight and he was smart enough to not get on that side of her.

"Nothing. Mayor's daughters are well protected, and everyone knows that they never have a chance with them. And I honestly didn't know you were one."

Jace couldn't keep it in. He laughed hard. It was crazy but he totally understood where Evan was coming from. Eva did not look the mayor's daughter part. All he had to do was think of his sisters and their craziness or any other woman for that matter, and Eva never would fit in. I think she knew that too. She was more comfortable with a sword in her hand and dirt on her clothes than doing whatever woman usually did, which come to think of it, Jace knew nothing about.

"Why are you laughing," Eva asked, but he could see the corners of her mouth turn up.

"I'm just trying to picture you actually hanging out with my sisters and enjoying whatever they usually do."

"Heck no! I hate that stuff. I only did it to appease your mom. I'd rather get sliced up on the training yard then get my fingers pricked by needles." Jace burst out laughing again.

"To remind you of what we were talking about," Eva said above his laughing, "was the fact that Evan is judging people before even knowing them."

Jace's laughter died, but he wasn't so angry as he was over Evan's previous comments. He got it. Everyone makes assumptions. Just because everyone does, doesn't make it right though. "Then let's agree," Jace stood and approached Evan, who visible looked sick, "that we all don't say things we don't know about each other, no matter if it is said out of anger or joking. We only speak truths and if we don't know, we'll ask."

"I like that idea," Eva nodded. They both turned their gazes on Evan waiting.

"Okay." He didn't look all that pleased but he knew that Jace could certainly hurt him at any point.

"Excellent. Now, let's hurry up and get our clothes dry, and that means you need to take yours off too." He smirked at Evan and turned back to walk to his stump. It's like Jace felt Evan's eyes roll.

"Yeah, yeah," he heard him mutter.

"And I'll go find water to refill our canteens," Eva scooped the containers up and trudged off.

"So," Evan began as Jace sat back on his stump with his pack in his hand rummaging around for a bit to eat, "have you been with a woman?"

Jace paused in his seeking and looked up at Evan, who was removing his cloak. "Nope." He went back paying attention to his pack.

"Eva?" He looked up again, but his eyes were slits. Evan saw them but put his hands up to placate his mood. "Hey, we just agreed to ask if we didn't know. And you two are awfully familiar with each other, so I had to ask."

"No." Jace didn't want to admit that for some reason. He already thought of Eva as his. She had even brought up when he was feeling jealous, like to her it was a foreign emotion. She didn't see how other men look at her. There had been several times that he wanted to rip a throat out or two from them just glancing her way. He did beat up one person, and he deserved so much worse, but he didn't.

This whole adventure they were on was ridiculous but at the same time revealing. It made him think about his feelings toward Eva and they were not at all subsiding. He felt like they were growing toward something. Whatever it was, it was going to be big, and they were going to be consumed by it.

Chapter 24
Guardian

Eva

Why are men so confusing? They don't even make sense half the time. Why would Evan joke like that? Or was he serious? Eva wasn't sure what she felt when thinking about Jace with other women. Angry for sure, but was it jealousy? All she knew is that deep down, if any other woman dared touch Jace, her life would be ended. Well, okay maybe she shouldn't out right kill them, but she will make them wish they never set eyes on Jace again.

She found a small stream not too far from where they had set up camp. She scooped up a bit of water and let if run through her fingers. She took another scoop and drank a bit. It looked and tasted fine. Nothing she could see that would indicate it being undrinkable. This will do.

It was hard for Eva to move around in just a blanket. The water-skins at least had a strap so she could carry them on her shoulder but bending down and filling them up while holding a blanket around her, now that was little trickier. Trying to fill it up with one hand was harder than she expected. She looked around her and seeing as she was out of sight from the guys and no one else was around either, she decided to ditch the blanket. No sense in making this harder for her.

With the blanket gone she was free to use both hands which made filling these skins much more efficient. As she waited for water to fill into them her mind drifted to the problem at hand. Evan's bound mind. There was this big block there, reminding her of a solid poured wall. At least a brick wall you can chip away at. Not sure if there is a weakness in the block that she could take advantage of. Not that she would know what she was doing anyway. And is the block only affecting his memories associated with Brosch, or more?

She had that feeling again that she really could do this, she could help Evan. But how to do it, and safely so as to not permanently damage Evan's mind, was another thing. She needed help. Oh Fates, she really didn't want to screw it up. She closed her eyes to center herself, but when she opened them, she wasn't at the stream any longer.

The Station still looked the same. Same clear bench and same white nothingness around her. Eva should just get used to this being a daily occurrence now. She seemed to be here as much as she was back in Hockland.

"You again," a voice chimed behind her. She turned and noticed who it was. It was the man who helped her with Mayor Jebrow. He was the first one she met at the Station. He helped her the last time when she needed it, so maybe he's here to do the same.

"I need some help," Eva admitted.

"Of course, you do," he stated like he already knew this. "That's my job. When the Sparks I'm assigned need assistance, I answer their call."

"That's what was up with the paper last time?" Eva remembered him checking a list of some sort or other when she met him before. It was a list of names.

"Truly the list is useless at this point because I've not seen another Spark in a very long time. It's been many, let's see, centuries since one of my assigned…well actually." He paused his brow scrunched in thought. "That's right, we haven't seen ANY Spark at the Station in centuries."

"You mean, people would come here all the time? Why aren't they coming now?" The man smiled, but it wasn't at all happy. Eva would say it was a sad smile, a resigned smile. He sat down on the bench patting the seat beside him, indicating for her to take a seat as well. He was still dressed in that white robe and seemed to have this otherworldly glow about him. As before, she didn't feel threatened at all by his presence. The feeling she got was like being with an old friend. Weird, since this is only the second time they have met.

She sat beside him, hoping that this time she'd get more information. She didn't have any rush to get back. Well, maybe so she isn't found in the state that she was in, probably frozen at the stream with an overflowing container of water, almost naked.

"Centuries ago, it was commonplace that Sparks would appear in this very Station to receive assistance from their assigned ones. It was a great honor to be placed in such a position."

"Why haven't I heard or read about this place?" Eva was curious by nature, but this place seemed so surreal. She still wondered if it was just her subconscious or a waking dream. But maybe not. Jace felt her 'gone' when she last was at the Station with Seraphim.

"It got lost through time I suppose. Or no one is worthy enough anymore to speak with us. Maybe they think they already know it all, not see what potential they could have. We are here to help you grow and learn. Maybe those are the reasons you are here. Are you a worthy Spark? What will you grow and become on your own? Probably nothing without our help."

"But who are you?" He just smiled at her with a bit of a mischievous glint in his diamond-colored eye. She had a funny feeling that she was not going to like his answer.

"We were given the label of Guardian. Although I really don't guard anything. I more 'guide' Sparks, but I'm not the all-knowing Fates so I just go with the flow."

"Were you always a Guardian?"

"No," he said. Eva was waiting for him to go into further detail, but it seemed that was all he was going to say about that. "Back to my question. Are you worthy, Eva?"

"How am I to be the judge of my own worth? I'm finding out I'm not a normal person with Might."

"Indeed, you are not."

"But, why? I don't understand. Why me?"

"The Fates do what they do best. Place people in the world that can influence it one way or the other. I don't want to say it's a game to them, but they let it all play out."

"Multiple outcomes."

"Exactly." She remembered when she had her vision about Sonya. She only saw one possible outcome, and she was able to change that outcome by interjecting herself as the victim instead of Sonya. Well, she didn't know she would be the victim at the time, but she was able to use her strength to avoid certain ruin and Jace was there, which he wasn't in the vision she had of Sonya. So, was she able to do that with all her visions? The event still happened, just not how the vision showed.

"Are some visions false then if they can be changed? Why send it?"

"Rules are meant to be broken at times. Maybe they wanted to see if you would," he said with that smirk of his. She was starting to not like that look on him. "Enough about what the Fates are up to. You said you were here for some help. That, I can do."

"I still have more questions though."

"All will be answered or revealed in time."

"I'd rather have them now," she mumbled.

"Patience, young one." He chuckled and tousled her hair. She felt a slight prick at the contact. Interesting, but probably nothing as she didn't feel any different. "You need assistance as a Manipulator."

"A what?"

"A Manipulator, one with control over the mind."

"What color aura is that?"

"Which one do you think it is? You have seen this aura recently." Eva thought about it. Yes, Willow. Her aura color was this deep violet. Not real dark but purple in color. Based on her Might ability, it seemed like she was doing something like mind control. Kind of reminded her of Jace when he persuades people. She wondered it if was similar.

"Purple?" He smiled in that way of his. It had that 'see I told you so' quality to it.

"So, you are needing to do some mind control."

"No, I don't want to control him, just fix it. Like, take the mind control away? I don't know if I'm describing this right."

"You can see something in a tangible sense when you go into his mind."

"Yes! Like a wall has been erected." He sat there stroking his chin in thought.

"Binding the mind."

"That is what I've heard it called, yes. Do you know how to fix that?"

"Not many have been able to do such manipulation. It's not very ethical to do unless the person agrees to the binding."

"I'm positive it was a forced binding."

"You wouldn't need my help if it was a voluntary binding, that's for sure."

"How do you mean?"

"That wall you said you see in this individual's mind, well, it would look different if it was voluntary, kind of see-through if you will. More made of glass, easier to break. Voluntary binding isn't necessarily permanent. And since the individual is aware that they asked for the binding, they know it was probably for the best. But, if they want it to be gone, then it can be undone, really, by any other Manipulator."

"So, with a forced one, I can't do anything?" This is starting to sound hopeless for Evan. They need the information he had to be able to stop Brosch.

"Do you think you can do something?"

"Yes," she was certain of it. That feeling that she could help him came back.

"Let's just say, maybe a voluntary binding can replace a forced binding."

"It can?" The man just shrugged. She narrowed her eyes at him. "You're not sure."

"Haven't heard it done before, so no. Just a theory."

"Okay, so I could possibly give that a try. How would I go about doing that though?"

"Trust in your instincts. You didn't come here for any help involving the mountain incident. I suggest the same approach. Use your strength, but not alone. This could be treacherous going into the mind, you need a grounding point." So, use Jace. With their connection, they were able to move a substantial number of heavy rocks. Literally felt like moving a mountain. She just had to make sure he was okay with evading Evan's mind. He didn't seem so keen on it when they discussed it the last time. Maybe if he was also involved, he would be more accepting of it. "Look at the time," the man said bringing Eva out of her thoughts. "I have to see to my other duties." The man stood and started to walk away.

"I still have questions."

"No need for worrying. Just 'feel' your Spark work it out," he said over his shoulder and continued, fading into the white nothingness.

"But I still don't know-"

In the next blink she was back at the stream. She instinctively stood from her crouched position and looked around her. Still the same empty forest around her. She looked down at the container clenched in her hand, filled to the brim. By the amount of light and possible direction of the sun through the trees, not much time had passed. Still, going to the Station left her vulnerable, and she hated that feeling.

Eva sighed and started replacing the cap on the water skin finishing what she was trying to say at the Station. "Your name."

Chapter 25
Travel Worn

Evan

At this point, he thought that dying would be better than this torture. Evan seriously did not get enough rest at the last stop. Was he going to argue with those two? Not a chance. Eva was very insistent that they needed to leave with a look that asked them to dare question her. Yeah, after seeing her fight, and her ability levels, there was no way he was going to cross her. And Jace, well, he was one scary dude. No need to go into details on that one.

He maybe got around two hours of rest because one, he felt groggy when he woke, and two, he was still weak feeling. Not like he has been 100 percent healthy from his time in captivity, but he certainly had better days. This was not one of those days. He prayed for just a full day. 24 hours of rest. Then, maybe he wouldn't feel like he was at death's door. Also, this running for his life did not help with his anxiety level.

Nor the prospect of Eva possibly rooting around in his mind. He knew that she had good intentions and only wanted to help him. Oh, he knew he had specific information on Brosch that could possibly lead to his downfall that she was also after. Just like Willow and the Rens, trying their best to force the information out of him. Well, they didn't understand why he couldn't tell them and treated him like the enemy.

The minute he met Eva and Jace, their treatment of him was quite different. It almost reminded him of a time long before he was taken by Brosch. They treated him as an equal. Granted, Jace mainly was giving him crap and giving him death glares, but it wasn't out of spite or where he had been before. Evan was the one with the issue, at least concerning Jace.

He looked over at the towering man who was currently stone-faced and slowly scanning their surroundings as if an attack could happen at any time. He was hyper-aware of everything and although Evan wasn't a small man, he looked small compared to Jace. If he didn't have to contend with Jace's muscles. Seriously, Evan was so out of shape it wasn't even funny. Not like he was worried about that before, but seeing Jace, he was worried about it now.

His real issue wasn't because Jace had more muscles or even was good-looking. It was the fact that he was a mayor's son. All the wealth and privilege that comes with the position. Only the first few years Brosch just took children no matter who they were, but now mayor's sons were given special treatment. Not like they would all have Might power, but they are in a position of influence. There were few strongholds that still opposed Brosch, but he hadn't pressed too hard on those individuals because they still give him what he wanted and go along with his crazy rules.

If only he was still a mayor's son.

"What's on your mind?" A soft quiet voice cut through Evan's thinking. Eva was looking at him from her perched position on her horse. He had not noticed at some point she pulled ahead and was now riding beside him.

"Nothing much. Thinking about a past I would rather not remember."

"That, I can understand." Eva always sounded so sure and if Evan was to admit it, he trusted her. Also, if she was who he thought she was. The fated first child that Brosch took, then she had more memories to bury then most. "But there are not always bad things in the past. I hope you don't think of me any less for, well, invading your mind, but your mother seemed like a very sweet lady."

"She was the best." Evan remembered only bits and pieces of her. Eva's dark hair and even her soft smiles reminded him of his mom. She was always a caring individual and believed the best in everyone. She laid her life down for him, literally. He tried not to remember what happened when he was taken, but it overshadowed a lot of his memories of his mother and that was the only one he could remember.

He openly winced and tried his best to push the memory away. Then he felt a little jolt on the back of his hand, and he pulled it away only to realize it was Eva's hand.

"Sorry Evan didn't mean to pry, you just seemed sad and, well, I don't like seeing people sad. I'd even take an angry person over a sad one any day."

"What was that?" He continued to rub the back of his hand.

"Oh, not sure. It happens most every time I touch someone. I try to avoid it as much as possible. But, to see what you were seeing," Eva shrugged, "I had to have skin contact. If that makes sense."

"You mean…"

"Yeah," she turned away and seemed to be looking off into the distance. Evan wasn't sure how he felt about Eva seeing his memories. She had done it before, but it didn't feel intrusive as he first thought. Even back in Kretz Swamp when she first went into his mind, he felt nothing. Like a thief, in and out without any notice. He didn't know if that was scarier then knowing.

"Just forget what you saw." It was his past and burden. He didn't need Eva feeling sorry for him. His story was the same as many children that were taken. Who would willingly part from their own child? Most of the Numbered parents were slaughtered. He could have saved his mom, if only they just let him go back to her. Ugh. He said he wouldn't think about it and now he was. He shook his head and chanted to himself that tomorrow will be a better day, tomorrow will be a better day.

"Tomorrow brings death. Only the true light of the Child can conquer it." Geez, here's for hoping it will be better. Evan glanced over at Eva with a questioning look. She was still looking off into the distance on her horse, but she didn't seem altogether there."

"Um, what do you mean by saying that, Eva?" She didn't respond right away. "Eva?" Her head slowly turned and if Evan didn't have a good grip on his horse he would have tumbled off because he legit was startled to the point of being extremely terrified. There was no mistaking what he saw. Her unblinking eyes were as black as a bottomless pit. He felt that if he stared into them too long, she might steal his soul.

Her eyelids fluttered and when she blinked, they came back to their normal hazel color. Creepy. Evan jerked his head forward and tried his best to avoid her stare.

"What's going on?" Jace asked in his gruff voice, pulling up along Evan's other side. Great, he couldn't get away now.

"Nothing!" Evan's voice squeaked out. Jace narrowed his eyes at him in suspicion.

"Jace, no need to be hostile toward Evan," Eva reprimanded him. Probably the only person Jace would allow to treat him like that. "Although his mood can be cantankerous at times, Brosch is at fault. Like most of us, he disrupted our lives, killing our loved ones. How would you feel if you must live without the people you love?"

"Eva," Jace's expression immediately softened, and his eyes held a pleading look. "It would devastate me. I don't think I would be the same man."

"And so, Evan isn't the same as if those people were still in his life. I know you can sympathize with Evan's situation, so don't be hurtful all the time towards him."

"It's not that. I could feel you were upset and wanted to make sure that it wasn't because of this guy," Jace jerked his thumb in Evan's direction.

"Me?" Evan looked back and forth between them, although he shrank just a little from Eva's stare, he still wasn't going to take the fall for something he didn't do. "I told you. I didn't do anything. We were just talking."

"Sure, you were," Jace looked skeptical.

"Honestly! We were just talking about the past, not at all a happy discussion, and then Eva started on with a depressing monologue. I was just asking what she meant by it."

"I what?" she asked with a raised brow, looking innocent.

"Seriously Eva, I was trying to think all positive thoughts about tomorrow, hoping that we would at least find some sense of safety at last, and you go and ruin it by saying 'tomorrow brings death' all creepy like."

"I did?" She seriously looked like she had no idea what Evan was talking about.

"Evan," at the sound of his name from Jace, he whipped his head away from Eva's confused face. "Did you witness another prophesy from Eva?"

"I don't think so. I mean, I guess it could have been. Now I'm completely unsure." Evan was paying attention and Eva's eyes were not the characteristic white when a prophesy was being uttered.

"What'd she say exactly?"

"She said the whole 'tomorrow brings death,' and then she said something about a child, a true light. I think, something about conquering it, yes, the true light of a child will conquer it."

"You don't sound sure."

"Am I supposed to remember what she said exactly?"

"You need to make a habit of it, because Eva isn't a typical seer as you have guessed, so anything she says needs to be remembered. Because she won't know what she's saying either when in a trance." Evan threw his hands up and looked up and mentally asked the Fates why him? Why did he have to tolerate such stubborn, slightly aggressive people?

"Is it that big of a deal Jace?" Eva asked.

"Prophesies are a big deal. I wouldn't joke around with them. It's inevitable that they eventually become true. They are certainty. Evan, just pay more attention next time. We don't want to lose any valuable information."

"What do you think it means?" Evan asked, moving his eyes between the two of them. "Tomorrow brings death and the way to conquer it is the true light of a child."

"Any child?" Eva asked with a raised eyebrow.

"You're right," Evan of course heard it differently. "You said *the* child. So, it's something that you can conquer Eva."

"I'm not so sure I'm this Child everyone is prophesizing about. Why do you believe I am?"

"Well-," Evan started to say, but Jace's hand shot out and they all brought their horses to a stop, abruptly ending his thoughts on the prophesy subject.

Evan watched as Jace hopped off his horse and slowly scanned around him. He crouched down and placed a palm on the grassy earth. He breathed in deeply and closed his eyes with a scrunched brow. Evan and Eva waited as Jace stayed that way for a few moments. As soon as he opened his eyes once more, Jace was up and mounting his horse.

"We need to move quicker," Jace announced. "If we don't, we'll be overtaken before we even reach Holds Stronghold."

"How are you even sure?" Evan asked with a confused expression on his face. Was Jace a Tracker? No, that can't be right, Jace didn't have any Might aura.

"You can trust me or not, but wouldn't you want to get there faster anyway?" Jace kicked the sides of his horse to a full gallop.

"Evan," Eva caught his attention. "He speaks the truth. I felt his sincerity. We need to hurry." She also kicked her horse and away she went galloping after Jace.

There was something strange going on with those two. Especially concerning the way they can feel the others' emotions. He had never heard of such a thing. But honestly, he really was tired of being out in the open and those were the only two who were going to keep him safe, so, he might as well keep up with them.

He kicked his own horse into a gallop following their trail. Hopefully whatever, or rather whoever, is tracking them doesn't succeed in their mission. Evan really didn't want to go back to Brosch Stronghold. After escaping, the treatment he would receive would be worse and Evan had a feeling he wouldn't live long once he was captured again.

Chapter 26
Strange Tracks

He was close. Not more than three hours ago they were here in this spot. 015 stood letting the dirt fall from his gloved hand. The embers of a fire were roughly scattered at his feet and were still warm to the touch.

Interesting choice going into these woods. They were known to be cursed, full of savages. By the scent of lingering blood in the air, it looked as if they had a little run in with the locals. It was strange though that no bodies were present. Plenty of blood trails, which he had a few of the men who were with him check it out. He was sure that it was only the savages who were injured, but how did only three people, one being a Healer, manage to scare them back into the woods? Something wasn't right.

"Sir," one of Brosch's cronies called coming up to him. As soon as his eyes landed on the man, he saw him cringe. They always did that. Maybe it was his eyes that did that to them, as they were solid black. Or maybe it was his stern expression. Whatever was the case, it helped keep them in line and they knew bad things would happen to them if they didn't follow his orders.

"Yes?" 015 asked gruffly.

"I came upon one of the savages. He had major blood loss and looked to be feverish. I questioned him on how he received his injuries. He wouldn't say, so I threatened him at sword point and even then, he said he didn't know. All he remembered doing this morning was his usual routine, wake up, wonder around the woods a bit, and at this point he said he would sneak into Tatter Stronghold, but he found himself lying on the ground bleeding instead."

"Are you sure he remembered nothing of what happened?"

"Yes, I'm positive." Another crony approached from a different blood trail that was followed.

"I found a bloodied savage as well," the man said, possibly hearing the last bit of the conversation. "And it was the same with me. He didn't remember how he was injured." Very interesting. Those two with the Healer weren't at all what they seemed. How were they doing it though? There hasn't been a Might who could hide their aura in a long time. One of the two traveling with the Healer had to be a Might and a Manipulator at that. There wasn't any other explanation. Could it be this famed 1?

He only heard snippets of her power from Brosch when he reminisced about his prize that would help him take over the world. Usually, it was when things would take longer than necessary, he would say things like, "if only 1 were here, she could cut them down like cattle with one look," or "pathetic Healers, if it was 1 doing the healing, my cronies could be back to full health within a day." Was she traveling with the Healer? He thought it was unlikely, but with how Brosch acted at the crossroads, maybe.

From the direction their horse tracks were leading, they were on their way to the only other stronghold in this area besides Tatter, Holds Stronghold. He was certain of it. Tatter was a weak stronghold, their defenses weren't strong and their leader wasn't much better. But Holds on the other hand, prime spot to have a stronghold. Buffeted by the mountains on one side and the sea on the other. Not to mention the large river that cut through his land and the only way to cross safely was one bridge. One heavily guarded bridge.

Still, they could be fooling him. Best to check out both. "We'll split here," 015 commanded. "Have about twenty men travel to Tatter Stronghold. Terrorize anyone necessary if they are unwilling to give us the information on any travelers that entered in the last 12 hours. Also send a small envoy back to Brosch Stronghold and request for additional men to be headed this way."

"How many additional men?" one of the cronies asked.

"As many as he's willing to send. This will not be a simple capture as I first thought. I will send a raven directly to him as he is currently in Nertman territory. The envoy should have their answer when they arrive in Brosch."

"Yes, sir."

"The rest will continue to follow the trail with me. If we can capture them before reaching any stronghold, then this will be easier. We will prepare for the worst. Go." He waved them off to do as he asked. They swiftly bowed and dispersed.

So, was he about to come face to face with the mysterious 1? She was the whole reason children were snatched up with the Might in the first place, him included. He could blame her for the reason he was taken from his home. But he knew deep down that she was a mere child just like him when she was taken. No, he knew who was at fault. But he couldn't think like that. Too many eyes and ears to report back to Brosch. They didn't call 015 the best Tracker for nothing. If he continued to perform at his best and deliver the needed results to Brosch, everything would be fine.

As he approached the gathering of horses, twenty or so were already heading out of the tree line toward Tatter Stronghold. He reached his midnight-colored horse. A rare beauty, completely black from nose to hoof. 015 was fortunate to have a bond with this horse. It seemed like the horse also preferred him too. He gave the horse a small loving stroke on his nose and proceeded to mount.

Once settled into the saddle, he looked around at the Chasers and cronies that were left. This pathetic lot did not compare to individuals with the Might. 015 pulled a thin strip of paper and quill from his side satchel, quickly scrawling down what he needed from Brosch. Basically, he was asking for an army. Once done, he rolled the paper into a small tube and tied it with a piece of twine that he also had stowed away.

He whistled, letting his notes float up into the air. Moments later a raven swooped down He held out his gloved hand and the raven landed. Taken the ends of the twine, he secured the note onto the raven's leg. He looked directly into the raven's eyes and spoke, "Nertman Stronghold. Brosch." He raised his hand in the air and the raven flapped his wings and took off, momentarily circled around above him, and then started south toward Nertman.

"We ride!" 015 commended. As a group, they started to move out of the forest with 015 in the lead. He always found who he was looking for, and hopefully this time he surpassed that goal. Then, there was no way Brosch would refuse his request.

Chapter 27
River Crossing

Eva

At last, they reached the river just south of Holds Stronghold. The sun was not quite out of sight, so they had a little light left. Now, how exactly do they cross? Eva thought maybe Jace could just flash one of his cards at the guards and they would just let them cross. However, Jace brought up the fact they would have to wait as the guards checked it out, delaying the crossing.

Eva had some not so friendly ways they could use. She knew that Jace had strong persuasive ability, the problem, she believed Jace didn't know he was using it, much like Newly not knowing he was using Might ability when developing his plans. They just used it instinctively. With Jace, she didn't know how he would react if she told him he had ability. She'd known for a while now because she had trained to block his persuasive nature from their time they spent together as children.

She always tip-toed around it and was still able to make use of his ability. But now that she knew that she also had a similar ability, did that mean she could just persuade the guards herself? Probably shouldn't chance it as the few times she's been in people's minds, other than Evan's of course, she tended to, well, end their lives. She really didn't want to do that with innocent people.

There was also one other possibility, and that was to forge the river and just bypass the bridge altogether. Good idea, but the execution of it, not so much. The river was fast moving and nearly all that tried to cross failed. The problem was the unseen undercurrents that could sweep even an ox up, carrying the large beast down river. In other words, it would be a nearly impossible task to cross, and the bridge was the only sure way.

Jace had his own thoughts on it. "Trust me, I think we can do it," Jace said assuredly.

"Really, forge the river? Do you have a plan that would allow a safe crossing?" Eva questioned.

"I have a plan," he had that darn twinkle in his eye, that mischievous one he got from time to time.

"I wish I could say that I am totally on board with this plan. But I'm not. We can just *persuade* the guards to let us cross. Then, we would for sure be safe."

"We are forging the river," Jace said. Eva could feel his ability caressing her mind, persuading her that forging the river was a good plan. She slammed down her wall blocking his ability and just shook her head.

"Yes, forging the river is an excellent idea," Evan chimed in. Apparently, Jace's ability was affecting him.

"See? Even this guy thinks it's a good idea," Jace indicated to Evan with a jerk of his thumb.

"Evan, you and Jace are out of your minds. This is not a good plan. Let's just stick to crossing the bridge."

"It'll take too long," Jace's brows pinched together in thought.

"Why Jace? Why can't we cross at the bridge?" Eva asked, curious as to what he was thinking now.

"A feeling I have. Hard to explain. It's like, the guards wouldn't be the only ones waiting for us." Ah. So, he was sensing something. Eva wondered if Jace was like her and that he had use of more than one Might ability. It was highly possible and usually if Jace had a 'feeling,' they really should follow it.

"Fine," Eva conceded. "But just to be clear, I still don't like the idea."

"Noted," Jace said with a smirk. Eva really wanted to smack that expression off his face.

As they neared the flowing river, Evan asked in a timid voice, "So, how are we crossing the river?"

"My thoughts were that Eva could use that push thing she does when she flings people out of her way and just does it to the river."

"Eva can do what?"

"Hang on Jace," Eva chimed in. "That's not going to happen. The river *moves and* takes up a ton of space. There's a lot of it and it's strong."

"I think it's worth a try," Jace shrugged.

"But I'm not willing to risk it, as it would take up too much strength, even if I borrowed some, I might possibly become unconscious. And I really don't like that."

"Okay, I can lend you strength, no problem. You moved a mountain; you can move a river." Such confidence Jace had in her ability.

"Wait, hold up," Evan held up his hands, trying to stall the conversation. "What's this about Eva flinging people and what's with you lending strength? That doesn't make any sense."

"How about condensing that push power into a little bubble?" Jace voiced his thoughts not even acknowledging that Evan spoke. "You can possibly create a barrier around us or something." A barrier? Eva thought about how that would look. If she was only concentrating on this barrier and making sure nothing entered it, then it could be possible that the water could just move around the barrier. She'd never thought of using her force ability like that before.

"I guess that might be an option. Never tried it before. I can do a small one to test it out once we reach the river." She wasn't willing to just create one on the fly around them.

"Alright, you have a little bit of time for a test one, but not much. I suggest thinking about the logistics now. You have about ten minutes until we get to the river." Jace informed her.

"Am I being ignored!" Evan shouted. When Eva looked at him, he did look a little flustered. "What the heck are you all talking about? I want my questions answered. You both have something going on between the two of you, don't you? Don't try to hide it from me!"

Eva sighed and smiled sweetly at Evan. It was a little complicated and since Jace really hadn't filtered the fact of him lending Eva strength, then she guessed it was okay for her to try and explain their link. "It's hard to explain Evan, but Jace and I have this connection. We can feel each other a little bit, like how we are feeling. That's why there are times he gets a bit worried when I don't exactly feel happy."

"I hate that you feel any other feelings besides happiness," Jace grumbled.

"I can't always be happy, Jace. That's impossible. You don't always feel happy either and you don't hear me complaining about it." No comment from Jace on that.

"Wait," Evan jumped in, "you can sense each other's feelings? I have not heard of this before. But, what's with this lending strength business?"

"When I moved the rocks back in place in the mountain, I could not do that on my own strength, I needed more. Trust me, I have plenty, but it was a large burst of energy I was using and well, I can only have so much on hand." Also, if she used too much, she started going down into that dark place, sometimes just to dream and other times suppressed memories. She shuddered at the thought of unending darkness. It had been a long time since the Tower, but she never wanted to be left alone in the dark again.

"That's some connection." Evan said. His brow scrunched as he thought on this new information. For the remainder of the ten minutes, they rode in silence, which was good because Eva really did need to figure out how in the world, she was going to create this barrier.

Her Guardian just told her to trust her instincts. Of course, they were talking about the whole mind binding thing, but the same concept could apply to this as well. How did she feel she could do this? Eva had learned how to direct this force in a single direction, not like when it first happened, which went out in a wide circle around her. She also wasn't emotionally heightened so that should help it not go awry.

For one, Eva needed to remain calm. She couldn't let emotions mess this up, especially because she was trying to do this for all three of them. What if she just did it individually? That would be easier. That makes more sense to have them cross one at a time. To make sure she had enough strength for each trip across, she will need to have Jace lend her some. She didn't think she would need it, but it was better safe than sorry.

Once she was in the right state of mind and had the grounding from Jace, all she needed to do was create this barrier. Maybe it was something that she could visualize happening. Just close her eyes and boom, there it is. Since it is force she is using, the barrier must continually push out anything trying to get in, so it needed to keep out the water rushing around the person. Right, simple enough. Maybe.

She didn't have any more time to think on it as they had now reached the river. It was moving at a fast clip, probably due to the rain that fell the day before and through the night. That would only make it slightly more difficult, as with a slower stream, the amount of force she would need to use would be less.

Jace stopped just on the edge of the river, Evan stopping on his left and Eva came to stop next to him on the right. They all looked down into the river, each harboring their own thoughts about this endeavor.

"Are you positive this will work?" Evan asked with a bit of skepticism in his voice.

"No," Eva immediately responded.

"Yes," Jace said at the same time as Eva. She just looked as him in exasperation. "Alright Eva, time to test this barrier out." Always so full of confidence. She never would have imagined even considering doing something like this. Jace had a way of convincing her, even without his persuasive ability.

Eva dismounted and started to scan the ground close to the river. There! A decent sized rock probably weighed about 5 pounds give or take. She picked it up and thought to herself this was the perfect test. All she needed to do was create a barrier around the rock that would force the water away from it.

She moved to stand at the edge of the river suspending the rock above the water in her hands. She closed her eyes and took a large calming breath. In, out. She started to see it in her mind's eye, a blue barrier radiating slightly out from the rock. She tapped into that thread in her Spark that was as blue as the sky, her strength. She fed the barrier, directing her strength down her arms to surround the rock. She made sure to visualize a tether that stayed linked to her so she could continue to feed the barrier.

Once she had this imagery in place, she let go of the rock. She was afraid to open her eyes to see if it worked. She only heard a thud. Did she miss the river? When she opened her eyes, there was the rock, sitting on the shallow edge of the river bottom. The water ebbed and flowed around it, but it didn't touch the rock. It stayed perfectly dry. She could feel the small drain of strength as the force did its job, repelling the water.

Eva mentally cut the tether and as soon as she did, water broke through the barrier and drenched the rock to where only the top of the rock was seen.

"That was cool," Jace said. Eva looked up at him and she could feel the awe and wonder he felt at witnessing the test barrier. He had a gentle smile on his face and generally looked good. She seemed to be staring a lot more at him lately, taking in his perfect features, from his sea-colored eyes to the sensuous curve of his lips. Fates, she wanted so bad to kiss him.

"So, we all going at once or what?" Evan asked, snapping Eva out of her obsessive staring. She was sure a blush had crept up her neck into her cheeks. She needed to get a grip on her thoughts. They had to be entirely blank for this to work.

"I'd rather do it one at a time," Eva answered.

"If that's the case," Jace said, "I'll go first."

"I'd rather put the barrier on myself first, as I would think it would be easiest," Eva countered.

"And I'd rather you not get swept up by the river."

"Oh? And you're less likely too?" Jace could be a bit stubborn at times. Also, she didn't want to hurt him. She didn't think she would, but she'd never done this before.

"I'm not saying this is a bad thing, but your skinny. At least with my bulk I can swim the current if needed."

"I'm a bit doubtful," she turned and looked at the churning water. Who knows what is under the surface? If her barrier failed, he could crash against unseen rocks.

"Stop worrying, I'll be fine. Will you be able to do the horse as well?"

"I can give it a try. But if it comes down to the barrier breaking, the horse is not getting the barrier back."

"Noted." Jace straightened in his seat and a stern expression fell over his features. "I'm ready."

"Alright. Lend me some of your strength. Just in case." He nodded, still concentrating forward. She reached out mentally toward him and there, she could feel him straining toward her. Before, she lent him strength, so this was the first time he had done so without touching some of her bare skin. She hoped the link was just as good as it was at the mountain.

She gently connected with the thread and as soon as it did, she could feel the grounding strength of Jace. She could sense that she could not tap as much as she would if they had multiple points of connection, but at least it was something.

"Okay Jace, I'm putting the barrier around you now." She did the same thing as she did to the rock. She closed her eyes, took a calming deep breath, and visualized Jace and the horse he was on surrounded by a barrier.

"Ease up a little Eva on directing any force in," Jace's voice cut through her thoughts. "Direct it out." Yes, she could see that some force in her barrier had also pushed into Jace and his horse. She had to make sure it went out, pushing everything else away. "That's better." Once her tether was complete, she opened her eyes.

There was a slightly shining blue encasing Jace and his steed. Now, for the real test. "Okay Jace. It's in place." She didn't want any distractions, so she solely focused on the force being fed in the barrier to push anything out.

Jace nudged his horse, a tad fidgety from the pressure. Just as his first hoof would hit water, it seemed the water was expelled, and dry river bottom greeted him. Jace kept urging the horse until he was fully in the river. It was working. She didn't know how the horse felt about it, but Jace made sure to keep a steady hand on the reigns and gently urged the horse forward.

As they got to the middle of the river, her strength strained against the amount of water being forced away. This was the deepest point as she could see only the top of the horse's head and Jace's shoulders and head.

Keep it together, Eva told herself. She needed not to panic. Its fine, Jace will make it. It's going all according to plan. The strain wasn't as much as they began to ascend to the other side. As soon as the last hoof was out of the water, she cut the tether. It felt like a big weight was lifted. She also felt more tired than she did. She needed to take more of Jace's strength for the next crossing.

Evan looked down at her from his mount with an eyebrow raised. "You alright?" he asked.

"Yes, I'm fine." She was just a bit tired, but no biggie. "Get ready Evan." He still looked skeptical but shrugged it off and faced the river. She did the same thing with Evan as she did with Jace, creating the barrier around him and his horse. Once the tether was in place she said, "Alright Evan, you are good to cross."

Evan was a little more hesitant and he didn't have the best control of his animal. It was like his agitation was also causing his horse to be a little more unpredictable. Although it was harder to maintain, she was able to hold it steady until Evan crossed to the other side. When she released the tether, it was such a relief. She absently rubbed her chest feeling a slight ache at her core.

Alright, now all she needed to do was cross. That shouldn't be a problem, right? She mounted her horse, and as she did, she could feel her muscles were a little more fatigued than before. No time to focus on that. She needed to cross. This should be easier in theory for her to do to herself. Let's hope that was the case.

Eva mentally prepared herself and imagined the barrier around her and her horse. She could feel the force gliding over her skin, almost like a crushing feeling. Was that what Jace was talking about? No wonder he mentioned to focus on sending it out, which when she did, the pressure on her body slowly dissipated.

Once her strength was tethered to the barrier, she opened her eyes and saw the faint outline of the barrier around her. *This is it,* she thought to herself. She guided her horse toward the river. She could feel the animal's movements underneath and the first pause of the step into the river. But as soon as they got past the initial step, the horse was confidently striding ahead.

It seemed to be going well at first, but as the water got deeper around her, Eva could feel the strain and the amount of effort it was taking to push back the water. It was different when she also had to guide a horse too. Her concentration wasn't all on the barrier and she saw it start to thin. Oh no!

Water was starting to seep through the barrier. At seeing this, it caused her to panic and the carefully placed tether snapped. The water slammed into her and her horse. She was immediately separated from the animal. She knew how to swim, but it seemed like the river was just too much and she started to slip under, being carried down river.

No, this can't be happening! She couldn't die like this. She wouldn't let this happen to her. She will make it, no matter what! In her desperation to breech the surface of the water for air, she let her strength flood out of her uncontrolled, causing her to push everything around her away.

Eva dropped unto her side on the rocky riverbed, feeling a sharp pain in her side. Her thoughts were a mess, and her strength was sapped so she could only guess that she landed on a rock. It wasn't long until she felt herself being lifted. A pair of arms wrapped around her protectively.

From the electrified touch on the back of her neck where the arm was, she immediately knew it was Jace.

"Eva," his voice was a gentle caress. "You can release it now." Her eyes were still shut. From the lack of strength, she just didn't have the energy to open them. But she didn't know what Jace was talking about. She forced her eyelids to cooperate. She blinked up into Jace's gorgeous face where his blue colored eyes swirled with green searched hers for reassurance. She glanced to the side where the river was flowing and noticed what she had done. It seemed that she had created a path from the spot where she had falling to the river's edge. She could feel the tether and that's when she realized she was siphoning from Jace's strength to feed it. She immediately severed the tether and the water whooshed right back, the raging river looking like it did before.

Eva felt like crap. Her muscles were stiff and the pain in her side was causing her breathing to be labored. Did she puncture a lung? She could try and heal herself, but she was just barely conscious. She didn't know if she could do it without completely succumbing to the feeling of the pain once again.

"I got you. No need to worry now," Jace gently carried her toward where his horse was. Evan had also dismounted, and his face popped into view above her.

"She's hurt. It's not life-threatening but it needs to be treated soon," Evan's gaze slowly traveled over her, assessing any more damage.

"Then treat her, Evan." Jace said on a growl, as his restraint was close to snapping. She didn't want any fighting.

"No, it's alright," Eva rasped out. Why was she hoarse? Did she scream? Take on too much river water? "I'll heal myself once I rest."

"You sure?" Jace asked, concern etching his brow. "I can feel your pain, Eva. It's killing me knowing that you're hurt." She laid her hand on his heart and breathed in his familiar scent. When had she noticed he had a distinct scent of pine and lilies?

She knew she was safe. She wasn't in the river anymore. There was this soothing response coming from their link. She did feel how crazy worried he was, but he also was determined to help. She didn't know what exactly he was doing, but the soothing feeling collected right in her ribs, where the pain was the most intense. Then a sort of numbing effect happened, like it started to ebb away. She was too tired to even process what was going on and her eyes couldn't stay open any longer.

"Rest, I'll protect you," Jace whispered to her. She decided to let go into the numbness, where her thoughts would turn off for just a little while. Jace was there, there was no need to worry. Sleep never sounded so good.

Chapter 28
Nertman Stronghold

Brosch

"I swear I didn't know they were there," the pathetic leader pleaded in front of him.

"I don't believe you," Brosch knew it was possible that he didn't know, as the Kretz Swamp extended quite a way south of the Nertman Stronghold. But he didn't care. It just gave him the excuse he needed to keep this newbie in line.

He forced the young mayor to grab the letter opener on his desk. Mayor Nertman's eyes grew large and fearful. Brosch fed on that fear and a malicious smile played on his lips. He watched as he forced the mayor's arm high holding the letter opener above his head.

"Please. Don't make me do this. I've told you the truth." He kept pleading, his voice growing increasingly higher as his arm rose over him. Brosch could see that he wanted to stop it, could even feel the resistance. But this mayor was nothing. He had no Might and could never overpower his ability anyway. There was only one who could.

Brosch smiled in satisfaction as he made the mayor stab himself in the top of his other hand that was placed on his desk. The wail from the young man was hilarious. Who would ever think a grown man could sound like that. Blood poured from the wound, and to make it more agonizing, he made the mayor remove the letter opener from his hand. After that, he released his hold on him.

Once Mayor Nertman was in control again, the letter opener dropped out of his hand and clattered onto the desktop. He used that hand to cradle his other damaged hand to his chest. The mayor was starting to look pale, and a sheen of sweat trickled down his forehead. Brosch was a tiny bit disappointed the man wasn't in tears.

"I know your men are trained to navigate the swamp so don't tell me you didn't know about these Ren being there. Someone in your ranks had to be helping them." He wanted to intimidate the new leader, show him that even if he held this place of power at this stronghold, it was not enough. Brosch would and will crush him if his orders were not followed.

"As I said, I was not lying. Although," the man paused, Brosch not knowing if it was from the stabbing or if he didn't want to say.

"Yes?" Brosch prompted. At his voice the young mayor twitched. That's right. Start talking or more stabbing will ensue.

"I remembered sometime last year when my father was still alive his military leader Boris told him he had some guards that defected. He was unable to track them down."

"Where can I find this Boris?"

"He also died, about 3 months before my father." Did he think he could be saved just because the people responsible were dead now? Someone had to be held responsible.

"It should have been your duty to make sure these defected guards were found. It is a major risk to your stronghold if they gave away the secrets of the swamp."

"I," the man was trembling, having trouble even speaking without stuttering now, "I, I just came into this position la-, la-, last week."

"A weak excuse. Loose ends need to be tied up. And it looks like you've let yours go rampant." He was just about to intimidate the young mayor again, thinking of using the lamp on the desk in some way, when Onyx's large form appeared at his side.

"I'm sorry to interrupt sir, but a raven just arrived," the large man said with no inkling of remorse for the interruption in his tone. Brosch could take offense at the tone of his guard's voice, but Onyx had always spoken that way. Straight to the point. The only time Onyx interrupted was for an urgent matter.

"No worries," he said to Onyx. "And you," he pointed a long finger at the mayor, causing the man to flinch, possibly thinking he was going to do something. He was, just not yet. "I'm not done with you."

Brosch turned and exited the mayor's study. Onyx was at his side leading Brosch to the drawing room just down the hall. There were two cronies stationed outside the door and when Brosch approached they visibly straightened to attention. One moved to open the door for him.

He strode into the drawing room and there perched on the mantel was a raven. Finally, word from 015. He needed to know that the Healer was captured. That old witch in the woods was right. It was getting worse. At least it was contained for now though. But if he didn't get the Healer back soon, his carefully laid plans to take over the whole of Hockland could be ruined.

He approached the bird and unfastened the paper from its leg. He unrolled the small missive and read.

Brosch. Runaway headed to Holds. Need back-up to attempt compliance. Suspected to be traveling with a Manipulator. No signature to confirm. 15

Brosch crumpled the paper in his hand and threw the offending thing into the fire. He watched the edge's catch and started to turn black and flake away as ash. Holds. He never liked the man. There were many attempts by Brosch in the past to take Holds down a peg, but somehow it never felt like he won against him. Yes, his stronghold sent the supplies that he demanded of every stronghold, more than any other. He had requested ridiculous things in the past to try and have an excuse to use his ability on Holds. But every time, that darn mayor delivered. It was frustrating.

Now, finally, there was a chance to bring that man to his knees. He was harboring a Might, one that has been numbered, and therefore his property should be returned to him. If Holds refuses, then yes, an army will be needed to breech his stronghold. He wondered what Holds would decide. He had his suspicions that he was working secretively to bring him down. He never had enough proof.

Now, this little tidbit that 015 mentioned about a Manipulator traveling with them, and one who could suppress Might signature, his eyes gleamed with delight. It had to be her. In all Hockland, she was the only one left who had that ability. It's to be expected, based on her linage. Her father was able to, so it made sense she was able to.

His prized 1 must be captured once again. It wouldn't be easy though. She didn't know what to do with her ability when she was younger, it acted instinctively on its own, protecting her. He was sure after this many years, she was able to control a lot of it. She was hidden well from him. Where had she been this whole time? Who had been training her? If reports from the attack on his cronies at the base of the Wedset Mountains was any indication, she could very much hold her own in battle. Just visualizing the sheer amount of damage she could do with just a flick of her mind, it was intoxicating. Dead in an instant if she so desired. That just made him want her even more. The more dangerous the better.

Nothing could stop him once she was at his side. If he really believed in prophesies, there was one he read about in his personal collection. He couldn't remember the exact words, but there are always two sides an event can take. For light or for dark. The old ways have been forgotten by many. The Fates weren't the only ones in control, this he was most certain of. He knew what the dark felt like, and if he was bound to 1, her power feeding the darkness, nothing would stop him. *They* would be in control, and he, the key. His power would know no bounds.

"Onyx. Send word to the Commander to have a quarter of our troops sent immediately to Holds Stronghold without delay. 015 will be in command."

"Consider it done," Onyx gave a slight bow and left to send the missive. Brosch still stared into the embers of the fire in the hearth, seemingly transfixed at the way the flames danced over the logs, slowly eating away at them until they turned to dust. Much like a body many years after death if no measures were in place to preserve it. If there was one thing he believed in, it was a way to avoid death. One wouldn't be afraid of it if it was no longer a possibility.

As much as he enjoyed torturing the new Mayor Nertman, it was time for him to return to his stronghold. He had a feeling that a major battle was about to take place, and he needed to be at his base of operations where he could access all his Numbered. He also had some unfinished business with 027. Hopefully by the time he returned, 015 will finish his mission on recapturing his property and also locate the Rens location. It was time that rebellious group was taken out.

Brosch turned his attention to the raven still perched on the mantel, patiently waiting for a reply to take to his master. He moved toward the desk set up in the room especially for his visit. He located a piece of paper and quill. He scrawled just one word, *Done.* He rolled it up and tied the little scrap of paper unto the bird's leg.

"You can return to your master." At his words, the raven cawed and took off out the window. Brosch's gaze shifted back to the fire. Let all that stand in his way, burn.

Chapter 29
Seer King

Jace

Dusk was settling over the stronghold. As Jace and Evan neared the walls, homesteads dotted along the path to town were coming to life, light blaring in the windows and the smell of heartily cooked meals drifted on the breeze. Jace's stomach growled. They hadn't had a decent meal since the night before at the crossroads.

"It's torture," Evan groaned from his steed. "Why'd we have to arrive at dinnertime?" Apparently, Evan was also feeling the same as Jace.

"It's better than the smell of rotting human flesh." Evan's reaction was priceless. It was like he didn't even know how to comment. Jace was only teasing, but a seriousness crept into Evan's features.

"True," Evan eventually said. Jace wasn't expecting that response.

"I don't know if I should just forget you agreed with that or worry about your soul."

"You, worry about me? Ha! I'd rather you not."

"I don't worry, trust me." He really didn't care about this Healer. But Eva cared. "I am just voicing Eva's opinion, if she was awake."

"Sure, you are." Of course, he didn't believe him. "How is she doing anyways?" As he asked, he pulled his horse next to his looking over Eva's sleeping form. Jace would think he'd be bothered by it, but for some reason he wasn't feeling his usual bout of jealousy. Maybe because Evan really wasn't leering at Eva, he was concerned about her. It was almost like Jace could feel Evan's intentions. Something in the back of his mind told him that he would never harm Eva and was concerned for her, as a friend. Evan was mostly scared of her and for her at the same time. Jace shook the weird thoughts away.

"She's fine. Albeit a little fatigued. I can feel a slow drain."

"Um, what now?"

"She's siphoning some of my strength."

"Oh." He could see the wheels moving in Evan's head. He was clearly thinking over something.

"What is it?"

"I'm trying to process this bond you have with Eva. With all the research I've done, I haven't come across anything like it. At least, anything that would be considered real."

"Whether it is real or not, you have heard of something like this then?"

"Yes and no."

"That is not an answer."

"I just vaguely remember a fairy tale my mother used to tell me before I went to bed at night. Of course, with all fairy tales, it goes beyond the realms of possibility."

"It could also be argued that fairy tales are based in facts. It just doesn't come from nowhere. Something influenced the tale, the person, an event."

"That could be one way to look at it."

"Which tale are you talking about?"

"Have you heard about the *Seer King* one?" Evan asked. As a matter of fact, Jace did remember this tale. It was one that his Nanna used to tell him. He heard it more than he liked to. It seemed to be her favorite one to tell.

"I have," Jace confirmed.

"So, if you remember, there is mention in the tale that the King's fated love he would be able to bond with her wholly." Jace did remember something like that. Nanna's eyes would get all shiny and she always seemed to speak in a sort of reverence to the bond that the King and Queen had. It was as if they were one person. Connected down to their very Spark. They could share everything with each other, love, happiness, pain, heartache. Life and death even.

"I remember. Seemed like a crazy idea."

"What's even crazier about the tale, is that the King's future Queen had the same ability as he. It was like they were meant for each other. And once they bonded fully, their ability reached its full potential. Of course, they had to have the rare dual ability and with their ability was able to heal like no other before them. Curing the incurable. I believe they also stopped a famine with their ability."

"I thought they used their combined strength to stop an invading country."

"Whatever the ability was, it still was fantastical. Seemingly unbelievable. Plus, a *male* seer? All seers are female."

"There is some truth in what you say. But say instead of it being a fairy tale, we believe it to be an historical account of an actual living King and Queen. Could it be believable, even possible? Most seers were able to track their linage. A lot of them found that they were distantly related, did they not?"

"I've heard that. Some belief that all seers stem from one family line? There's no proof. I wish that some of the early history of the country was better recorded, but that's not the case. It's all speculation at this point." When it came to the history of seers in this country, Evan was right. There was no written account.

"Speculation aside, is it out of the realm of possibility that a male could be a seer? If it's in his family line, he at least carries the gene. Maybe it's just dormant in males. Like, they have no way to access it?"

"Interesting theory there. Not sure if that's how it works. I mean, you are correct that it necessarily does not need to pass from mother to daughter. I've even heard it skips generations as well."

Jace had not realized that they had already reached the fortified wall of Holds Stronghold. Evan's musings about his and Eva's bond plus the possibility of a male seer distracted him. He didn't get distracted easily. "We'll talk later. It's not something to be discussing in public."

Inside the wall was much different from the outside. Even as night closed in, the streets still bustled with people. Carts where people sold their wares were still open, trying to sell a few more items before the day ended. Music and chatter filled the streets from open tavern doors, inviting all to join in the merriment. Unlike some strongholds, Holds was very prosperous, being able to balance the demands that Brosch made to keep him happy and be able to provide for the people calling Holds their home.

Jace's father was an old friend to Holds and they had travelled back and forth many times. Before he was forced to go to the Lous School for Boys, his father would take him on his trips to familiarize him with the country. Jace now understood that wasn't his father's only objective. It was also to teach him who was to be trusted. Thankfully when Eva mentioned coming to Holds Stronghold, it wasn't much of a concern. This stronghold could not easily be accessed, and it was well guarded. The citizens have much need to protect what they've built here. All male citizens were required to receive combat training in case of an invasion, there were plenty that could and would defend in case of an attack.

The Jebrow Stronghold didn't have that requirement. They left it up to the men if they wanted to receive training, and most did without being forced to. Jace didn't want to brag, but his father Kalvin was very skilled on the battlefield, so it would make sense if there was an opportunity that he was conducting the training, the men would practically jump at the chance to train with the best.

It was too late to ask Holds for an audience, so it was probably best to find an inn to get some rest until morning. He had already passed several, but they just didn't feel right, until he spotted the *Marvel Inn*. For some reason he had a good feeling about this place.

Jace signaled to a lad by the door who immediately came over and took his horse's reigns. Still holding Eva, Jace dismounted, trying his best not to jostle her too much. The lad must have realized Evan was also with him and was grabbing onto his horse's reigns too.

"We are stopping?" Evan asked, a look of utter distaste on his face. "And here?"

"I don't want to be rude and show up to Holds unannounced at this time of night. And what do you have to complain about the state of where you sleep?"

"But," he lowered his voice to a whisper, "aren't we being followed?" Jace thought about it for a second. They were indeed still being followed, but the threat has dropped for now. Probably re-strategizing their approach now that they had made it into the stronghold.

"We're fine. I will inform you when it's not. Come on then, let's get inside." Jace flipped two small coins toward the lad, who expertly caught them like he was used to it and began walking toward the entrance. Evan dismounted from his horse, Jace hearing him grumble a bit under his breath. It did bring some satisfaction that Evan was uncomfortable with the whole situation, but in all honesty, he was starting to like the guy.

He made his way into the inn and looked around. The open area where patrons were sitting, eating and drinking had a warm friendly feel to it. It was well cleaned, and the atmosphere was relaxed, unlike the tension he felt at the last inn they had stopped at. He made his way over to the bar where a lanky teen stood polishing glasses.

"Evening," Jace greeted.

"Goo' day sir," the teen said in his wobbly voice. "Whatcha needing?" Well then, was this the owner of this establishment?

"Two rooms and meals delivered."

"Alright," the lad responded. He set his glass down and turned to a table behind him that had several keys atop it. He plucked two from the pile and proceeded to shout into the back room, presumably the kitchen. "Hey love! Show these gents and lady to rooms 2 and 3 will yea." He turned back to Jace and handed him the keys. "My mum Gertie will be up with the meals. That'll be 3 farthings please." Jace took the keys and placed the coins with a couple extra added in.

"For the excellent service that I know will come." The teen quickly grabbed up the coins and bobbed his head several times.

"Anything ya need, just give a holler." Jace smiled at the lad and moved on toward the stairs to the rooms above. When he reached 2, he handed Evan the key.

"Arrange for our packs to be brought to this room and Eva's brought to room 3."

"And what will you be doing?" Evan asked.

"I'll settle Eva into room 3," he said with a hard look towards Evan to try and test him on the decision. Evan raised his hands in surrender, but Jace swore he saw a smirk on his face as Evan turned away to gather their things.

He unlocked the door and continued to carry Eva inside. He would have thought people would find it strange that he was carrying someone around, but nobody paid much attention. The teen, who he presumed was the innkeeper's son, didn't even flinch and none of the other patrons even looked their way as they made their way to the stairs.

He stopped just inside the threshold, scanning the darkened room. Nothing felt out of sorts, so he continued toward the bed. He placed Eva gently on the bed. He got to work lighting a fire in the hearth to make sure the room was warm enough. After he had finished ensuring the fire was not going to die out any time soon, he made his way back over to Eva and sat on the edge of the bed next to her. A few locks of her hair had fallen on her face. He brushed them away and his fingers lingered near her cheek.

Jace could feel that she was fine. There was no draw anymore from his strength. He marveled at the length of her eyelashes and how they lay along her cheeks as her eyes were closed. It was rare that he had ever seen her asleep and she looked so peaceful and vulnerable at the same time. It brought on a surge of protectiveness within him.

"I'll be waiting, Eva," he quietly muttered. He leaned forward and gave a brief kiss to her forehead. He stood and made his way to the door. Before exiting, he turned back for one last look. He was very tempted to stay, but he had to do some strategizing for tomorrow and even if he didn't want to, he had to include Evan.

As Jace shut the door, he vowed that no one was going to hurt Eva. If that included Eva herself, well, he would just have to figure out how he would make that happen, if it's just the fact that he comes to terms with having a possible fated connection, then it is what it is.

Chapter 30
Memories

Eva

"Come on this way!" She walked as fast as her little legs could take her. Her hand was being tugged to the point that she was certain she would start to be dragged. Shouts and sounds of fighting could be heard toward the entrance. Night had just fallen and not all the lights were lit in the house. They had traversed a few unlit halls before coming to the farthest room from the attack.

The woman holding her let go of her hand to open the door. She quickly scanned around inside and immediately gestured for her to enter. "Come quickly!" She hadn't realized two others were with her too. Her siblings? They moved in ahead of her and she followed after them. Once inside the tall woman shut the door and slid a long board in place. A lamp was lit on an end table across the room by her sister. There was not much to the room as she looked around. Many things had coverings over them. It was sort of like a storage area, but with no windows.

"Argon, come help me move this." She assumed her brother, went over to the woman and began to help move a heavy piece of furniture in front of the door. It took them a little effort as they strained and pushed until the item was in place.

The woman, which now she thought had to be her mother, went across the room to a very unsuspecting wall. Nothing seemed special about it. Just an old bookcase with a scattering of dusty books laying on its shelves. Her mother reached up into one of the shelves' corners and the whole bookcase moved revealing a small hidden alcove.

"In you go," her mother gestured to her and her siblings.

"No way! It's too dark in there," her sister whined.

"We don't have any other choice," her mother whisper shouted. "I will not lose any of you."

"Let me stay and fight," her brother chimed in. "I can help!"

"Absolutely not! You are too young, and this isn't child's play. They will not be lenient to you because you are children." A jingle of the door latch startled them, and she heard a sharp inhale from her sister.

"I'm scared!" her sister huddled closer to their mother, trying to make herself small behind her. A thud on the door made her squeak.

"Hush child!" her mother shushed her. "All of you get in the hiding place now!" The banging became louder, and voices were heard as well.

"I'm not leaving you out here by yourself mom!" her brother was arguing.

"It's too dark in there!" her sister cried. Her mother started to pull them toward the hiding place. The door started to splinter. Her sister cried harder. Her brother still urged her to stay out there with her.

"Listen to me!" her mother's voice raised slightly. "There is not enough room for me in here as well. And Argon, you need to protect your sisters. Do you hear what I'm saying? If anyone gets past me, then you are the only one who can protect them." Her brother wasn't happy, but he finally started to withdraw, pulling our sister with him. Her mother turned back to her with her hand outstretched. Even with the door starting to come down, her mother smiled gently at her and said, "You too sweetie. Time to stay safe."

As she was placing her hand in her mother's, she watched as her mother's eyes grew wide and her body jerked. Her eyes moved to her mother's shoulder where an arrow protruded out.

No.

"No!" Eva gasped as she sat up. Wait, was she just lying down? She looked around the room and there was a familiarity to the place. She had been here before.

What kind of dream was that? Did that really happen? It seemed very real to her. Real enough that her heart was pounding, and a slight ache appeared at the base of her skull. A memory then?

She slowly eased herself out of bed rubbing the back of her head. She made her way to where a basin of water was set to splash some water unto her face. As she let the water drip back into the bowl, she looked up into the mirror. It was still her, but she could pick out some features that matched the woman in her dream. The same small nose and sharp eyes. Although the woman's eyes were a sparkling blue, Eva's eyes were hazel and tended to change with her mood. Her blonde hair was so unlike

Eva's dark raven locks. No matter, it was hard to deny it. That woman she saw was her mother.

What was her mind doing? There were memories best left forgotten. That was just the beginning for those painful memories. To think about her family, why now? What was the purpose of reliving that event in her life? No matter, she needed a distraction to take her mind away from these dark musings.

She dried her face with a towel and took stock of the room. Nothing had changed since she had been here last with Newly. A different comforter on the bed, but the furniture looked the same. It was even in the same arrangement. That means they made it into Holds Stronghold without incident. Thank goodness! She needed to stop passing out.

She exited the room and made her way to room number 2. She knocked once and opened the door without waiting for a response. There just inside the door was a table laden with food and no surprise to her, Jace and Evan sat there, looking toward her with food suspended in front of them.

"Don't let me stop you from eating," Eva smiled. Shutting the door behind her and settling herself in the other vacant chair at the table. Jace smiled back and continued eating. Evan placed his food on his plate and looked at Eva with concern.

"You alright?" he asked. "We were worried."

"I feel fine," wait a minute. She felt a little too fine. She absently rubbed her side as she remembered having landed hard on the river bottom. She didn't feel any aches or really any pain in that location. Hold on, that's right. She felt a numbing effect just before she passed out.

She looked between the two men, Jace having continued with eating and Evan still looking at her. "As a matter of fact, not just fine, but healed."

"I did gather that from my assessment," Evan said. Of course, Healers can see the extent of the damage.

"But I didn't heal myself."

"Wait, come again?" Evan was about to chomp down on a chicken leg but stalled with his movements when Eva spoke.

"I don't think I did. I know what healing myself feels like and I am most certain I did not. I do remember feeling something before passing out. Some sort of numbing affect."

"Well, as much as I was compelled to try, I didn't lay a finger on you. Honest." If it wasn't Evan, then who healed her? She slowly turned her gaze to Jace, who seemed to be ignoring her and Evan completely.

"Jace," Eva said, trying to get his attention. He glanced up like he was caught doing something wrong with a large chunk of food being chewed in his mouth.

"What?" he said around the food. Seemingly looking innocent but Eva knew better.

"Why, are you eating like that?"

"Huh?" He looked at his hands with a slightly confused look, but then he shrugged like it wasn't a big deal. "I feel like I haven't eaten in days. I don't know if it was because of our connection thing and you taking my strength, but I was famished. I could probably eat everything on the table and not feel bad about doing it."

"Okay. Makes a bit of sense. I'm hungry too." *Just not that hungry,* she thought. She grabbed a piece of bread and started to spread some butter on it. "Do you remember feeling anything else by the river after you pulled me out? Not just me siphoning your strength?"

Jace sat back a bit, thinking in that way of his. Eva took in his handsome features. What she would give if she could have a taste of his lips. Whoa there, where did that come from? He must have felt her desire because she felt hers flare again, probably because she was feeling Jace's too. His eyes locked with hers and a slow predatory smile graced those very kissable lips.

She could feel her heart beat just a little faster at the prospect of his hands and lips on her. If there wasn't a table separating them, she would probably jump him right now. The suspense was slowing killing her.

"That's it. If you guys are going to be doing something I shouldn't be here for, then I'm out," Evan's words jogged her out of her staring contest with Jace. Geez, this was embarrassing. Her face felt on fire.

"Sorry, Evan. No need to leave," Eva said. She turned her attention back to Jace, "As for you, we were talking about what happen down by the river."

"Right," he said like he just didn't forget. Eva could only roll her eyes so far. "As Evan said, we were both worried and you know I don't like feeling you in pain. So, I took it." He nodded and went back to eating.

Eva's mouth dropped open. Did he do what she thought he did? "How?"

"Not sure. I felt how you were taking my strength, which I don't mind you doing by the way. Just to be clear on that. So, I just applied the same feeling to the pain I was feeling inside you. I thought with our connection thing, maybe I could. I gave it a go, and it worked."

"That's, interesting." Great. Now that theory of hers looked like it might be true. Did Jace have more than one ability? Eva suspected, but this was the first she had seen, other than obviously exhibiting strength and persuasion.

"Hold up," Evan said. "Back up a second. Did you just say you took her pain?"

"Yes."

"It's not possible," Evan started to get that weird look about him again. His eyes stared wide at Jace but then a smile started to curve his lips and then a twinkle came to his eye.

"What's with the look?" Jace asked with a hint of uneasiness. "You should probably not smile like that. It gives off creepy vibes."

"Your connection with Eva, the multiple powers Eva has, I'm wondering Jace. Do you have ability?" Jace stilled in his eating eyeing Evan like an annoying insect.

"No."

"Are you sure? I'm being serious now. I'm starting to figure out this weirdness between you, but there was always something missing in the puzzle."

"He doesn't know," Eva blurted.

"What don't I know?" Jace asked with brow raised.

She released a slow breath. She sat down her bread in her hand and looked back up into Jace's eyes, his were waiting intently for her response. "You do have ability."

"I knew it," Evan clapped his hand down on the table.

"Eva, what are going on about? I would know if I had it, wouldn't I?"

"I don't know Jace, Newly didn't." Shoot, she wasn't supposed to say that.

"Wait a second, Newly has the Might?"

"Forget I said that."

"Highly doubtful at this point."

"Did you ever suspect that you did Jace? Any inkling?" Evan asked as he waited in utter joyful suspense. Jace was right, that smile was a little creepy.

"Well," Jace lowered his eyes, thinking about it, then raised them slowly to look back at Eva, "I was wondering how Eva was able to show me auras when I supposedly didn't have ability. I didn't think anything of it at the time, you know, because we were in a precarious situation. But it was something Willow said that made it sound like only people with ability can do that. So, to answer your question Evan," he turned his eyes on him, "that's when I doubted myself. Whether or not I had ability. Mind you, I wouldn't have a clue what ability that would be."

"I got a theory," Evan said singsong like.

"Please Evan, we are so looking forward to hearing this theory," Eva said in the most deadpanned tone she could manage. Looks like it didn't faze him though.

"I mean we were just hypothetically speaking but maybe you were right. What if the story of the *Seer King* is truth?"

"You think I'm a seer?" Jace asked.

"No, not that part of the story. Unless there is any indication you've had visions we don't know about?"

"None."

"Right, thought so. The other part of the story talked about him meeting his match. They had the same abilities. The reason that they could bond so closely is their Might made them able to. The only explanation at this point that I can figure out with this connection you two have, is that you were fated to be together."

Wait, was this the same story Seraphim was telling her at the Station? She did mention something about the pair having the same ability.

"So," Jace surmised, "you are suggesting that I have the same abilities as Eva. Which includes pretty much all the ones she's displayed so far? That, sounds unlikely."

"Yes, almost a fairy tale, don't you think?" Evan was still ecstatic.

Jace lowered the food in his hands, gave Evan a hard stare, and said, "What aura color am I?"

"Umm…" Evan's face turned to confusion. "I can't detect one."

"Right, I forgot," Jace was seemingly saying to himself. He turned his gaze on her. "Eva, what aura color am I?"

"Why are you asking me?"

"Because you can see anyone's aura color, not just people with Might."

"Wait, what are you talking about?" Evan said off to the side, but Eva wasn't paying attention to him now. All her focus was on those ocean-colored eyes that were looking at her in anticipation. Should she tell him the truth? Was it the right moment to tell him?

"You don't have a color Jace."

Chapter 31
Might All Along

Everything that he'd learned recently and everything he had known before, did not prepare him for the information he was just given. Jace could never tell if Eva was joking with him before, but with their connection, he could feel what she felt when she said those words. It was a combination of regret and worry. Maybe a touch scared. What does Eva have to fear? Especially from Jace.

"What does that make me then?" Seriously, if Jace didn't have an aura, but supposedly had abilities, did that really make him equal to Eva?

"I've always known Jace, since I met you the very first day I arrived at your home," her voice was small, not sure on how he would react.

All he could do was stare because he really wasn't following. He usually was pretty good about picking up on Eva's doubtfulness and figuring out her meaning, but this time, he needed a little more information. She had to feel his uncertainty and continued.

"After leaving the tower, those dark auras were all that I was surrounded with for years that seeing any other color was, spectacular. Knowing what an aura really should look like. And your family's auras were so bright, the brightest I've seen. Except for you. I've never seen your aura and it has always been a question of mine as to find out why I couldn't." He remembered that day. Her look of fascination, he thought it was with what he was doing, not with what she was seeing, or not seeing in this case.

"That first day," Jace smiled in fondness, "I thought you were going to be just like my sisters. Boy, was I wrong."

"You told me to go away."

"Yeah," he rubbed the back of his neck, "I did. But you refused to, just stayed there staring at me like you were determined to go against anything I said. Which you usual did, come to think of it."

"Let me rephrase. You tried to *persuade* me to go away, and I sort of blocked you from doing it."

"What now?"

"I've always blocked it Jace. I could feel when you were using it on me, so I just didn't let it affect me. I know, I should have told you sooner, but you weren't hurting anyone."

"Wait, so you are saying I've been using ability on you? Since the first day we met?" She nodded slowly. Well, that certainly changes things a bit, but then it also made things make a lot of sense. He never understood most of the time why people were so agreeable with him. He just thought it was because he was the mayor's son, but now. Now he wasn't so sure it was because of his station in life.

He sat there absorbing Eva's words, thinking of the times in his past he told people, no what was the word she used, *persuaded* people into telling them to do certain things. Was that why his roommate at Lous School for Boys never ratted him out? Or why Devon didn't tell anyone who beat him up? Or all the times he told his sisters to do this or that, and they did? Was any interaction he had with anyone ever genuine?

"I don't know if you two are ignoring me on purpose," Evan's voice cut through his thoughts. He can admit to Evan that he certainly did ignore him at times. It wasn't intentional this time, but in all honesty, he probably knew more than Eva and him, so he should do better to include him. If Eva trusts him, then he should too. "But I have a lot more questions now, and I think I'm also scared for my very life."

Jace had to admit that Evan did look like he was about ready to bolt. He had done a complete one-eighty from excitement at him and Eva being a fated pair to now, who knows what was said that changed him to be utterly frightened.

"Evan," Eva interjected, "why do you look like you are going to run off as fast as possible?"

"I'll admit that, just because I do highly value my life."

"You're more useful to us alive. Your logic behind us taking your life is inaccurate." Eva, ever the practical one.

"Yeah Evan, what made you scared anyway?" Jace continued, "You were all happy just a second ago about the prospect of Eva and I being fated to be together."

"Oh no, don't get me wrong. I am still excited about that part of it. I just forgot the whole thing about not seeing your aura, but if Eva can see *all* auras and you don't have one either, just like Eva, then it is highly possible you could have multiple abilities like her. Which is scary because you're a scary dude Jace!" Right, Eva isn't projecting an aura either. He was wondering why that was, but maybe Evan's theory about the multiple abilities is messing with what color aura she would have. Well, what both would have.

"And what the heck Eva?" Evan continued. "You can block ability? That is hard for a Might to master. But people can only do it from others with that same ability. If another Healer doesn't want me to heal them, they can essentially block me from doing it. With your seemingly limitless ability, you probably can block anyone from using ability on you. Not saying that you should let someone use their ability, but you have just become a force to be reckoned with. And you can see everyone's auras? Not just people of Might, but everyone?"

Jace could take a guess, but that wasn't something that everyone could do. "Since you seem to be a wealth of knowledge on probabilities, what is the likelihood that other people can see everyone's aura as well?" Jace asked.

"I have never heard of such a thing before."

"Rare then."

"No, it's unheard of."

"Well, then, it's ultra-rare. Unless that status changes if you know two people can."

"What?" Evan looked like he was struck, jumping back, and trying to create distance from the two of them. Yeah, Jace liked seeing

Evan more on edge. He didn't know why he liked messing with the guy. He felt this sort of comradery. He couldn't explain where he got the feeling.

"I can see all the auras. Eva showed me and I can do it now. I only see them if I'm concentrating though." Evan just stood there was his mouth agape.

"So, you believe me?" Eva asked tentatively.

"I can feel you are not lying to me Eva. And honestly, I probably always known myself, I just didn't realize it. Like you said, using it without knowing I was."

"You're not mad?"

"Of course not. You can feel that I'm not. It explains a lot of situations I was in before." He could feel the worry seep out of her, but then again, he was using their connection again to take it away.

"So, Evan," she turned to her eyes on him, Jace didn't know what Evan saw in Eva's eyes, but he cringed and tried to shrink in on himself. "About that block in your head from Brosch. You still want us to give it a try?"

"Wait, did you say us?" Jace asked.

"Yes." She didn't even turn to look at Jace. "I already was going to be using Jace even if he didn't know that he was contributing. But now that he knows, he can be in on the plans."

"Don't ignore me woman."

"Think about it Evan," and she was ignoring him. "If we are really this fated pair and Jace and I are supposed to perform miracles with, well, whatever this connection is, then don't you feel like the odds are that we'll succeed?"

Eva did bring up some good points. But Jace had this feeling that it wasn't just the connection they needed. They were missing something to make whatever they were about to do to poor Evan work.

"Ah, that's what you were thinking about," Evan spoke. "For a moment, I thought you changed your mind and was thinking of scalping me." Jace snorted. This guy.

"I only want to help Evan," Eva sounded hurt.

"I know, I know," he said, sighing and tension releasing from his shoulders. "I don't want to get my hopes up. Just in case it ends up not working. And every day I'm with you guys you seem to change my mind anyways."

"That was just Jace persuading you. You're probably still scared out of your mind."

"I don't know what to think about that." Jace didn't either.

"We've had a rough couple days. Let's just relax tonight, get some rest, and then worry about all this tomorrow."

"Okay," Evan bobbed his head in agreement.

"Jace," Eva finally looked at him with amusement in her eyes.

"What?"

"Evan, he just persuaded you."

"He did?" He generally looked confused, but Jace was confused too.

"And how would you know that, Eva?" Jace asked.

"Because you were trying to persuade me as well. I blocked you."

"Right, that blocking thing you do. But I didn't feel any different when I said it. Should I be feeling something?" She shrugged, generally not knowing an answer. Jace turned to Evan.

"You manipulated me?" He looked hurt.

"Not intentionally." But then he saw it. Evan was playing him. "I am supposed to feel it or not?"

"I would say yes, but I don't know with Manipulators. I'm a Healer. I must feel it because I'm taking it from them. Sometimes I give a little too, but I'm always feeling the pull from somewhere."

"I agree with Evan. I feel that when I do any healing and when I had changed my appearance, but it wasn't as big of a pull when I did that. When I pulled all the rocks in the mountain, yeah, I felt that."

"Well, I felt that too, but that's because you were taking from me at the time."

"True. I know I really don't feel it when I'm fighting."

"You use ability when fighting? I mean, I know about the force thing you do."

"If we are entertaining the idea that I have all the abilities, then maybe the reason I wanted to learn how to fight and do exceptionally well at it is because I have ability."

"A Warrior." Evan supplied. Both he and Eva looked at him to explain further. "That's what the Might are called with heightened fighting techniques, strength, swiftness, even leadership."

"You don't win all the time," Jace smirked.

"Which means what Jace?" He waited. Eva's eyes sparkled. If he was feeling what he was feeling, she most definitely liked the idea of a fight. He did too. They never knew which one would win in the end, sometimes it was draw. The supreme satisfaction of defeating an opponent was exhilarating. Defeating Eva, beyond euphoric. Pleasurable even.

"He's a Warrior too," Evan answered for him. "That makes sense now. The seeming ease he had leading everyone on the whole boulder moving incident. Sticking with the Elites, Willow uses that term instead of Warrior, and moving the boulders. That takes a lot of strength."

"Eva helped with that through the connection."

"You still were moving the boulders after she passed out." True, he did.

"We are getting off topic." Eva stated. "I should have never brought up being healed."

"And let me miss out on all this?" Evan threw his hands out to indicate the topic they were just discussing.

"I'm not saying it's un-important. We need to plan on how we are going to fix your memory. Since you did come to me because you hold the answers we need." All Evan could do was shrug, because honestly, maybe he did, maybe he didn't. "We also will need to meet up with Penn as well."

"Penn?" Jace gave her a questioning look.

"Holds."

"Great, that sounds exciting. Not." Evan finally was relaxed enough to slump back down in his chair.

"He was in my vision. He needs to be included."

"Okay, just expressing my thoughts out loud. I'll try to keep them to myself. Not used to people being around me." What a sad thought. Was he mostly alone at Brosch's Stronghold?

"You never talked with anyone when you were a Brosch's?" Jace asked.

"Not that often. There were more of us when I was younger, but eventually they either died or fell in line. And his cronies never talked to us."

"Never talked to us," Eva mumbled. She had some turbulent emotions. Maybe Jace should change the subject before she started to have any painful memories come up. Those seem to be the worst feeling ones to date.

"Alright, plan is to sleep, we aren't in any immediate danger. We will talk to Holds sometime tomorrow. And we can do any other planning or whatnot for invading Evan's mind tomorrow as well."

"Invading?" Evan started to get that panicked look again. It just made Jace smile even more.

"Sleep. Okay, that sounds good," Eva said, almost as an afterthought. She stood up and started to leave.

"Where you going?" Jace asked. She didn't answer, just opened the door. "Eva?" She was out of the door and was shut before he was even able to catch up with her. He stayed at the door though, not sure if she wanted him to follow. Her feelings were, well she wasn't in pain, and he did feel that she was sad. He wasn't really feeling anything. Maybe she really did need sleep.

"Ahhh," Evan yawned. "About time for a rest. I am beat with all the escaping I've been doing." Really Evan? Jace looked at him like he was being a little dramatic. "The bed calls to me and I accept it's call." What a weirdo.

Jace just shook his head. As Evan made his way, still mumbling to himself, to the bed, he thought about what he should do.

Should he stay in here, as is the proper thing to do, or should he join Eva in her room? By the Fates, he really wanted to go to her room. When did he ever get the chance to do that before? She always visited his room. Not that anything happened anyway. Yet, this time he wasn't so sure.

He rubbed the back of his neck trying to figure out these thoughts. What was driving him to act like this? His thoughts are only ever on Eva lately. It's like this consuming need. Something is not whole, finished. It was only the start and has yet to become complete. He could tell it was getting worse. Maybe that isn't the word for it. It wasn't bad thoughts, but at the same time anyone in proper society would say they were.

He slowly made himself back away from the door. Not tonight, he wouldn't be able to stop himself. Eva was too tempting, and he knew she felt the same. He has never reacted like this before. Yes, he's always been protective of her, missed her when he was gone, excited to see her, obviously, but this lust. This need to make her his, where was it coming from?

And why as the days go on, he felt like it was a mighty fine idea?

Chapter 32
Hesitating

Eva

Why was she standing there at the door? It was probably locked, and they were sleeping, at least Eva could tell Jace was sleeping. Could she sleep? Nope. She didn't feel fatigued at all. Probably because she had just awoken after passing out. She needed to get in control and not have that happen again. It's happened way to often for her liking.

There was this emptiness inside her that was urging her to be with Jace. And not just in a friendly plutonic sense. Even imagining Jace's soft touch on her skin and lips dotting her flesh was causing her body to go haywire.

Not that she didn't appreciate him before. He was a fine specimen, tall, muscular, handsome, strong, and let's not forget his fierce protectiveness. He made her breath hitch and her heart flutter. She was probably blushing right now. Hands to her cheeks, Eva looked around to see if anyone had seen her.

She needed to get it together. Pacing outside his door wasn't going to do her any good, but she didn't want to go back to her room and sit there uselessly. She had to do something.

Eva decided to venture out and around the stronghold. It's been several years since she was here last. There were few patrons left in the inn, a sign that it was well into the night. She stepped out on the street and surveyed the area. Not too much change from her memory. The streetlamps were new and illuminated the cobblestone roads that led throughout the stronghold.

As she began to walk, she took in the familiar areas she remembered Gene had showed her. There were still a few stragglers but as the night went on, she seemed to be the only one. The lamps also grew dim, probably running low on whatever was powering them. She knew at that moment that she was safe and even if someone thought they could mess with her, they were in for a rude awakening.

She tried not to have her thoughts run rampant, but they continued time and time again to drift toward Jace. What was it that kept pulling her in his direction? If he was truly her match, was there something that could connect them further? How was that even possible? Eva wished she had more answers. The one book that might touch on it was back at the Jebrow Stronghold. Better yet, she could go to the Station. Her guardian dude would know the answer, the problem, she didn't know how to get there.

How was she supposed to make her Spark call for help? Is there some sort of process or were all the visits to the Station up to the Fates? Try with all her might, she couldn't quite remember any feeling when she was transported to the Station. Her physical body stayed firmly on this plane, so it was all a mental thing, or something. Jace said he could feel it when she was gone.

Scary to think that her Spark, her very essence, could freely come and go. Would that mean another Spark could take up residence in her body? Nope, not going there. Eva was not going to entertain such notions. Anything is possible, but she would rather play ignorant with that possibility. Not something to forget, but not something she needed to think on anyways.

Just before the sun began to rise beside the mountains in the distance, she made her way to the highest point within the stronghold. It happened to be a small courtyard and in the center was a large oak tree with branches reaching high into the sky. She easily scaled the tree and peeked out above to get a view of the sun's warm rays blushing the sky.

She always loved the early dawn. Seeing the plants liven up as the sun touched their leaves. Trees brightened; flowers opened as if they couldn't get enough. Every little ounce of sun they try to gather to recharge. It reminded her of her own struggles at a young age. No, it wasn't fair what happen to her, but she wasn't the only one taken. Evan was a Numbered too. The one big difference though, he wasn't locked away and the only natural light she saw was from a small slit at the top of her dungeon.

Does it matter anyway? They both suffered. It really wasn't a competition on who had it worst. Eva was sure of one thing though. She would help Evan, make sure that Brosch never messes with his mind again. He could be himself again, or at least, gain some of his old self back, whatever there was left of it. She knew the struggle all too well.

Before it became apparent that she was away, Eva made her way, reluctantly, back to the inn. As she passed by homes, she saw people stirring inside. Doors opening as people exited to go about their day. Some of the small shops she passed were getting set-up for the customers that might come and view their wares.

As she made it to the inn, she could feel Jace was awake. He seemed content. He must have slept well. He most certainly needed the rest. Good thing she did restrain herself last night. She was so tempted to knock, even contemplated picking the lock. A skill she might not have told anyone she had. That wasn't any ability, just simple trial and error and practice. She wasn't going to be locked up again.

Before she went back upstairs, she made an order for food to be brought up. She noticed as she got closer to Jace and Evan's room, her heart sped up. She could also feel Jace's excitement. Why was he excited? Just as she was about to knock the door opened and there stood Jace.

Eva took in his appearance. His hair was still messy from sleep, shirt seemed to be pulled on hastily as some buttons were undone showing some of his pecs, as her eyes slid down, she noticed he was barefoot. She didn't know why that made her smile, but it did. To think that she should be used to seeing Jace in many states of undress, but lately, it seems he had too many clothes on.

Her eyes slowly made their way back to his face where he had his customary smirk and that, *I know what you're thinking,* look. She had the realization that she missed him. And she got the feeling that he felt the same way. The excitement, the rush, the longing for his touch. What was stopping her exactly?

Before she could act on any of those feelings, Evan spoke. "Morning Eva," he said with a big yawn. "Is it late already?"

"Still early," she confirmed. She felt slightly annoyed with his interruption, and apparently Jace was annoyed to.

"I think I could sleep longer, but I'm too hungry."

"Lucky you, I already requested food to be brought up," Eva said as she stepped into the room. Jace barely letting her pass, which meant she brushed against his chest. She shivered from the contact. She quickly made her way to the table and sat.

She chanced a look toward Jace, who was still standing, holding the door open. His look was that same smirk, but a twinkle entered his eye. She nodded her head toward the door in answer to his staring contest. Without even looking away, he gave the door a little push and it was shut. Their exchange didn't faze Evan at all, oblivious of what was transpiring.

As Evan made his way to the mirror to freshen up, he started up the conversation. "So, the plan today is what exactly?"

Jace finally moved his gaze away from Eva to turn his attention to Evan. "We meet up with Holds and update him on what we know," Jace said. He finally moved and made his way over to the table and sat in the chair next to Eva. Did he just move the chair closer?

"What do we know exactly?"

"We are most certainly being followed. We don't exactly know what that could turn into, but it can't be good." Eva had a vision that a battle was to take place just outside the stronghold. But of course, she didn't share that with them. Visions aren't finite usually, so she wasn't all too comfortable sharing it. But she knew there wasn't anything she could do to stop it, so it was probably inevitable anyways.

"I'm not sure if I'm ready to share why I was kept in the tower," Eva put in. Jace clasped her hand on the table. He sent her reassuring thoughts and, a warm feeling. What was that?

"I'd rather we keep anything to do with your abilities on the down-low for now. We don't need everyone knowing your capabilities. Or mine apparently."

"Agreed," Evan said, finishing up at the mirror. He came over and sat down.

"You remember some of your experiences at the tower, maybe that would be enough," Jace supplied.

"I don't know how that would help in any way," Eva said. She really didn't want to share, but it could be important. Even the information she hid from herself could be, but she wasn't sure if she was strong enough yet to face the past.

"And then we have this guy," Jace indicated Evan with his thumb.

"What about me?"

"All that information on Brosch just waiting to burst free."

"Right, the mind invasion thing you guys are planning," Evan blew out a breath and fixed a blank stare on the wall.

"We want to help. Yes, the information about Brosch would be helpful in finally putting an end to his tyranny," Eva reached out across the table and squeezed Evan's hand getting him to shift his gaze to her, "but you shouldn't be shackled by him any longer. Body or mind. You need to be your own person."

A small smile tugged at Evan's mouth, "That would be nice."

"Plus, we need your abilities. I fear we will need them sooner rather than later." A slight knock sounded at the door. Eva released Evan's hand and placed it back on her lap as Jace opened the door and took the food tray from the serving maid that had knocked. He promptly shut the door and placed the food on the table. Evan didn't even hesitate. Just before the tray reached the surface of the table, he was already grabbing for the bread and cheese.

"I can go on ahead to Holds and announce our arrival after breakfast," Jace said and grabbed a plate and heaped bacon, eggs, biscuits, and gravy onto it.

"We should all go with you. I don't want to be left out." Jace looked like he was going to argue but Eva gave him a hard look of determination. She was not going to be on the sidelines for this talk.

"Fine," he sighed, giving in. "Not like there is anything else to check on or whatever anyways. I'm sure you are at least somewhat eager to meet him again after all these years." Jace's brow pinched in thought, but he shook it like whatever he was thinking was ridiculous, but Eva did catch a hint of the jealous emotion again.

"Well, not really, since the news we have to share isn't all that good," she grabbed a strip of bacon and began munching on it.

"Do I have to come along too?" Evan asked. Eva could see he was practically pleading with his eyes to not be included.

"Might as well. You're the reason we're being followed," Jace answered with a shrug and tucked back into his food.

"You don't know that for sure though, right?"

"It's highly unlikely they are trailing Jace and I," Eva supplied the answer. "We don't give off any Might signature. The only likely explanation they are following us is they picked up on yours."

"But I haven't used it, isn't that the only time it can be picked up?"

"What's this 015's ability like? Could he be able to sense Might signatures long after the person has left the area? I can see them clearly enough around people and see when it's being used, so let's say it's not out of the realm of possibility."

"He wasn't called the best Tracker for nothing," Evan grumbled. "Alright, so maybe I am a little bit at fault for that."

"So," Jace cut in, "it's settled. We are all going to Holds and updating him on what we know. If you remember, we also need to discuss breaking Evan's mind."

"You are trying to scare me at this point, aren't you?" Evan narrowed his eyes at Jace.

"I don't feel like it's the right time to do this before our meeting with Penn," Eva said. There was a feeling when she thought about helping Evan that she wasn't equipped yet to handle that big of a fix. But why?

"Agreed," Jace said. "I'm positive Holds will offer his home to us just like Newly did. Since Holds didn't know we were coming, I wasn't going to be walking up to his door last night. Plus, a mayor's home does have a little more privacy than an inn, no matter how good of an inn it is." She could feel his hesitancy through their link. Did he also feel something was missing?

"Great, more time to hype myself up," Evan said deadpanned.

"Right, so we have a plan," Eva concluded.

"Yes, we do," Jace smiled.

If only the plan wasn't fraught with insecurities. She needed to figure out that missing piece quick or having Evan along with them was for naught.

Chapter 33
Lous School

Brosch

"You will be most impressed by the young men graduating this year. They were very receptive to your proposed curriculum." Brosch doubted that.

The headmaster of the Lous School of Boys was always prostrating, trying to stand in good favor with him. It was true that he was threatening many people most of the time. Who was he kidding? He threatened people all the time.

"We will see in time. Even keeping them away from their families doesn't mean their opinions will stay manipulated." He did like keeping a close eye on the next generation, hoping he can garner some loyalty and not have outright opposition once these key youngsters take their places as mayors and lay leaders.

Brosch wasn't keen on staying long, only as a stopping point to get back to his stronghold. The school was just on the way through the Jergon Forest and a convenient resting place. He didn't engage with the students directly. When the headmaster had a student that seemed exceptional, they were sent to him. None of them had ability but they were useful in serving other ways around his stronghold.

"As you have instructed, we do our best to encourage them to your way of thinking." With a big emphasis on *encourage,* Brosch knew exactly what he meant. There weren't that many Manipulators about, as it was a rare ability. He couldn't even deny its usefulness in his interrogations, but it also protected him from other Manipulators. It was also troublesome when asserting his influence on other Manipulators.

"That's good to hear." They stepped into a small office, lined one side with shelves laden with books in a haphazard mess and the other a desk strewn with papers. A man was sitting at the desk absorbed in a book, but at the entrance of the headmaster and Brosch, the man hastily closed the book and shot to his feet, knocking his chair back in the process.

"Sir," he said and bowed his head slightly. He was a small man with unkempt brown hair, his clothes didn't fit well and quite frankly Brosch never understood why someone like him was ever gifted a rare ability. He held out his hand and raised his brow. The man, his name Brosch frankly didn't care to remember, stared at it for a second and then jumped into action, digging amongst the paper on his desk until he produced a single sheet and handed it shakily to him.

Brosch glanced at the list which had four names on it. "These are the most recent boys who have ended their education and have been sent back to their families," the man said. As Brosch scanned the list a name caught his eye.

"This one," he pointed to the name. "Jebrow. As in Mayor Jebrow's son?" He vaguely remembered the boy starting, but nothing stood out and no reports the past few years brought the boy in any light.

"Yes, I believe so," the headmaster confirmed.

"And your impression of his schooling? No push back?" Not that he had any trouble with Jebrow, even with the higher demands, they never balked, so he never had any reason to go back. Rarely did he travel south of the mountains.

"He completed the activities. I wouldn't say any stellar performance, but adequate. He never caused any trouble with the other students," the headmaster supplied.

"I don't recall any issues in my classes," the frazzled man said. The man's meaning, there didn't seem to be any issues when as he was using his ability on the students.

"If I remember correctly, Jebrow was a sizable man. Good with a sword, even with no ability," Brosch commented. "Was his son the same?"

"He was a large lad," the headmaster confirmed with a nod.

"Yes, he was, wasn't he?" the teacher said.

"He didn't seem threatening then?" Brosch asked. "Didn't push anyone around with his size?"

"He was always very respectful," the headmaster supplied.

"And when you say large, do you mean he was tall? I know the school was tailored to instruct the students in a certain way and some extra curriculars were no longer offered so there really wouldn't have been an opportunity for this boy to build his strength. But your wording doesn't seem to fit a tall description."

"Well," the headmaster's brow scrunched, "he was tall, but I can say he was broad."

"How much compared to the other students?"

"I could say with certainty he was twice the size as some of the lads." What now?

"And you weren't threatened by that at all?" That sounded very peculiar to Brosch. This boy, why he sounded like he could rival his personal bodyguard, Onyx.

"Never."

"I can hardly believe that he would become that size just because of genetics. Did you notice any weird patterns he developed? Any activities outside of class that seemed suspicious?"

The headmaster was shaking his head and the teacher had started tapping his chin in thought, and then he did say something, but not what Brosch was expecting. "He liked to go for walks in the woods."

"In the woods?"

"During the lunch hour, he would take his food, walk out the door to the woods, and then return just before class started."

"You didn't suspect he was doing anything other than taking a walk?"

"That's what it looked like to me. He always came back, so I never gave it much thought to exactly what he was doing. I really thought it was just walking." Well, apparently this lad pulled one over on the headmaster and this teacher if they honestly think that was all he was doing in the woods.

Before he could have one of his men do a small look in the woods surrounding the school, the headmaster pointed at his face, "ah, sir. You're bleeding."

Brosch lifted his hand to his nose and sure enough, blood was smeared on his fingers. Dang it! This was not the time to have this happen. He could NOT look feeble in any way. His supply he got from the witch had run out last night. He needed more now, but he knew once the bleeding started, within an hour, he wouldn't be able to move as easily. He needed more of that concoction before he even attempted to move. That would cost him a day.

Brosch turned away and stalked out the door, the headmaster played catch-up behind him out the door. "I have matters to attend to that don't need your supervision headmaster."

"Of course," the headmaster nodded, but had still dutifully followed him. He stopped abruptly and turned toward the headmaster with an assessing eye.

"You will STOP following me," he laced his words with conviction. "You have seen NOTHING. Go about your business and pay me no mind for the remainder of the day." He watched the headmaster's eyes dilate and immediately turned in the other direction and walked away without another word. Now that the headmaster was out of the way, he can attempt to fix the problem he was currently having.

He made it back to the room he lodged in when he visited the school. Onyx was sitting just inside the door, ready at a moment's notice. "Onyx. I need you to personally travel to that witch and get me some more of that, whatever crap she gives me." He snatched up a towel and pressed it to his bleeding nose.

"I will see that it is done." Onyx never questioned his orders, he just did. And that's the way he liked it. He did have some business to take care of, and the sooner that happened the better. Whatever leverage he might have to keep that traitorous 027 alive, well, that was well and truly used up. Besides, by the time the one person who might still care about her realized she was no more, they would have already been too busy doing his bidding.

Chapter 34
Holds Stronghold

Jace

"So, let me get this straight. You are the ones responsible for sending the whole of Brosch's army to my doorstep?" Well, when he put it that way, it does sound bad.

Holds was aware of Brosch's cronies' movements but wasn't quite sure how it came about. As glad as it was to catch up with him, he wasn't too happy to find Eva standing before him along with the escapee. Jace knew that it was a bad idea to bring them at first, but he knew if Eva put her mind to something, it would be hard to sway her any other way.

"I wasn't aware of this, and I do apologize. Truly I do. I was heading to the most logical place at the time," Jace tried to offer.

"Yes, right. By coming to my stronghold. Why not your father's stronghold? Or better yet, camp out in one of the small villages or the nearby forests." Holds did have a point there.

"I encouraged everyone to come here Penn. So, if there is anyone to blame, it's me," Eva spoke up, feeling a little guilty. Jace could tell she didn't mean for this to all happen the way that it was unfolding. And she was very adamant we had to come here. Jace suspected she saw something but wasn't willing to share in that vision.

Holds sighed, running his hand down his face. He pushed off his desk where he was leaned against and strode off to the window to look out. "As much as I want to blame you all," Holds started, "it was probably going to happen anyway." He turned his gaze on each of us with an uncomfortable smirk. "I've been pushing back as much as I can. Secretly for years with the people we recovered from his stronghold. Even now, I wish to refuse certain resources that were asked for that I clearly could not provide. I am thinking about the people who call this stronghold their home, and I don't want them to suffer just to appease some tyrant."

"But if we didn't bring Evan," Eva motioned to the escaped Numbered that most everyone in Hockland knew by now that Brosch was looking for, "there wouldn't have been a solid reason for them to come."

"The truth Eva, I haven't even received a missive stating the release of this man. They are coming with an army, a show of aggression, and it looks like it will all come to head in the morning."

"That soon?" Jace asked.

"I've been preparing my men for years. That doesn't mean I wanted to go through with an all-out battle."

"This is my fault," Eva said softly to herself, looking at Holds with so much remorse. "I knew this could happen, and I let it happen by coming here."

"No one can predict the future. It's up to the Fates to only know that." And this is where trying to explain why Eva made the comment she made was tricky. She had visions. She received some messages from the Fates. Whether they are good or bad, it really is up to her to decide what to share. Our little trio already decided not to share with Holds that she was a seer. As for her ability, she looked over at Jace with her head tilted just so. A silent question on whether to indulge in her ability. He just raised his eyebrows and shrugged, basically leaving it up to her.

"I cannot guarantee any outcomes to anything that would have not occurred yet, but I am able to offer to join you and your men to defend your stronghold," Eva's voice carried with a note of certainty, even as Holds expression became very uncertain.

"Absolutely not," he stated. "We didn't rescue you all those years ago just to put yourself back in danger."

"And many years have gone by that I haven't been able to properly thank you for that. Getting me out of that tower."

"Anyone could see that you were harmless." Holds statement was based on her appearance and demeanor before, but he didn't fully know the reasons why she was in the tower. Jace could see the resolve on her face. She was finally going to reveal the reason she was placed into the tower.

"I implore you not to think any less of me about the information I share with you. That goes for you two as well." I already knew the gist of what happened, but I didn't know the full extent of the situation until she began to speak to Holds.

"I can't tell you how many years I was held in the tower, but I do know why I was put there. In my young mind I wasn't exactly sure of the reasoning, maybe just to block out the tragedy that had occurred. But you have already witnessed some of that reasoning yourself Penn. With the guards."

Holds stood there for a second, blinking as if not sure what she was talking about. Eva continued, "You wouldn't have made it down to the tower cellar without the guards being taken out first. You wouldn't be alive today if they didn't die first." As she finished that sentence and understanding took hold in Holds face. More perplexed than anything, not really believing as of yet.

"So, are you saying, you were the one to take care of the guards? Is that what you want me to believe? You were in a locked dungeon Eva. It's hard to believe that it was you."

"I am able to take a person's spark from them," she said softly.

"I've never heard of such a thing."

"I can say with certainty that I have ability, and part of the ability I hold can literally take a person's life. And I have done it before. That's the main reason I was locked in that tower." She looked away from everyone in the room, feeling ashamed. But that isn't what she should be feeling. Jace told her before, and he would tell her again to make sure she knew she wasn't in the wrong.

"You have every right to defend yourself Eva," Jace pronounced along with coming up to her and lifting her chin to meet his eyes. Jace can send her all types of good vibes through the link but if she wasn't willing to believe it herself, then there is no amount of support he couldn't give that would make her change her mind. Direct eye contact was the key for her to not only feel but see that she wasn't a failure.

"Maybe the first time, but –"

"No buts," Jace cut her off. "The first time was just your instinct. You either killed them or you would have been killed. Those men at the tower tortured you for years. You didn't kill them in all that time. You killed them because they were going to kill other people. The people you saved went on to save so many people from Brosch's clutches. Look at what those actions amounted to. Was it extreme, sure. Death is final, but at what point was life an option? Would the same outcome occur if you didn't go that route? I have never thought of you as a violent person, and we are all put in situations in our lives where we must make difficult decisions. You just have had to make those decisions at such a young age."

Jace brushed the small whisp of hair that had fallen into her eyes. He looked deeply into them, sending her all his love. Truly this woman had more strength than anyone he knew.

A small tear escaped the corner of her eye and Jace felt an echoing warmth through the link. She still might be unsure, but at least he let her know that she was loved no matter what, and Jace was certainly feeling that love reciprocated back at him. He hugged her and didn't really give any thought in the moment to the people around. She needed him, and he realized he never wanted to leave her side. He wanted to always be there for her. He could also help to stand up for her decisions as well.

He pulled away and turned to Holds to express his opinion on her participation. "Even without her ability, she's the best fighter there is. She also won't be alone." Jace still had one of his arms around her waist, not willing to let go of her yet.

Holds was thinking, running his fingers over his mustache and beard. At some point he caved, Jace could tell in his posture and the small shake of his head.

"Fates only know why I'm allowing this," seeming to say that to himself. "Alright, if this does end up becoming a battle, then you can join in. You better believe I will try to negotiate."

"Evan can't go though, so what else could compare?" Jace asked.

"Then, it looks like I'll have to prepare the stronghold. Feel free to move your things in my home. Just outside the study, Roy can show you to your rooms." He eyed Jace's arm around Eva. He pursed his lips and looked between the two of them. Jace could have dropped his arm and stepped away, as he should have to indicate that he and Eva weren't a couple. But that just didn't feel right. She was his and he wanted people to know that. Holds was older, but he was still single and Jace couldn't let anyone else claim her.

Eva must have felt the tension, so she slowly stepped away, but not before Jace could feel her appreciation and adoration. She took the high road on this one. "We appreciate it Penn," she said. "We can use the training grounds as well?"

The move seemed to appease him and he smiled warmly at Eva, "Anytime. Now, I must get prepared. If you are willing to share more of that ability you got Eva, that could help with the strategy we use in this battle." She nodded her head with a small smile.

Holds left, leaving the trio again on their own. Surprisingly Evan remained silent through that whole encounter. The whole killing people thing that Eva could do was something he didn't know, but maybe he took that in stride.

As soon as the door closed behind Holds, Evan spoke, and boy did he have something to say.

"The more I learn about you Eva and what your ability can do, the more fascinated and frightened I feel. You can be as destructive as you wish to be with these abilities." Jace could see the slight terror in his eye thinking about those possibilities. "And yet," Evan continued, "you choose to use them to help. You would think I would be discouraged at the prospect of you rooting around in my mind, but you make anything possible. I'm already broken. You can't break something again. I might still have some uneasy feelings about it, but I'm more then sure now. I'll let you fix me up. I can only hope that your ability can do that. And yours too, Jace."

Eva gave Evan a soft smile. Jace could feel how grateful Eva was to hear those words. She had to hear from someone else that she wasn't a harbinger of death. Jace grasped her hand and squeezed slightly to emphasize the need to stand beside her, whatever decision she had to make.

"Let's get our bags to our rooms," Jace said. Eva nodded and they both headed toward the door, still holding hands. Evan trailed behind them out the door.

As Holds said, Roy was standing just outside the door. Jace reluctantly let go of Eva's hand to pick up his and Eva's bag. Eva looked to protest but Jace just shook his head stating with that movement that he was carrying her stuff. She let out a huff and rolled her eyes. Fates, she was beautiful even when she was annoyed.

Evan picked up his meager supplies and Roy gestured them toward the stairs. When they were led to their rooms, Roy bowed and moved away back down to where they came from.

"A room all to myself," Evan sighed and opened one of the three rooms they were given. "I can't remember a time that I could call a space all my own. Even if this one is borrowed for a bit."

"Enjoy," Eva said. "But don't get too comfy just yet. You'll come down to the training yard in an hour."

"What's that now?" Evan looked most confused.

"I can't let you on the battlefield without some way to protect yourself."

"I wasn't planning on being in any battle, now or ever."

"You have to be there." Eva's expression broached no argument.

"Did you see him in your vision at this battle?" Jace asked. "I know you haven't told us exactly what your vision was about, but I'm going to take a guess that had something to do with a battle, because I agree with Evan. He wouldn't need to train if a battle wasn't going to take place."

"Okay," he could feel that she was about to be stubborn about it, but she relented. "So, I might have had a vision that a battle would take place here at Holds Stronghold, and I saw everyone that would be involved, including you Evan."

"We know visions don't always turn out the way they are given. It's changeable," Evan said.

"I don't think I could with this one. It was different than others I had, more of a foretelling of what was to come."

"Oh, that's just great," Evan threw-up his hands in exasperation. "You could have warned us sooner you know."

"I didn't think it would make any difference. It was going to happen either way."

"Eva, you are very frustrating at times, aren't you?"

"Just go rest for an hour," Jace cut in. "You'll get some basic training and then afterward, we'll see about making sure you are useful for the battle."

"And by useful you mean?"

"Getting that ability of yours back."

"Fine." Evan turned and shut the door on Jace and Eva. Did Jace just use his ability on him again? What did it matter at his point? He was glad to finally be alone at last with Eva.

He looked down into her eyes, marveling at the flecks of color. The bags dropped to the floor of their own accord as he reached out again and found her hand, this time twinging his fingers with hers. She wasn't going to get away from him right now. There was no way he was going to let her be all by her lonesome self in a room.

This need rose like a tidal wave. There was no way of stopping it. Honestly there wasn't. It's like the air around them even halted to see what was going to happen. He didn't see any reason to stop, and Eva seemed just as eager.

They crashed together, arms flung around each other, his around her waist and hers around his shoulders. When their lips finally touched it was electrifying. It was everything and more than he hoped. When she responded by parting her lips at his exploring tongue, a moan escaped him. Slightly aware they were still in the hall, he backed up slowly toward the door, feeling for the handle without releasing his hold and lips. Kissing her was all he could think about, and he wasn't going to stop now that they started.

He was able to pull open the door and they both stumbled their way into the room. The movement had separated them briefly, both staring at each other with breaths sawing in and out. A heat came into her gaze that practically melted any lasting resolve away. Without looking away, he felt for the door and pushed it shut, hearing it latch.

He took a step closer to Eva, he could feel the overwhelming lust inside him, pouring out of his soul and crashing into and merging with whatever feelings she had, which were exactly the feelings he had. All it did was amp him higher, taking another step.

Eva shivered. But from the expression on her face, it wasn't from being cold. As he reached her to pull her gorgeous body flush against his, she jumped, springing toward him in a surprising move. He caught her effortlessly. She twined her legs around his waist and that was all the encouragement he needed.

He kissed her again with a ferocity that matched her own. Her hands tangled in his hair, his held her tight around her waist. He longed for this, agonized over it, talked himself out of it for so long. Why exactly did he do that?

He made use of his legs and found the bed, hitting it and crashing down right on top of Eva. She seemed to not mind at all. She pushed him away for a second and before he could protest, she reached for his cloak, undoing its tie and pushing it off his shoulders. He shrugged it off and she was now working on getting his tunic off him.

"You sure?" asked Jace, still a part of his brain telling him that he shouldn't be doing this. She grasped his chin and made him look at her.

"Do you want to stop?" Heck no he didn't. His face must have said it all because a slow smile came to her mouth, and she continued with removing his clothes. He helped by pulling his tunic over his head. A small gasp escaped Eva as she greedily spread her hands over his chest.

He made swift work of her cloak, and practically ripped her tunic off to expose her creamy flesh underneath. Her breasts were bound but that didn't stop him from sliding his hands over her flesh. His hands splayed across her stomach and crept up to the cloth. As he started unwrapping her, he brought his mouth to hers, giving her as much tenderness in the kiss as he could.

He was in love with her. He didn't know exactly when that feeling manifested itself in his heart, but it was there. Maybe it had always been there. Jace hoped that in every caress and kiss that he gave Eva that she would feel just how much he adored her.

He was in awe of her and at this moment, nothing was going to stop them from basking in each other's love. He knew it in the depths of his soul, his very life essence, his Spark. He could feel his insides overflow with a light he never knew was possible. And it was all because of his dark-haired beauty, his friend, his love, Eva.

Chapter 35
Non-comply

It was midday and the sun glared down on the open plains. Just in the distance Holds Stronghold was visible, nestled at the foot of the mountains and the sea just beyond. 015 stood there surveying the land as Brosch's cronies settled in behind him.

A messenger was sent with an ultimatum. Holds hands over the Numbered he was harboring or Brosch's cronies would use force to retrieve these individuals. Depending on what response was sent back, which 015 doubted that Holds would comply, then Brosch's army could do what they did best. Destroy and conquer. Once the army defeated and overwhelmed this stronghold, who's to say that Brosch couldn't do it again?

As much as this was a necessity to retrieve the Numbered, it was also strategic on Brosch's part. If his force can take on a powerful stronghold such as Holds, then it shows the other strongholds that he wasn't messing around. Brosch didn't tolerate disobedience. You obeyed or you were dead. It was cut and dry with him.

The army marched through the night and had arrived at high noon. 015 could see some weariness on the cronies' faces. He had already decided that they needed to recuperate their strength and that if any fighting was going to take place, tomorrow morning was going to be it.

Sure, he could surprise them and just barrel on up there tonight, but who would that benefit? Although it would certainly be a surprise, that doesn't mean the stronghold wouldn't be ready. The cronies would be at a disadvantage, not being at their best, and that just won't do. 015 couldn't take the risk of failing. He has failed too much in the last few days.

He didn't know how they did it, but they forged that river. Seeing the mighty waters churn, and the dead horse on the bank, he thought better then to risk his own life. If they crossed, they were on Holds' land. Even if they hid out in a hut at the edge of the sea, it was still Holds' responsibility.

Instead of staring, waiting for the messenger to appear again, he made his way to the tent that was set-up for his use. He ducked inside and in the middle of the tent was a table with a map atop it. There were rough scribbles of the surrounding area him and the cronies currently resided in. He made his way over to a small cot that was set off to the side and sat down.

Did he like the wait? As a Tracker, it wasn't in his nature to want to wait. If he didn't fulfill his obligations and held to his word, then Brosch might, no. That would never happen. He needed to stop that line of thinking. Everything will work out.

"Sir," a crony appeared in the tent entryway. "The messenger has returned."

"Have him enter." The crony gave a slight nod and headed back out of the tent. 015 stood and walked over to the table, looking down at the map with the surety that the pieces which lie unused on the side, will be placed soon enough.

The messenger entered with a grim expression. 015 could already guess Holds response. "Well?" 015 asked.

"The mayor will not release any known or unknown Numbered that might be on his lands."

"What about specifically the two Numbered that were mentioned in the missive?"

"He said he had never seen 034 or 1. No branded person has come on his lands to his knowledge." So, was it possible that he did not know they were on his lands? As 015 thought about the probability that a few people went unnoticed by Holds and his people, well that just didn't make any sense. He had sentinels scattered about his land and he usually is very aware of any new arrivals.

"He could be telling the truth; he could be lying for all we know. No matter. Either way you look at it, they are on his land. If that means we go searching ourselves, then that's just what we will have to do."

"And if he defends?"

"Then we will know that he was lying. Send in 021 and 046."

"It'll be done right away." The messenger left to do his bidding.

Was there doubt? Oh 015 most certainly doubted. He doubted that Holds knew what was going on. Doubted that he wasn't going to be ready for an attack. Doubted that Holds would stand a chance against Brosch's army. Doubted that lives would be spared.

As we waited for the Strategists, we thought on all that was taking place. 015 did this from time to time, weighing the outcomes. What could happen? Well, one outcome was Brosch's army would succeed in combing Holds lands, killing as many people that stood in their way, and retrieving the Numbered. Another outcome was Brosch's army came up against Holds army, if he had such a thing, and Brosch's army would have significant losses but, in the end, triumphed and claimed the Numbered while slaughtering the rest of the inhabitants of the stronghold.

And yet another outcome came to mind, one that he didn't entertain very often. Brosch's army is defeated and 015 fails to capture his target. In any other instance before with Brosch's cronies, he would say no one stood a chance. But with what happened at the Wedset Mountains with the Ren, he had those doubts creep in.

If hypothetically 1 was in that stronghold and took part in the battle, it was probable that Brosch's men could lose again. Never had there been a force that changed the tide as the small skirmish at Wedset. He could say it was Brosch's weakness, being overconfident. There were people that openly opposed him, and they just showed him they could win.

What 015 believed was unstoppable now possibly wasn't the case. And deep down there was something trying to break free. It felt trapped, waiting for the shields to be lessened. And every time, an opposing force clouded it and the feeling dissipated, but not before unsettling 015. He was having an internal battle; one he had dealt with before. This time though, it lingered just a little, making all those old doubts come back to the surface.

No, he wasn't that scared little boy anymore. He wasn't small and weak. He had a special ability that no other could match. He was not useless. He will survive. He just wanted to be accepted for who he was.

015 shook his head, trying as he might to forget those long-ago memories. They just brought him pain, and right now that was the last thing he needed. He needed surety and confidence. None of this about a small helpless child. He was a grown man that could make his own decisions. They were his.

And yet, that doubt crept in again. Were they really his?

Chapter 36
Visiting the Station

Jace

As Jace opened his eyes, he was standing in the most unusual place. Did he dose off? All around him was white as far as the eye could see. He heard some voices behind him. He turned and saw Eva, standing next to…another Eva? Jace rubbed his eyes. He couldn't be seeing double. As he opened his eyes again, sure enough, both Eva's still stood there, except, the other was fair and had blonde hair.

So, not another Eva, but someone in her likeness. He approached the pair who seemed to be in conversation. The blonde woman looked over and her eyes widened. As he came closer to them, Eva turned to see what startled the woman and even Eva's eyes widened. They were standing next to a clear bench. Wait a second. Was this that place Eva was talking about?

"Hey there," Jace came up and raised his hand in greeting to the blonde woman. He went next to Eva and placed a small peck on her head and snaked his arm around her.

"How are you here?" Eva looked him up and down, an expression of disbelief on her face.

"Here? In this dream?"

Eva stepped away. "This is not a dream."

"Okay, so if I'm not making this up, then where are we?" He truly did not know.

"Eva, who is this man?" the blonde woman asked. She tilted her head studying him. Jace glanced down but all he saw on his person was a plain white tunic and trousers. Nothing spectacular.

"Yes, this is Jace," Eva indicated an arm his direction. "Jace, this is Seraphim," she nodded over to the woman.

"And we are?" He prompted Eva to answer his original question.

"At the Station." Oh yes, that was the name of the place she had talked about in the past.

"This is quite fascinating," Seraphim chimed in. "I don't think I've ever heard of this before. I certainly never experienced it before."

"Experienced what?" Jace asked.

"Well, when I've come to the Station, I am only here with one other Spark. It's not to say that there might be other Sparks there too, but whoever we are connecting with at that moment, well, that's the only other Spark that is present. But as you can see, there are three of us."

"Not normally something that happens. Well Eva, it seems like everything that isn't normal is our normal," Jace joked. But his jovial mood dampened with Eva's look. She wasn't mad, at least he couldn't tell that she was mad. Then again, he really didn't feel anything right now through the link.

He touched his chest instinctively, realizing he was missing something there. Eva's hand went to her own chest and her eyes widened, seemingly also noticing the change.

"I can't feel you," she whispered.

"Same," Jace confirmed.

"Eva," Seraphim interjected. "What is it dear?"

"I'm supposed to be able to feel Jace, like his emotions." Her hand dropped and a slight panicked look came into her eyes.

"Oh my. Can it be?" Seraphim looked between the two of them and then a large smile spread on her face. "It is. This is such wonderful news!" She hugged Eva.

"What news?" Jace asked. Before he could stop her, Seraphim turned and embraced him. Okay then.

As she pulled away tears sprung to her eyes, and she held her hands close to her heart. Well, the tears were very joyful, so nothing to be concerned with.

"You are matched! Oh, this is so exciting. I waited many years myself, but unfortunately, it didn't happen for me. I've only known a handful of couples in my lifetime that found their match. It's a wonder in this day and age. I would love to hear all about how the two of you met."

"Wait, slow down Seraphim," Eva held up her hands to halt the woman talking. "I don't know what you are talking about."

Match. Found his match. Hold up. Didn't his Nanna say something to him about that?

"Your match is when you find the person who matches you in every way. Your abilities, your Spark, everything! Well, except for the obvious difference of anatomy. Your souls were not complete until you finally came together."

That's exactly what they did in the physical sense. He's going to be in trouble with his father over that. He saw Eva blush a little and rub the back of her neck.

"Right. So, that means Jace can do all the things I can?"

"In theory, yes. But also, much more. You are essentially one person. There's no separating you two now. Whatever you were able to do with your ability before, double its strength. You two will be packing quite a wallop when you use ability," Seraphim explained.

"We merged," Jace said absently, thinking about his Nanna once again. *Jace. One day you will meet your aura's match. Nothing will be able to stop you once your auras merge.*

As he looked at Eva once again, he finally understood what his Nanna was talking about. He reached for her hands and held them while looking into her eyes. How did he miss it this whole time? If he had just paid more attention to his Nanna's words. She obviously had a vision about the two of them and told him about it. He always just nodded and played along, but he really discredited what his Nanna said. He was such an idiot.

"My Nanna said when I met my aura's match that we can do anything once our auras merge."

"Right, you told me about that once," Eva remembered their brief conversation when talking about auras just before they left on their journey.

"Your Nanna mentioned that?" Seraphim questioned.

"Yes. She was a seer and had visions all the time. I just didn't realize that when she was telling me stuff like that was because she had a vision."

"Remarkable. You have seer's blood flowing inside you." He guessed when she put it that way, he did.

"This is all very interesting," Eva said. "But how was he able to come here with me?"

"Well, you two are merged, as Jace said, so you aren't you anymore. Your Spark isn't all your own. They've combined. So, wherever your essence goes, Jace's goes and vice versa."

That's wild. He just stared at Eva like this was all just a dream. They'd wake up and he'd tell her about this craziness, and she wouldn't know what he was blabbing on about.

Yet, it's like he knew this was real. He couldn't feel her right now, so he had no idea what she was feeling. But the look in her eyes told him that she was in awe just like he was.

They claimed each other. From the first day they met, they had a connection. They were young, so they didn't know what was going on, but it was always there. If he was sure of anything, it was that they belonged together, and no one was going to separate them.

"It seems like a fairy tale," Eva whispered. Jace couldn't agree more.

"We'll talk again some other time Eva, I don't want to keep my love waiting," Seraphim gently spoke. He was so used to Evan's abrupt interruptions that he almost felt bad for ignoring Seraphim.

"Of course, no need to stay here," Eva released Jace's hands. She gave Seraphim a warm hug. That's when Jace really took a look at what Seraphim was wearing.

"Are you getting married?" he asked, because she looked to be wearing a traditional wedding dress.

"You are preceptive, Jace," she released Eva and opened her arms to give him another hug. Oh, might was well.

"Congrats. He doesn't know how lucky he is." Seraphim laughed and stepped back after releasing him.

"Thank you again Seraphim for your wisdom. You know I have so many more questions," Eva spoke.

"I know dear. Have faith that we will meet again." She waved a final goodbye, and she faded away right before them. Just as he was going to say something to Eva, she was also gone too, and just like that, the white world faded away before him.

Chapter 37
Agreement

Evan

Evan stepped out into the training grounds, after having to ask several people to point the way. He would have knocked on Eva's door, but he didn't know which room she took, plus, both doors stood ajar anyway. Seeing as they were not in their rooms, that meant they had already decided to head down. Without him.

They did say an hour, and he most definitely took that much time to relax. He wasn't overly stressed or anything. This was the first time he wasn't being chased down since he escaped Brosch's Stronghold. Well, they were essentially still being chased, but it seemed like they weren't actively being captured, or escaping, or being attacked, or trying to cross a river.

The sun was just starting its path down into the sky. Dinnertime was close at hand, and he most looked forward to the food these days. There was a bit of activity on the grounds, mostly people gathering supplies, but he spotted the two people who currently were his, friends?

Had he ever really had friends before? He tried to think back to when he was younger, and he just didn't remember playing with many children. He certainly didn't have friends at Brosch's. He didn't take kindly to them forming any attachments with each other.

Well, anyway, his friends were in a conversation when he stepped right up to them. His movement caught their attention as they both turned, like it was choreographed in his direction. Okay, that was different.

"Hey there you two. So ready to start this training," he said with a pained smile on his face. He wasn't looking forward to this.

"For a second there a thought you weren't going to show up," Jace teased him.

"I thought about it, but then I was like, I don't want to die, so I came."

"Ha! I wouldn't hurt you." He could though, and that's what scared Evan. "So, what should we teach him," he directed his question to Eva.

She looked over at Evan, scanning him up and down. He squirmed a little under her scrutiny.

"Knives," she said. "Just in case anyone gets close. We'll just always keep a couple other people with him." Jace nodded in agreement.

"I'll let you get to it. You were always better with knives," he smirked over at Eva. She raised her eyebrow at him but had a small smile on her own face. "I'll go help move supplies." He moved off to help but not before he noticed the small wink, he gave Eva. What was that about?

"Come over here Evan," Eva gestured him toward a table and as he approached, he saw that the table was covered with very sharp objects, from small throwing knives to large axes. She picked up a pair of knives that were each as long as his forearm.

She held out the handles to Evan. "Here you go." He tentatively took the knives and held them in his hands, feeling the smooth wood grips against his palms.

Eva was already walking away from the table, so he hurried to catch up with her. She turned back toward him when she was part way into the open yard, he stopped just a few feet from her. He didn't notice that she had something in her hand. It was a hip sheath. She approached him with the item.

"You'll have to get used to removing them too. Put this on." He looked at his hands that held the knives and then the sheath. "Oh, for Fate's sake." She came over and started attaching the belt to his hips. She did it with little fanfare and stepped back as soon as the belt was on.

"Let's get started." For the next half hour Eva led him in a series of drills that involved just handling the knives. Then for the next hour after that, they worked on a few defense moves over and over again. His arms where well and truly tired at the end of the time.

"That's the basics to help you stay alive," Eva said. That sounded encouraging, not. "You'll be primarily focused on healing so we will have a couple fighters near you to protect you. This would be as a last resort if anyone got through them."

"Right, healing," Evan said as he sheathed his weapons. He had to say it did make him feel a little bit better he had something to protect himself. "And when is this mind breaking business occurring?"

"After dinner," Jace announced as he strolled up to them. His hulking form very much in contrast to Evan.

"You'll get all feed, and then take a nice soothing bath, get you some nice clean clothes, and have you all cozy by the fireplace," Eva put in.

"Um, that all sounds nice," Evan wasn't exactly sure where she was going with all that.

"To relax you," Jace put in. "Although you have stated that you are all fine and dandy with this mind invasion thing, it'll still be a better go for us if you are as relaxed as you can be. We don't want you to be nervous at all." And just by saying that, Evan did feel a tiny bit nervous, but not in the way they probably thought.

Yes, the whole mind entering thing was not in his list of activities he overly enjoyed. He was more worried about it not working and if they are messing around in there and something does happen, well, he wasn't sure he'd be alive at that point.

Eva touched his arm and gave him a warm smile. "I know it's hard. And I'm not going to say it'll be easy by any means. But we want to help you." He believed Eva, she said that so much over the last few days and even though at times she was scary with her whole eye-changing business and brutality with fighting, she still had this warmth to her. Her general attitude of care.

She didn't want to bring trouble to people. She was very remorseful of bringing Brosch to the Rens and now to Holds Stronghold. She was trying her best to do what was right, even if things seemed to be falling apart along the way.

Now, Jace was a different story. Did he trust Jace? As Evan looked over at him, Jace had a similarly warm smile too. Odd, he never thought Jace would care that much. He was always fooling around with him and picking on him, and since Evan was thinking about it, that's what he really liked about Jace.

Maybe it was his way of showing he cared. Either way, if they both had this ability and were going to try this mind stuff together, then he couldn't think of two better people.

"Alright guys. I'll go fill by tummy and relax. And then we'll get to the part where I get to be the Healer I'm supposed to be," Evan gave them a small smile.

"We'll come to your room when it's time," Eva said as she stepped to Jace's side.

"Off you get Evan," Jace shooed him away.

"Yeah, yeah, I'm going." He started to move across the field back inside but not first looking back at the pair. They were a very odd couple.

Over the past week with them he had witnessed the tension between the two of them and it was getting to the point that Evan seemed to be a major interruption. But as he looked at them now, he didn't see that underlying tension.

They were both relaxed, happy, and was Jace holding her hand? Something changed between them. Evan didn't want to know what that was, but he was glad that the atmosphere around them was pleasant.

He needed to find some information on that bond of theirs. Maybe he can ask Holds to browse his library. Never can tell what can be found.

Eva

"We're actually going to do this." Eva was still apprehensive about it but with her Guardian's information and now this deeper bond she had developed with Jace, she was as ready as she was ever going to be to attempt it.

"Yes. Stop worrying. I have complete confidence in you," Jace brought his arms around her and rested his chin on her head. Her hands landed on his chest, and she breathed in his scent of pine and lilies. Why that scent comforted like no other, she didn't know, but she was so thankful for Jace's support.

The slow circles Jace was rubbing on her back made her relax but other thoughts crept into her mind, mainly from their private interlude earlier that day. She knew a blush adorned her cheeks and as she looked up into his eyes, she could see the adoration in them.

He bent and gave her the sweetest and tenderest kiss. Just barely any contact, more like a soft caress. She pouted a little as he withdrew.

"Not now, love. We must get Evan's mind fixed up for him."

"Oh alright," she could concede to that. He already waited this long, might as well get to it.

She reluctantly left the enclosure of Jace's arms and headed out their room towards Evan's. Jace was right behind her as she knocked on Evan's door. She heard movement and steady footfalls until the door was opened and there Evan was, looking very well rested.

"Greetings. So, its time?" he asked with an eyebrow raised.

"Yep." Jace said behind her as she bobbed her head in agreement.

Evan opened the door wider and moved off to the chair that was set by the fireplace. They both entered and Jace shut the door as Eva came over and grabbed the chair before Evan could sit in it.

"What are you doing?" By Evan's expression, he was curious as to what prompted her to take this seat, which clearly was where he was heading to. Without answering him, she moved it and placed the seat facing the sofa. She scooted it as close as she could to the sofa and then sat herself down on the sofa.

She felt amusement. She touched her chest and looked over at Jace. Turned out that the connection they had didn't go away. It just didn't work at the Station. It was the weirdest thing, but as soon as they both came back, the link on their emotions remained. They also seemed to be deeper and stronger.

She smiled, being affected by his own feelings. Feeling each other's emotions seemed to remain the same, but there was something else there now. It wasn't just feeling them, but also influencing her own emotions right back. His happiness made her happy. Just like, he could feel her worries and was also worried. They could still be worried or happy over different things though.

Now, this would be the first test in this newfound merged ability business. Maybe it was something that they should mention to Evan before they got started.

Jace didn't hesitate and sat down beside her facing the empty chair. He glanced over at Evan and did a grand gesture toward the seat. Evan's eyes narrowed, but he slowly made his way over and sat down in front of them.

"You ready?" Jace asked.

"I think so," Evan said, but there was something Eva was picking up in his posture. He was worried about something.

"I don't know if this will make you feel better about the whole process," she looked to Jace before she continued. He gave her a small smile and shrugged. His way of saying might as well. "But Jace and I are merged now."

"Okay," Evan's brow arched.

"Like the *Seer King* story," Jace added.

"What? You must be kidding me. It's a joke. Right?"

"Nope," Eva answered. "We were told the strength of the ability we use is doubled, now that we are merged."

"Told by who?"

"Long story," Jace supplied. Yes, probably not the time to talk about Seraphim and the Station.

"In any case," Eva went on, "you should know that whatever you have going on in there can't be more powerful than our combined ability."

"Are you sure you two can control that much? I mean, you both aren't slouches when it comes to your abilities."

"Eva's worked hard to control and master hers," Jace's confidence tickled at her own. She was sure she could do this. Jace on the other hand, might not be able to. It'll be more instinctual with him, but she didn't believe his ability will go haywire or something. He was controlled in the sense that he really didn't know how to use ability.

"And you Jace?" Evan asked. "Do you think you can control your ability?" She could see Jace looking at Evan, thinking about that for a second, but she didn't feel any bit of confidence dip, it instead grew a bit.

"I might not have acknowledged my ability in the past, since I honestly didn't know about it, but I can control it. I will control it. Better yet, I'll make a deal with you Evan. We will only do exactly what you agree us to do in that head of yours."

"Meaning?"

"Meaning," Jace elaborated, "We make it contractual. A guarantee." Yes, that felt right. Eva's guardian said, if she had permission to build a barrier from the individual, in this case the individual being Evan, then it might be enough to replace the other imposing barrier placed there without permission.

"Let's say we replace this barrier of yours with one that is more suitable to your needs," Eva interjected.

"What kind of barrier?" Evan's eyes narrowed.

"One that will freely let you do what you want, sharing knowledge we need, your memories, using your ability, anything you'd like to access, but at the same time leave things out that need to stay out. Like a certain someone putting a barrier on you in the first place."

"You could really do that?" Eva's eyes widened. She could tell just the idea of it was exciting.

"We'd certainly like to do that for you," Jace replied. "All we need is your approval. With the reassurance that is all that we'd do. No locking up that mind of yours again."

Evan stroked his chin in thought. He lowered it, looked at the two of them and nodded his head firmly that he approved.

Jace held out his hand and spoke the words, "Evan, former Numbered. You agree to allow us to enter your mind and place a barrier which you will have access to as much as you require and at the same time not allowing any other people in to do any more damage." As he spoke, Jace's eyes started to sparkle, like he was channeling something, but Eva couldn't imagine what. "We will only perform the necessary actions upon your handshake as the approval."

As Evan was about to shake, Jace pulled back and said one more thing. "And in case of an emergency which might threaten your life, you give us complete access to our abilities to save you in any way we deem necessary."

There was no hesitation. Evan placed his hand in Jace's. As soon as they shook their hands, there was this glowing light that sealed their hands for a second and then seemed to seep in, like it was accepting what took place.

As Evan let go, he looked down at his hand, trying to figure out what happened. "What was that?" he asked.

"The agreement was sealed." Jace said. "Now the real work can take place."

"I didn't know that was a thing."

"I honestly don't know what the whole glowing hands was all about, but I got a sense that it will hold us to our agreement."

"Yeah, I think you are right."

"Shall we?" Eva asked.

Evan straightened up and had a look of determination on his face. "I'm ready."

Eva took Jace's hand. They both looked at each other for a moment. Looking into his eyes was like looking into herself. They were one person now, and she believed they could do anything. Just like his Nanna said.

Chapter 38
Breaking Walls

Jace

This was the real test. Jace was going to purposely go in and manipulate another person's mind. Here's to hoping the first time wasn't a bust.

Eva reached up to Evan's temple, and Jace did the same on the other side of Evan's head. He wasn't sure what to do next, but there was this tug to come along. That must have been Eva. He let the tug take him and sure enough the next he knew he wasn't sitting on the sofa anymore.

In front of him stood this wall. It looked solid, made of a material stronger than bricks or stones. It was black as pitch and reached as high as he could see. He looked over to where Eva was standing, also looking at this wall. Their hands were still connected. Probably best to make sure they both channeled the ability properly.

"And here it is. The wall," Eva murmured.

"When we were saying barrier earlier, I wasn't expecting an actual barrier," Jace pointed out.

"This is what I saw when I was in here the last time. It's specific to who I was searching for. This blocks my way when I am looking for information on Brosch."

"Is that so? Is there a different block for his ability?"

"I think they are somehow tied together. I don't know exactly how that can happen, but it seems that this is binding multiple things, his memories and physically what he can do."

"If only it were bricks."

"I thought the same thing. This must have strengthened to what it looks like now over time. A constant application, layer upon layer. I don't think a wall like this could happen the first time."

"Maybe for us it can," Jace said hopefully.

"Right, but our wall is going to be totally different from this one."

"It is, but it still will have to be stronger if it needs to keep people out."

"True." Eva studied the wall again, trying to determine the best way forward.

"Let's just walk along and see if we notice any cracks. With him being away from Brosch, maybe one appeared."

"That sounds like a good idea." So, they both walked together, searching the wall as they went. It probably would be better if they split up to cover more ground, but he just didn't want to let go. They were so tightly connected. It was hard to think of going in any other direction than the direction Eva was going in.

The time seemed to stretch on, but suddenly Eva pointed at the wall. "There, I think I see one." They approached cautiously and inspected the wall. Sure enough, there was a small groove the size of a baby gardener snake that appeared along its normally pristine surface.

"I see it too."

"So, what, we just start chipping away at the wall? Take this whole thing down and replace it?"

"I think we need to do this from the inside."

"You mean on the other side of this barrier?"

"Yep." Okay then. Eva continued. "We chip a hole big enough for us to get into and on the other side. After we can take stock of what we are dealing with, and feel it, then I think we'll be able to replace the wall."

"Replace? So, what are we supposed to do with the wall that is already there? Not destroy it?"

"It'll come to us, I'm sure. Let's get to chipping." Jace was not as sure, but he did trust Eva. If she said they will know, then they will know.

"So how do we chip away at it?" Jace asked. Eva looked at her hand for a second and clenched her fist. Then seemingly out of nowhere, a pickaxe materialized in her hand. "How'd you do that?"

"We are essentially in an alternate space, and we can manipulate it to suit our needs. Like, needing this," she held up the axe. She handed it to Jace. It felt real enough. As he looked at it and felt it's weight, Eva created another one. "I think it'll be alright to let go right now." They were still holding hands.

Reluctantly, he released her hand. He waited just a beat, but nothing seemed to change. Good. Now it was time to get to work on this crack. They both started swinging their axes and little chunks of the wall fell away as they went. It seemed like tedious work, but their rhythm was steady and soon enough a hole started to form.

The bigger they made it, the harder it was to chip away the pieces. At one point, it seemed like the hole was starting to shrink.

"Quick Jace!" Eva shouted. "Climb through!" Without any hesitation, he started climbing through, it was tight and seemed to tighten around him, but he sucked in his chest and squeezed himself through, landing on his side after he got through.

He looked back to see Eva scrambling through as well, but the hole was closing. He reached toward her and grabbed her hands and pulled as much as he would dare without hurting her. He could feel that she was held up, but with one more tug, she was through and sprawled right on top of him.

They both looked back at the hole, but there wasn't one. When their gazes met, both had their eyebrows raised. Yep, that was a close one.

As they rose, they took in their surroundings. In the center was a light that flashed periodically. If he looked closely, he could see shapes and images of people, places. These must be Evan's memories.

He started to approach, but Eva stopped him with a hand on his arm. "Remember, we are only here to take care of the wall." Looking into his memories wasn't in the agreement.

"Good call. We don't want to be kicked out of his mind now that we got this far," Jace commented.

"Agreed." She faced back toward the wall, looking up to the very top. As Jace looked, he realized it was a dome. There was a ceiling to this place. Evan's memories where truly enclosed.

"What are the ways to take out a wall?" Eva asked.

"Well, you can set explosives, shoot cannon balls at it, use your ability on it like from the mountain," Jace supplied.

"I mean I could give it a go."

"But it doesn't seem right, does it?" Jace could see her apprehension. Something he also felt as well. They would have to know exactly how to construct their wall quick if they took this one out, but it would cost them a lot of their strength.

She touched the wall, studying it. As he also looked at the wall, he also thought what she had done just on the other side of it.

"You just manifested axes out of nowhere. What's to say we can't change the wall what we want it to be because we said so?"

"Just think it, and it will be?" she asked with a smirk.

"If this is some alternate place that doesn't have normal rules, then sure, why not?"

"You do have a valid point." He thought so. "Alright, let's give it a try." She held out her hand.

He grasped it and they both stared at the wall. All they had to do was change it. This wall didn't exist anymore. Their wall was going to be stronger and better and let Evan make his own decision. He felt his will merge with Eva's but before they would apply it to the wall a voice cut into his concentration.

"Whatcha doing?" They both were startled and turned toward the voice. There before him stood, Evan?

"Umm, trying to take this wall out." Jace gestured toward the imposing force. Evan nodded his head and looked over at Eva. She stared at him trying to understand what in the world this was. Jace was in the same boat. How was he here? It was his mind, but wasn't he already present on the other side of the wall? Was this just a manifestation him and Eva somehow created?

"I'd say it's impossible, but I've been saying it for years," Evan said. He looked Eva up and down then said something totally unexpected. "You are a sight to behold. I wouldn't mind you staying awhile." He winked. Legit winked at Eva. Jace pulled Eva closer and glared at Evan. He didn't know what he was trying to pull, but Evan knew better then to try anything with Eva, especially with Jace present.

"Do you know who we are?" Eva asked. What kind of a question is that? Of course, Evan knew.

Evan scratched his head and then shook it. "Never seen you before in my life. I think I would remember if I met you." He smiled again at Eva. Jace was just on the verge of enacting some violence.

"I'm Eva, this is Jace."

"What are you doing?" Jace asked Eva out the side of his mouth. "Evan knows us."

"Maybe this is part of Evan we don't know. Trapped here in this barrier," she suggested.

"Well, I don't like him."

"Right, of course you don't." Eva just shook her head in exasperation. Addressing Evan once again, "We are here to try and fix this thing so you can do whatever you want."

"Really?" Evan looked generally interested. "Well, I've been here so long. I do have to say seeing other people in here is a first for me."

"Maybe you can help us," Eva suggested.

"No way," Jace said. "What does he have to contribute here? He's only a Healer."

"I'm a very powerful Healer, thank you very much." Evan puffed up his chest and putting on an air of respect for his position. That wasn't a trait Evan had at all. Seriously, who was this guy?

"Maybe that's exactly what we need to make this work," Eva said.

"How do you figure?" Jace asked.

"This wall is what is binding Evan's mind. He's not able to use his ability on anyone else besides Brosch. What if the reason he can't tell us those memories is because they all relate to him using his ability on Brosch. Why keep a *powerful* Healer?"

"Because Brosch needs a Healer?"

"But it's not like he's participating in any of the battles recently. If there is no way for him to get injured, then why have a Healer on standby?" She had a point.

"Okay, so Evan's been healing Brosch of something," Jace surmised.

"So, Evan's really powerful," yes, she said that already.

"Where are you going with this?"

"Brosch doesn't seem the type to broadcast anything personal. Because we know of this block on Evan's mind, we know he has ability. But which ability? Remember there are two mind abilities."

Yes, Jace remembered, the Scholar and the Manipulator. "I'm going to go with Manipulator. Scholar doesn't seem to fit because they are just good at remembering things, like facts."

"Fascinating stuff," Evan chimed in. "How can my healing help the wall?"

"Brosch made you use your own ability to strengthen the wall. By forcing you to use that ability, you essentially helped to block yourself."

"How'd you come to that conclusion?" Jace asked.

"How else could Brosch put a block on his abilities *and* his memory? We only see the same block. Which means,"

"I did this to myself?" Evan asked.

"He made you do it to yourself," Eva continued. "He forced you to put it there and then he somehow can still use your ability for himself."

"That can't be right, he used his ability on me," Jace mentioned. Eva turned to him and had that question in her look.

"When did that happen?"

"Right after we closed the mountain. He came up to me and placed his hand on my arm and I had some of my strength return."

"I remember that!" Evan exclaimed. "I found myself healing some person I didn't remember healing before. It was only briefly though. That's when that crack appeared."

"Jace, did you say something to Evan that might have been a command?"

"Well, I might have." Jace remembered saying something to Evan. Okay, so he remembered exactly what he said to him. "Okay, I said if either I or Eva need healing, you will heal."

"But he didn't heal me."

"Oh, I remember bits and pieces of your face," Evan said to Eva. "I couldn't use my ability on you because you were already healing yourself. It's harder for a Healer to work on another Healer anyway." Yes, Jace remembered him saying that much.

"Do you know what this means Jace?" Eva asked. He just shrugged and looked at her to explain. "It means your manipulation is stronger than Brosch's. You can overpower what he's placed on Evan's mind."

"I did that outside of Evan's mind. How am I going to apply it in here?"

"I got a plan," Eva continued. She explained how Jace was going to use what she called persuasion, which was the fancy way to say manipulation, Evan was going to use healing, because apparently we were dealing with the Evan that had no problem using it inside the wall, and Eva was going to bolster both with her strength, which Jace would also be lending to, and then with a last punch of her own manipulation to place the approved barrier in its place.

"I got to say," Evan said, "I'm a little doubtful this will work."

"You'll have no choice because I'm going to make you do it," Jace glared at him.

"You're not making him do anything Jace, that wasn't in our agreement with him."

"So how am I using my ability?"

"You are going to use your persuasion on the wall. You will persuade it to become something new. Something better. Exactly what Evan agreed to."

"I don't remember agreeing to this," Evan said.

"The other Evan did," Jace said.

"Oh, and what did this other Evan agree to? What if I don't approve?"

"Fine, you want to also be a part of the agreement." Jace stuck out his hand and repeated the words he said to Evan on the other side of the wall. He repeated every single word, including the bit about life threatening circumstances.

This Evan looked at his hand, then looked up at him. "There will still be a barrier though."

"Not really," Eva explained. "The barrier we are putting in place is to keep people out. You won't have any restrictions and there won't be anyone in the future who could put a block on you again."

This Evan thought about it, but then eventually he did shake Jace's hand, then same glowing effect took over and seeped into their connected hands.

"Well, what are we waiting for? Let's get started!" Evan said with a pained expression. Ah, there's there Evan he knew. Not too sure but willing to try anyway.

"Okay, I feel that it would be best if we were all holding hands in a circle," Eva started by grabbing Jace's hand and then Evan's. Jace reluctantly took Evan's.

"Don't worry there bud, I won't start chanting *Blessed Be the Fates.*" Joking now, are we? We needed to focus.

"Everyone should be concentrating on the wall," Eva said. "Close your eyes and let your ability seep into its foundation." As she spoke, Jace did just that, trying not to think about who he was holding hands with, but letting his ability do what it needed to. He looked deep inside himself and saw a small little glow. When he got there, it was like a little string just waiting there to be used, glowing a deep purple color. He grabbed the string and was yanked across space.

For a second, he didn't know if he was still in Evan's mind or not, but he looked up and realized this impossible force being pushed on him. The wall? It must have been. He had to persuade the wall to not be

Brosch's wall any longer. It was Eva's wall, no it was *their* wall. This barrier wasn't going to hold anyone or any ability in anymore. He felt a tingle alongside him, an orange light floating there. He had the impression that was Evan's ability.

Yes, that needed to be in here, he started to see where his ability was intertwined with the original wall. Deep within him another ability swelled. That was Eva's part, or rather, their part. They were one, weren't they? They could do anything. This was possible and Jace was going to do everything he had to make it so. He never quit when the going got tough.

He pushed everything out of him at the wall, while also making sure Evan's ability rode along with the push too. And before his eyes the wall was turning.

The wall felt lighter and was brighter. Clear walls started to take place. He watched as the whole space lit up and then as it reached the very dome, which seemed to be the last of the imposing darkness, it finally released, but that wasn't right.

It was hurtling down from the top. All that black was originally trapped in the wall, but Jace thought it was only a color. He didn't realize it was something. Something that seemed familiar, but what was it? What was coming at them?

Chapter 39
Child's Light

Eva

What in the world was that? As the dark strange mass fell toward them, all Eva could think to do was get out of the way. She pushed herself at Evan and Jace, trying to knock them out of its ultimate path. They were too stunned at what was happening to even think to move.

Her efforts finally had them stumbling back to move away from the object. She glanced up to see if they were moving fast enough to escape it. It didn't look that big before, but when she looked it seemed to spread out, which meant they would be caught by it.

"Sorry about this Evan," Jace said before he placed a hand on their companion and pushed with ability flinging the man far enough away so he wouldn't be caught by this dark mass. That meant it would hit her and Jace.

He already knew what she was thinking and beat her to it, scooping her up and tossing her. She felt the push of his strength ability and she was flying. In her disoriented state she couldn't do anything for Jace.

As she landed on her backside, she saw the thing hit Jace.

"JACE!" she screamed, reaching a hand out to him.

Jace

All he could think about was that he saved them. They weren't going to be hit. That meant he took the brunt of the whole thing. But it wasn't a normal tangible thing. When he threw his arms up to protect himself, all it did was block out everything around him.

He was standing in total darkness, not able to see Evan or Eva. As he tried to figure out how to get out of it, a figure manifested itself from the shadows. It didn't have features, its body shifted like they were made from the shadows, and it floated instead of walked.

Jace wasn't afraid of much, but this thing, well he didn't know if he should be scared. He could admit it did creep him out a bit.

"You will join us," a voice that wasn't just one voice. It sounded like multiple voices together. The way the being spoke sent a shiver down Jace's spine. Alright, he was scared.

"Join who?" Jace looked around but all he saw was the one shadowy being.

"We've always existed. Our presence lingers in the world, and we accept the deaths that are offered us. They strengthen us."

"Whatever you all are, I've never heard of you."

"But your soul calls to us. We cannot ignore the darkness." His soul? He didn't call anyone. All he was trying to do was help Evan. This place wasn't real. This isn't real.

Jace tried to think, manifest something like Eva had. He just had to concentrate hard enough he could have a sword in his hand to defend himself. Try as he might, it wasn't working. Nothing appeared and the being still floated ominously closer.

Yeah, no thanks. He needed to get out of here. He turned and started running. The only problem was that everything was dark around him. He didn't know where he was going, only hoping he was running away from that floating shadow creature.

He stopped and glanced back. He almost jumped out of his skin because he was expecting to be far away from that thing, but there it was, floating there like he never left.

"What do you want?" Jace asked. Maybe if he figured out what was going on, then maybe he might find a way out of whatever was happening.

"Death."

"Mine?"

"You will be our instrument. The collector of Sparks. Continue to feed us these blackened souls and you will be rewarded."

"Um, no thanks. Very much not interested in helping anyone do that." As it floated closer yet again, Jace took a step back, but like before it was like he didn't even move. Alright he was beyond freaked out now. He needed to try to get out of this being's presence and fast.

"There's darkness in your soul. It needs death to grow. Feed it. Feed us." They came closer.

"Stop! Don't come any closer. I don't have anything for you. Just leave me be!" He put his hands up in front of him to try and ward off this creeper.

There must be something he's missing. Think. He needed help. *Please help,* he cried out with all his Spark!

Where'd he go? One second, he was in the weirdly dark space and now he was in a small kitchen. Wait a minute. He moved off to the adjoining room and peeked in. Sure enough there was a fireplace just where he remembered. A familiar grey-haired woman was sitting in the rocking chair next to the fireplace. A small child sat on her lap. No. That was him.

Jace slowly came closer, but the two seemed to not know he was there. As he approached, he saw the older woman smile. His Nanna. How he missed her every day. He crouched and looked up at her, much like his younger self was doing just now.

"Can you tell me a story, Nanna?" his younger version asked.

"If you'd like one deary," his Nanna said. He smiled at hearing her sweet voice.

"Once there was a young man, as tall as any man I have ever seen. He was very strong and kind."

"Did he have ability?" His Nanna tapped her chin and smiled at the boy.

"Yes. But sometimes strength isn't always seen. It can lay hidden inside," his Nanna touched the boy's chest. Jace touched his own, he vaguely remembered this story. She continued. "The man had come against an enemy that seemed impossible to defeat."

"But he was very strong. He could defeat anything!" the boy exclaimed.

"I love your spirit," she tousled his hair. *"The man had no weapons, just himself. And yes, I know you are going to say that he could take them on with his bare hands. This wasn't an enemy he can grasp unto. This was an enemy that usually didn't show itself. It sneaks through the shadows."*

Shadows? Wait, was she talking about what he faced now, that being that wasn't really anything? It did just come out of the shadows.

"Then, how did he defeat them?" young Jace asked. Yes, how did the man defeat them? His Nanna told him once.

"Can I ask you a question?" she leaned close to the boy. He nodded his head eagerly. *"If the fire were to go out, what would happen to this room?"*

"It'd get cold."

"What else?" The boy's brow scrunched as he thought. He shrugged when he didn't come up with an answer. *"It would become dark."*

"Oh yeah, it would."

"Maybe dark enough that you couldn't see anything. If you started to walk around you might run into something," she tickled him, and he laughed. *"So, what would help you find your way through the dark?"*

"Start the fire again. Or I could get a candle! Well, unless I was cold then a fire would be better to warm me up."

"Indeed, a fire would warm you up. And a candle would produce the light you would need to see. For darkness cannot stay if there is light. Light chases away that darkness and you can see again."

"Like the sun! It gives us light."

"So, what would you do if there was something sneaking in the shadows?"

"Shine a light at it! It wouldn't be able to hide then."

"That's right Jace. Shine your light. It has much more power than you think." Nanna looked up then and stared right at him. Like she knew he was there. That this story wasn't just another bedtime story for little Jace, but exactly the answer he needed.

That memory world dissolved away and there he stood back with that shadow being. It seemed to arch and possibly take the last remaining steps to attack Jace. How it would attack he didn't know.

It can lay hidden inside. His Nanna's words echoed in his head. He concentrated on looking inside himself, to the place where his Spark resided. As he reached, he could feel it's warmth. It wasn't just warm but blinding. A light brighter than he could imagine.

The being jumped and Jace just thought of grabbing that light and throwing it. He saw that blinding white light escape his person all around him. Illuminating him in this otherworldly glow.

When the shadow touched it, it screeched a Fate's awful wail and shrunk back from it. There was a slight sizzle, like he had burned the thing somehow.

It has much more power than you think.

Well then. So long creepy shadow being and your world of darkness. Jace wasn't even going to give it any warning. He let himself take a deep breath, basking in the glow of his Spark. Not just his. Both. Eva and Jace. They were one now.

He embraced the light and let it glow brighter. The being shrieked out of existence as the light exploded out of him. As the light dimmed down, his eyes grew heavy, and he fell to the ground.

He just wanted to open them to see if he made it back to her.

Eva

When Eva opened her eyes, she was staring up at a ceiling. Just a normal ceiling, in a normal house. She sat up but her head was pounding.

She realized then an orange glow was against her skin, she was going to push it away, until a voice reached her in her fogginess.

"Hold on, let me help. If you push away now, I might not be able to again." It was Evan. Was he healing her?

Her head started to clear, and her eyes could focus more on him. Now that she could think and get her bearings, she looked around and saw Jace on the floor next to her.

"Stop," she forced Evan's ability away and blocked anymore from affecting her. "I can take care of myself. You should help Jace."

Evan jerked back like he was slapped. Well, she did shove his ability back at him, so that might have physically hurt him, but she didn't care. She needed Jace to wake up.

As she threw herself at him, she was already getting her own healing ability to assess what was going on with Jace. He seemed okay as she tentatively looked him over. Nothing obviously wrong stuck out. He was breathing.

"I thought you two were dead," Evan said. Eva whipped her head around and looked at him.

"What do you mean?" she asked.

"When I felt different, like I was reconnecting to something, both your hands dropped, and you slumped forward. I was able to catch you before you hit the ground, but Jace did a face plant."

"Why'd you think we were dead?"

"You weren't breathing, I couldn't feel your Spark right away. You guys did it. I have access to my ability. But I was afraid that it killed you. Like I thought that binding was going to kill me eventually."

Right, that weird darkness thing. Was that why Evan was worried? "Jace pushed us out of the way to take it on."

"What, death?"

"No, some darkness thing. It was in the barrier that Brosch put in your mind. It attacked us."

"Sounds bad. But before I could really dive in with my ability, you both started to glow, which took me off guard for a second. As it started to get brighter, I got the sense to hightail it out of there. I got myself behind the sofa and closed my eyes. I could have been blinded. I was momentarily. Thank goodness I was able to heal myself."

"Alright, well, why isn't he awake now?"

"You both are drained. You should be resting too. I was just trying to give you a bit of strength so you can recuperate the loss. I didn't know you were going to wake up on me."

"You mean, we used up our Spark?"

"Probably what that light was all about. You were both breathing, but I could feel it low, like critically low. Didn't want to take the chance of you dying on me. Especially since this time, I could save you," he smiled. He was truly glad that they were both still alive.

A groan came from Jace, and Eva's attention immediately returned to him. She gently stroked her fingers down his cheek and his eyes started to open. Blinking a few times, he reached up and grasped her fingers.

"Eva," he breathed. Smiling up at her with those blue-green eyes of his. She smiled back and let her fingers slip out of his. Just so she can give him a slap across the face.

"Oi!" He grabbed his cheek and started to slowly sit up. "What was that for?"

"Don't you ever do that again."

"Alright, you don't need to hit me for it." She stared at him for a few moments longer and then launched herself at him, hugging him like if he tried separating them again, she would slowly wither away into nothing.

"You scared me Jace," she shakily whispered to him. His own arms wrapped around her and squeezed a little.

"Ditto," was his response. She pulled away and he brought his thumb up to wipe a rouge tear that escaped her. Stupid emotions.

"Thank goodness, Jace. You're not dead," Evan said.

"Surprised you cared," Jace looked over at Evan who was standing there. Really looking out of sorts as to what to do with himself.

"Cared? No, well. I mean Eva was concerned. It wouldn't be right if I just didn't try to make sure you were all set. You know. It would be devastating for her."

"Right," Jace looked to Eva with a crooked smile. "So, it worked? I didn't just try and sacrifice myself for nothing, right?" She hit him again on his shoulder. "Ow," he said as he rubbed it.

"It appears that Evan has his ability back," she said to him. She turned to address Evan. "The question is, did we unlock that information you have on Brosch."

Evan stood there, pondering that question for a moment. Then asked, "What would you like to know?"

"You were healing him. What were you healing him of?"

"Oh yes, that," Evan said and pulled at his collar. "My specialty deals with the incurable. And, well, Brosch is afflicted with a rather nasty disease." After he said that, he put his hands over his mouth like he could take the words back. Surprise shown on his face, but then full happiness glittered in his eyes.

"Fascinating," Jace said. "But I'd rather ask questions later. I'm tired and we have a battle to be well rested for. Or did you two forget that."

"No, no, of course we didn't forget," Evan nodded feverishly.

"Right, we can all discuss this in the morning. Eva, let's go get some rest." He slowly rose, Eva tried helping, but he just swatted her hands away.

"I got this woman," he grumbled.

"Just like you handled whatever the heck happened in Evan's mind?"

"Fair enough." She helped him to his feet and they both shuffled their way slowly to the door. Evan ran around them and opened the door for them.

"I cannot thank you enough for what you two did for me," Evan said. "I just wish I could do more for you. You know, healing-wise."

"You've done enough Evan," Eva said. "You need to rest too."

"So, you do still want me at this battle?" If Evan was trying to get out of it, he lost that chance.

"Yes. Rest. We'll talk with you in the morning."

"Right, of course. I'll rest in my room and try to prepare myself for tomorrow. For the battle." As Eva passed, she could see the stricken look on Evan's face. She couldn't do much for his fear now. She was not at her optimal strength to even walk down the hall.

"Good night, Evan," Jace said as they passed by him out the door.

"Right, good night. Sleep tight. Don't let the crazy be right." Before Eva could ask what on earth he was saying, he had closed the door.

"Another time, Eva. Let's get to bed." Bed. Why did that sound so good right now?

"Okay, bed it is." Tomorrow was a new day. No one knew what Fate had in store for them. What would the outcome be after this battle? Would they go on to save Hockland, or doom them to a worse fate?

Chapter 40
Battle

Holds

"I honestly didn't want it to come to this." Holds stood there in the open field just beyond the gates into his stronghold. The villagers were still streaming in since he had them evacuate to the stronghold at dawn. Brosch's army had already breached the bridge and was assembling. So much for wishing they'd just wait until midday.

There were his own men, young and old alike, wearing whatever army they could get their hands on and holding weapons of their choosing. They were coming out of the stronghold and gathering just at the base of it. Half of the archers stayed inside the stronghold where they would take their spot along the wall.

Holds also ordered a set group of men to also guard the stronghold's only entrance. Well, the only known entrance. After the women and children were inside, the heavy wooden doors would be closed and sealed. Just on the other side would be the last defense. If it came to that. He prayed it wouldn't.

As he was directing his men to their various positions on the field, he spotted the trio that arrived yesterday. All he could think of was that they were a bunch of kids. They had no business fighting in this battle. They were the ones that Holds and his supporters were fighting a better future for. So much for trying to unconvince them.

When he was in his study earlier this morning, the three of them came in and began changing up his already established plans. The nerve of them. But he couldn't argue that their plan was solid, and it would probably save lives, on both sides.

What surprised him most was what this Evan person knew. He spoke with him privately after Jace and Eva left to give the orders to his men. Evan might be the key to Brosch's downfall at last.

He could have argued to keep him locked up in his home and hide him away so no harm would come to him. That's what Holds wanted, but that's not what was best for his stronghold. He was a Healer. Apparently powerful enough to heal that dreaded disease Brosch had. Holds had asked him why Brosch never had him cure it outright. "He couldn't risk what would happen if it came back. He wouldn't have another Healer." Right. Evan would have died, and then who could Brosch use to cure his illness?

Fates, Jace was an imposing man. He took after his father. He was glad to have a Jebrow on his side. Even though he was against Eva participating, she looked just as confident and deadly. The things she said she could do with her ability. Better ally then foe.

"There you three are," Holds hailed them down. "You really think this is going to work?"

"Better than not trying anything," Jace shrugged.

"Sir," one of his men came up to him. "All the villagers are in the stronghold."

"Then shut the gates," Holds said in a commanding voice.

"On it," the man ran toward the stronghold to give his order.

"Come," he motioned for the trio to follow him. They made their way through his men. Along the route, he gave encouragement where he could, patting men on their shoulders, a handshake here and there, an encouraging word to the younger men. He ordered most of the newly trained men to be the defense in the stronghold, but there were some talented individuals readying to battle. He knew he needed every advantage to win against Brosch's army.

Once they finally made it toward the front of his men and stepped out in the open with the trio right behind him. He eyed up his enemy and the formation they were taking. The numbers were close.

He could say they were evenly matched, but he wouldn't really know. Brosch didn't play by any rules, and he used whoever at his disposal. They were going up against a small portion of Might. Well,

Holds would have said that his men would be at a disadvantage, but he couldn't really say that now that these young'uns appeared.

Eva stepped up to his left side and placed a hand on his arm. "You're a good person Penn." He patted her hand and nodded.

"No one should suffer like the two of you had," he also inclined his head toward Evan.

"What happened to us was wrong. We could go in hiding, with the Ren. But even if we did that, we'd still end up in this war. Might as well jump in at the start."

"Was peace so difficult?" He asked the wind. Why were there people like Brosch in the world who thought they deserved everything? That they were better and stronger. Well, he appeared to be stronger, but he was as weak as any one of them. No one can outrun their own ending. No one can live forever. They didn't call themselves mortal for nothing.

"It'll come again," Eva said, hope coloring her voice. She was right. Peace can happen and it started with standing up to the one person who was disrupting that peace.

"Then we fight. Not just for my people, but for all Hockland."

"That sounds great. So, who else was supposed to be with me so I don't die?" Evan asked just behind him. This idiot. He had the worse timing.

"I'll go get them," Jace said and ambled off.

"Also, I thought you might want to know you have my support once you take your men and go across Hockland to dispatch Brosch."

"Who said I'd be doing that?" Holds wasn't thinking of doing that at all. And who was he to offer such support anyway?

"No one of course. Just if you do decide."

"What support could you give me? Your ability?"

"Well, not just that. I hope I still have a few connections back home. It's a long shot since I haven't been there in years."

"Thank you, Evan," Eva cut in. "We'll keep that in mind." So, she was talking for him now? "They are on the move," Eva said with a nod of her head. Sure enough, Holds looked over at the opposing side and they were starting to march this way.

"Positions!" Holds yelled behind him to his men. And so, it begins.

Eva

Eva looked across the field, scanning Brosch's army. The tainted auras she saw made her in the past see them as the enemy. Now, she only had pity on them.

What if they all had been corrupted by Brosch? Some darkness that lurked inside that made their auras change the way they did. When Jace explained his encounter with the shadow being, it seemed to make a bit of sense that Brosch had been manipulating his people a lot further then they wanted to. Essentially making them into mindless shells. Following orders of a madman.

Eva would have argued in the past that they chose to participate in heinous acts, but what if that wasn't true? What if they were all puppets? Their strings were being pulled and they went through the motions, not really paying attention, or can't change their course.

Evan was truly an exception. After pondering on what made him different, it was his ability. His ability somehow protected him from being completely succumbed by this darkness. A portion of himself fought back, yet it still wasn't enough to totally dispel it.

Now seeing Evan in all his glory, he was one powerful Healer. His aura shown brighter, and he held himself higher. Free to say and do whatever he wanted, now with the confidence that his mind would be his alone. Her and Jace made that possible.

Maybe she could make it possible for them too. Eva knew that there would still be losses. The instructions she gave to Holds and his men were to injure only. Then they would detain as many as they could where they would be healed and then hopefully, cleansed of the darkness. Eva and Jace were trying to figure that part out, but that was for later. Right now, they had an army to save.

"Advance!" Holds shouted beside her. As Holds moved forward, she kept pace with him and Jace flanked her on the other side. A line of men followed along behind them.

It was a dreary morning, with the sun behind the clouds. The wind was unpredictable, becoming gusts on and off that played in her hair. A fitting mood for a battle. *Fates, I hope this is what you wanted,* Eva thought.

She removed her sword from her back and flexed her muscles, loosening them. Remember, only injury. When Jace told her what the shadow thing said about there being darkness in his soul, it wasn't his soul they were looking at.

Their Sparks were combined now. That darkness, that must have been living inside her. Every time of intense anger, that was what fueled it. This need to kill and bring death to all that wronged her. Yet, she didn't always take that route.

Jace reminded her the other day in Holds study of that very fact. Whatever the darkness tried to get her to do, it failed more then it succeeded. If Evan held off the darkness, then she must have been holding it back most of the time too.

She honestly didn't know if it was still there now, after Jace's light display. If it swept away the darkness in Evan, then it was possible it also took whatever darkness that was in their Spark.

Brosch's cronies charged. As she picked up speed, Eva focused on the objective at hand. Save as many as she can. Her sights finally set on a man coming straight for her. And as their swords clashed, so began her task.

She expertly batted his sword away and sliced a cut in his stomach. He fell grabbing his middle. Hopefully that was enough damage, yet not too deep to not be able to heal. She did a quick assessment and was satisfied that he wouldn't die, but he would be incapacitated.

Another charged her way. She parried a few times and got around to the back, where she slashed right across his shoulder blades. The man cried out and fell. She caught Jace out of the corner of her eye, slashing a man's hand and his other arm, essentially making his arms useless.

They continued through, only injuring the men that dared to challenge them. She knew that it wouldn't be much of a challenge unless it was someone with the Might.

That's when she realized there really wasn't anyone on the field on this side with it. Not even some Warriors. Holds even thought that they would at least encounter some. But as she looked around, there were none. And as she thought back to the battle at the Wedset Mountains, they didn't have Might either.

Was Brosch playing a trick? Making everyone think he has this unbeatable army because he had his Numbered. Eva was starting to think his Numbered didn't get let out of the stronghold often.

Holds men were making an impact and gaining ground. After taking a handful more men down, that's when she started to see the panic in their faces. They were still advancing, but not in the least bit happy to do so.

Then she found something unexpected. A white aura amongst a sea of darkness. She cut her way through, literally, dropping bodies as she went. Still being very cautious of not killing them.

She hadn't seen it at first because it didn't project off his body. In fact, it seemed to be stunted, kind of like Evan's had before they unbound him. She was close enough now that one of Holds men he was fighting with fell to the ground at his feet. He looked up and locked eyes with her.

Eva raised her hand and pointed at him shouting, "Stop right there!" He smirked and went to move, but as he tried to take a step, he couldn't. Even though it was instinctual, she effectively made a barrier around his feet with her ability. She marched straight toward him, and he looked none too happy about it.

015

Fighting wasn't 015's strength. Even though he was part of the planning with the Strategists, he wasn't going to lead anyone. He had a very specific job that needed completed. If this battle would help him finish his goals, then he made sure he contributed, but just far enough away that he could still have a chance if this all went sideways.

About twenty minutes into the battle his doubts about the whole thing surfaced. Holds was prepared and his men were no slouches either. That meant Brosch's army could possibly lose.

It also meant he was harboring the Numbered. He caught a glimpse of an orange aura on Holds side. There he was, out in the open. One of his targets. Either Holds had no idea he was Might, or he had a strategic reason to use him in the battle. Possibly to lure 015 out in the open. He wasn't going to take the bait.

When his gaze caught on a woman, her dark hair billowing around her and her eyes sparkling like jewels, he had a sneaking suspicion of who that might be. "Stop right there!" she shouted at him. As he went to move toward her, he found he could not.

Of course, that was something she could do. Hadn't Brosch mentioned that she could do whatever she wanted. Controlling him, making him respond to her demands. Whatever torture she could think to drum up, he wasn't going to crack.

He still had use of his arms and as she closed in, he slipped a knife out of his sleeve and as swiftly as he could, threw it at her. Right before it would hit its mark and bury in her chest, it bounced of an invisible barrier he had not seen. She didn't even flinch.

Her hand came up and his arms immediately clamped to his sides. It felt like they were in a vise and no matter how hard he tried to move them; they wouldn't budge. She didn't stop until she was toe to toe with him.

She looked him straight in his eyes. He tried his best to show exactly how he was feeling, all that anger inside him. He directed it all at her. Instead of fear, or even backing away from him, her eyes softened.

Was that pity? She reached toward him, but he couldn't jerk his head much further away and she touched his cheek. What was her plan? What was she looking at? What was making her have that expression?

"Let me help," her voice was a soft caress against his skin. He blinked slowly trying to understand what she was asking of him.

"Once I have use of my legs and arms, you will be helping me by letting me capture you and take you to our master."

Her eyes narrowed. "I'm not property. I'm a person." Her eyes had that pitying look again. Her hand came up to rest against his temple. "And so are you."

Her eyes changed a brilliant white and as he tried to process what that meant, her image melted away and he was standing in an unfamiliar space.

It was dark as night. Nothing could really penetrate the gloom that settled around him. As he moved his head to take in everything, he realized he wasn't immobile any longer. While taking in the darkness, a pinprick of light cut through, like there was a small hole or something.

As he made his way over, the hole grew, and when he peered in, he wasn't expecting what would happen next. The light burst toward him. He closed his eyes and covered his head with his arms. He didn't hear any noise and wasn't sure if the light would hurt him.

He slowly lowered his arms and opened his eyes. There before him was a wall of moving images. He couldn't help himself. He approached the wall and touched it.

All at once, these images flooded his mind, one after the other. Seeing one woman repeatedly. An image stuck out of him stretching his arm toward the young woman shouting "Fanny!"

015 shook his head and as he did, he was back on the field with the dark-haired woman.

"Brosch lost this fight," she began to say, stepping away from him. "He won't stop, even when he will lose." Brosch. Yes, the man that kidnapped him. He stole him away from his family, along with his sister.

"You must hurry back," she said.

"Why?" He was all confused. Didn't he have something to do? Some job?

"Save her," he jerked his eyes to hers and there he saw them stark white. His eyes widened. The went back to a hazel color when she blinked. "He intends to do her harm. Free her and then find us."

Who was she talking about? As he thought about the question, that face of the woman surfaced. Fanny. It was Fanny. He knew exactly where she was. Just before leaving Brosch Stronghold, he found her in one of the dungeon's cells again. He slipped her some food and said his goodbyes.

"How do I find you?"

"Are you not the best Tracker there is? Go south and pick up our trail. Go now, before anyone notices." She was letting him go. He could move his arms and legs again. He would have said she was crazy but if a seer was telling him to do something. He better do it.

015 dipped his head slightly saying, "Until next time." He turned and made his escape back toward the army's camp. He wouldn't stop until he reached the stronghold.

Fanny was his only concern now. He didn't know if he could fully trust the dark-haired woman, but there was no way he was going to deny her vision. The Fates gave her the vision so he would know and do something about it.

I'm coming, Fanny.

Epilogue

He started coughing again. It seemed to send him in these bouts where he couldn't get enough air. When he finally stopped, he looked down at the cloth that he had held to his mouth. The red color shown starkly against the white.

Nothing was going right. Brosch just received a missive that his army was defeated by Holds and only a handful were able to escape. That shouldn't have been the case. He had the best trained people, and his Strategists were the best.

It was all *her*. She changed everything. She's the one who disrupts his plans. At least when she was locked in the tower, he had control. Molding her how he wanted.

He winced, feeling a tinge in his chest. He slowly rose and shuffled his way over to the fire. He tossed the bloodied cloth in the flames, and he unsheathed the knife at his side.

He twisted it this way and that in his hand, looking at his reflection within the blade. Pathetic, weak. He had bags under his eyes and his face looked gaunt.

He slashed his wrist, focusing on the pain to drown in a little bit of sorrow. He murmured the ancient words, and he watched as the blood seeped out of his wrist and hit the floor, sizzling like his very blood was on fire.

The world around him fell away and he was in a large chamber. The walls were obsidian and the glow of the fire in the scones didn't seem to penetrate the dark. He made his way through the chamber to the three thrones at the end.

As he made his way to the raised dais, three figures emerged from the very shadows, each residing on a throne. He came to the foot of the steps and stood looking up at these beings.

"What have you called us here for?" The middle being asked. Brosch was never able to make out their faces, only that their eyes each held a distinct color. This one's eyes glowed red and on his shadowy head there was a shadowy crown. Slightly higher than the other two. Brosch always assumed he was the one in charge. The one on his right had glowing orange eyes and the one on his left, yellow.

"I need more time. I'm close to my goal. All I need to do is capture her, then I will be able to take over – "

The shadow being on the left cut him off laughing. It wasn't a friendly joke. It was truly a laugh that left him wondering what he could have said to offend the being.

"Your time is long overdue. We've been looking so forward to your death."

"I thought you wanted an alliance," red eyes said. "Then you go and delay it by being healed."

"I never said I wanted to die for this alliance."

"That was always going to happen." Fat chance Brosch was going to allow that. He wasn't done yet with his plans.

"If you would just stop this sickness, I can finish what I started."

"Oh, I think you've done enough. If we don't step in now, all your progress will go to waste."

"What do you mean? I did everything you asked."

"Yes, but you also took advantage of it. Did you give us the credit? Very much a mistake on your part."

"Fine. I will let everyone know that you are the true kings and you're the ones that hold their mortality in your hands." The being on the right tsked. He stalked a little closer until he was just in front of Brosch. His shadowy robes seemed to seep darkness, and some snaked its way out and down.

"We wanted a chance to corrupt them, yet you let them merge." Brosch didn't understand what the being was telling him.

"What my companion is saying," glowing red eyes came up alongside yellow, "is that you had your chance with the Mighty. But you were too blind to see that to truly be the One, there had to be two of them."

Brosch shook his head. That stupid prophesy again. It meant nothing and the people who believed it were ridiculous. "What do you mean by two?"

"We try our best to disrupt the path our brothers so delicately lay out for these mortals. To say that they have an upper hand is an understatement. The One could destroy us!" Red hissed out at him, causing him to shrink away slightly.

"I'll do anything to stay alive," Brosch pleaded.

"Anything?" The last of the beings came forward and stood next to the others.

"So long as I don't die." That was the only thing he wasn't going to agree to. He didn't agree to death the first time around either. They tricked him with that.

"Hear this," they all seemed to speak at once. "Death will rise out of the Shadows. The Kings of Darkness will claim mankind for their own."

"What would you have me do to make that possible?" Brosch asked.

"Target the Might. No hope is left once they are destroyed. If you accomplish this, then we will let you fight for your life."

The Rens. Fine, he will take them out. They were a bother to him anyways.

"Thank you, sirs. Let me depart and complete my task."

"You can certainly try." The middle waved his hand in dismissal and Brosch was back in his room at the Lous School.

He looked down at his wrist where a fresh scar puckered his skin. He sucked in a lungful of air and slowly released it. Yes, that was better.

"I will do everything I can to win. I'm coming for you, daughter of Capton."

Author Biography

W.W. Morse is naturally a creative person. Creating stories and being able to share them has been an eventful journey. Morse lives in the Midwest and is happily married and has two adorable children. The family goes on many adventures together, especially to their cabin in the woods. They raise chickens and grow vegetables in their garden at home. Morse is currently a project lead yet still finds time for family and working on other hobbies. Some hobbies include playing Horn, gardening, reading, bowling, and baking. Morse was always busy at an early age, and it's no different now. "I thank my parents who allowed me to buy all those books from scholastic book fair when I was younger. If I wasn't surrounded by books at a young age, I don't think I would be the writer I am today."

Stay connected with W.W. Morse

 https://www.instagram.com/webmorse/

 https://www.facebook.com/w.w.morse

Child Prophesy
Read Book 1 in The Might Series. Available as eBook and in print.

Vanquishing the Darkness
Book 3 in The Might Series coming 2024!